The Pearl at Black Diamond Bay

BLACK DIAMOND ROMANCE
BOOK THREE

DL WHITE

BOOKS

Editing by: A. Kaitesi Tibandebage

Cover by DL White. Image courtesy Depositphotos.

Full wrap print cover designed by AuthorMya.

❀ Created with Vellum

Contents

For Kay. ;)
Inspired by my grandmother, Pearl Chaney.

BEACH THING

Ameenah Porter, a young woman from a successful New York restaurant family, moved to Black Diamond Isles to pursue her dream of opening her own smoothie and coffee shop called Tikis & Cream, much to her parents' disapproval.

Wade Marshall, a famous music producer working with hip hop star Gage Coleman, came to Black Diamond for the summer to focus on his music away from distractions in New York, especially the reappearance of his estranged father Ruben. Wade and Ameenah had an inauspicious first meeting but quickly developed an attraction.

Despite agreeing to keep things casual as a summer fling, Ameenah and Wade fell deeply in love as they spent time together on the island. However, with Wade set to return to New York at summer's end, they worried a long-distance relationship wouldn't work out.

Ameenah's parents visited Black Diamond to convince her to move to Houston and help open a new restaurant. She refused, asserting her commitment to Tikis & Cream. Meanwhile, Ruben tried to use Wade's name to book a performance in New York. An angry Wade confronted Ruben and cut ties with him for good.

Ameenah and Wade confessed their love for each other. With Ameenah getting Tikis & Cream to a point where she could travel back and forth to New York, they decided to continue their relationship beyond just a beach fling. The summer ended with their love stronger than ever, ready to build a future together.

ELYSIUM

Athena Wilcox, a travel nurse and single mother, was intrigued when entrepreneur Vance Griffin sent her a flirty private message on social media. Their casual flirtation soon blossomed into late-night conversations, bringing a yearning for more.

Vance invited Athena to join him on a work trip to Black Diamond, a stunning island resort off the coast of Texas. He promised she could relax on the beach while he conducted business, sparking hope that their online relationship could translate into a perfect real-life love affair.

Despite her initial hesitation and the concerns of her son Darius, Athena decided to take a chance on love and accept Vance's invitation. She flew to Houston, where Vance picked her up, and they began their journey to Black Diamond.

On the island, Vance and Athena's chemistry was undeniable. They indulged in the resort's luxuries, from poolside cabanas to yacht excursions and intimate dinners. Their connection deepened as they shared personal stories and dreams for the future.

Athena unexpectedly had to put her nursing skills to use when a local singer, Sabrina, collapsed at a performance. This event prompted Athena to consider starting her own concierge nursing business on the island.

Vance, meanwhile, was contemplating buying a condo at The Pearl and making Black Diamond his permanent home. He and Athena realized their feelings went beyond a casual fling and decided to plan a future together.

After their magical time on the island, Athena and Vance drove to her home in South Carolina to pack up her belongings. Despite Darius's initial coldness towards Vance, he eventually came around and accepted his mother's happiness.

With their love stronger than ever, Vance and Athena set

off on a new chapter together, ready to build a life on Black Diamond filled with passion, resilience, and the promise of a lasting love.

Author's note

I have a few words to prepare you for this book:

This book depicts a family in the throes of parental loss, refers to drug use, the criminal justice system, and features adult language and situations, including vivid descriptions of consensual sex. If you are sensitive to any of these descriptors, please proceed with caution.

All others, pack for undeniable sparks and a warm, sandy feeling in your heart.

I *love* to hear how much people are enjoying my books. Please send any "GIRL, HE DID WHAT?!" to me on any social media site or to my **email**. Post any criticism in your review at your fave retail or review site. Warn the others!

Want to set the mood? Visit my Spotify playlist here.

I appreciate your time and good opinion and truly hope you adore this novel.

xoxo,

DL White

The Pearl at Black Diamond Bay

One

DAVIS

"There is no excuse for a miss like this, Mr. Hudson."

The general manager at Breakers on the Bay stood in a collared, short-sleeved shirt with the restaurant's logo embroidered on the left side and khaki shorts, hands propped on his hips. "I know, but we—"

"Where's your end-of-day procedure? Do you regularly open this restaurant without ensuring you have everything you need?"

I dropped a stack of inventory pages onto a long shelf near the busy kitchen, which was in a barely controlled crisis. "What's the sense in tracking inventory if you let something like flour get so low you can see the bottom of the barrel?"

"It's these storms lately," Tim offered. "The weather is killing us." He lifted a hand to grab his earlobe and pulled it. I recognized this move as a signature—he pulled his ear when he felt pushed into a corner.

I took note and stepped back. "Running low on flour points to *weeks* of mismanaged inventory, not the weather report. We cannot afford a preventable miss like not having a staple in this restaurant."

"I'm aware. But as I was about to say, it's been a long winter and a longer spring. With the bridge always closed for some storm or flood or traffic jam, my orders get held up, which puts us behind, and we eat into our reserve. Yesterday was supposed to restore us, but it's been raining for days, and it's jacked up my delivery schedule."

Tim was correct, I acknowledged, noting that several deliveries to the hotel had been delayed because of the recent storms, including linens and equipment. Employees had been late, citing traffic as the excuse. Black Diamond had seen an explosion of growth in the last few years. It was now jam-packed with homes and businesses from one end to the other.

Though there were roadways through Black Diamond, there were only two ways on or off the island—the ferry, which only carried people, not cars, and the bridge across the water to the Texas mainland. Recently, that point of entry and exit had been ruining spring business.

"So…" I sighed, rubbing the pads of my fingers over my eyelids. "We have no flour anywhere on the property?"

Tim cleared his throat. "We've been scrounging here and there. The Cupcakery and The Bistro borrowed from us last month and we clawed back what we could. If that truck doesn't get over the bridge today, dinner prep will be an issue."

"It's sunny today," I noted, glancing across the restaurant at the rays brightening the dining room. "The trucks should run. Will your delivery arrive in time?"

"In theory," quipped Tim. His pallor had deepened to a crimson red. "I've got reports that there's already a backup at the bridge."

"In theory," I repeated, scratching my temple and suppressing a sarcastic chuckle. "If you run out of bread today, it will be ugly. And embarrassing."

"I thought we could call over to—"

"Come in, Mr. Scott." A rough, age-worn voice crackled through a two-way radio clipped to my belt.

"You could call…" I reached to turn down the volume on the radio.

"Clinks, maybe?" Tim suggested, referencing Black Diamond's five star beachside restaurant. "I know the manager over there and his chef stays stocked."

"We should hire his chef," I muttered, then pulled out my phone to tap out a text to my assistant. "Justin will arrange for a courier to pick up what they're willing to lend. We'll deliver the repayment once we've received ours. I want to see an improvement in how you manage supplies and staples. Flour is a necessary item to run this restaurant. We should never run low. We can always send someone across the bridge. Don't let this happen again."

Tim heaved a relieved breath and picked up the phone on the corner of his desk.

Breakers on the Bay had become famous for its buttery, crusty, flaky bread, which the restaurant baked all day, even leaving ends and pieces for guests to sample. A day without bread would be disastrous, and Breakers had quickly earned enviable ratings that it couldn't afford to lose.

I paced between two stainless steel prep counters just outside of the kitchen, where Chef Stephen Gramble orchestrated a world-class breakfast like a symphony.

I began each day with exercise, a tall glass of water, and vitamins. Then I showered, dressed, and completed my morning rounds of the property, always stopping at Breakers before heading to my office in the main building.

My usual breakfast was two pancakes, turkey sausage, scrambled eggs with a slice of bread and black coffee. When one of the wait staff mentioned offhand that I should get my bread while I could, I headed straight for the kitchen to find Tim.

"Mr. Scott, come in."

I snapped the device from my belt, brought it to my mouth, and pressed the button to talk. "Is there an emergency, Mr. Palmer?"

"I'd say. Got a call from a guest in Elysium, fifth floor," answered Gavin Palmer, maintenance supervisor. "She said water was pouring into the bathroom in her suite from the ceiling."

My shoulders sagged as my arms dropped. I pushed out a hard breath and brought the radio back to my mouth. "What's going on in the suite above her?"

"That's where I am now. A little boy has been busy flushing all kinds of things down this toilet." His voice turned hollow, sounding far away. "When he tried to flush a stuffed animal, he finally found something that wouldn't go down. Bathroom started flooding, he got scared and ran off. Nobody knew anything about it until 512 called it in."

I heard Tim hang up the phone behind me. "Could you send my usual to my office, please?" He gave me a thumbs up and walked around me, heading to the kitchen.

I made a beeline to the hotel administrative offices. "Can the toilet be fixed?"

"I stopped the water from running, working on unclogging it now," Gavin answered. "But that ain't even the big problem. Half of the suite is under standing water. We've got to move everything out and run a fan over these floors. This wood will rot, and mold will grow."

"Grab a crew and get started. That's a room I can't book until it's put back together."

"I'm on it. The guests are packing up and want to know when they're going to be moved to a different room. They have plans for the day."

I paused my trek across the property and stared at the radio like it had bitten me in the ear.

"They have *plans*. What were they doing while little Bobby was flushing their suite down the toilet?"

"I'm just trying to fix this here toilet, Mr. Scott," said Palmer, his dry, flat affect crackling over the line. "Guest business is your forte. That's why I beeped you."

I let out a frustrated grunt, my eyes rolling in exasperation. "Let me know when the toilet is fixed and everything in the suite is dry."

Plans. They're lucky I don't sue them for damages.

———

"The day just started. How do you already look beat down?"

Vance fell into step with me as I headed to my office. Back in college, people often mistook us for brothers because of our similar appearances. When I moved to Black Diamond to run The Pearl, I knew I could count on Vance's travel expertise to help bring in guests.

"Would it be too much to ask to go a single day without an issue? My very busy flagship restaurant might run out of bread, which would be a nightmare, in case you didn't know. Then one of my guests let their son flood a unit and they want to know how soon they can be moved to a different room. I should shove them to a cheap hotel up island, but that's sure to hit the grapevine, and I don't want to hear Calhoun's mouth."

"No, we don't want that," said Vance, as if he'd ever met Calhoun. He had only lived on property for a few months since he and his fiancée, Athena, bought a condo a few floors above me. She served the growing population of Black Diamond and Corpus Christi as a travel nurse, while Vance ran a thriving global travel agency from his suite at The Pearl.

Vance trailed me to my office, where neat stacks of work awaited my arrival. Financial reports, summaries from departmental staff meetings to review, property improvement plans, and occupancy reports all begged for attention.

I was hungry, which was throwing me off. I couldn't concentrate. I reached for the phone to dial Tim to ask about the progress of my meal, but the main line warbled a soft alert, the name *Harlan Calhoun* scrolling across the screen.

"Shit," I hissed.

"Must have conjured him up." Vance chuckled. "Can I sit in?"

I shrugged, punched the blinking line, then set the phone to speaker before sitting in my desk chair. "Good morning, Mr. Calhoun."

"Good mornin', my ass!"

Vance suppressed a laugh.

Without the usual pleasantries, Calhoun launched right into a rant. "I've got a bone to pick with you, Davis. You're supposed to be turning my property into some big damn deal like you did with those hotels you worked at before. Why in hell am I still in the red?"

His country twang did nothing to hide the tone that came across loud and clear. I'd heard Calhoun took his calls with his feet propped on the corner of his Texas-sized desk. Not for comfort, but so people could see his expensive custom boots.

Whether it was by luck or skill, I'd transformed a few mid-range hotels into classier five-star residences. When the opportunity to take the helm at The Pearl dropped into my lap, I convinced myself that I was ready to take on the challenge of running a boutique guest and residence property. I wish I had known what a mess the place was in before I arrived.

The Pearl, which had a lackluster grand opening, was just turning the corner.

"Sir, it is my every intention to bring the same success to The Pearl."

"I'm not seeing enough action, Davis. We're treading

water, and it doesn't make a lick of sense! The Pearl was built to be a spectacle on that little island out there. It's mild in winter, hot as hell in summer, and you don't need a passport to vacation on Black Diamond. There's no reason for the property to be empty, but there are tumbleweeds blowing through the guest suite floors, and don't even get me started on the condos."

I blinked, suppressing an indignant scoff. "I don't sell the condos, sir."

"Condo owners use amenities at the resort. Their experience is your responsibility. I'm scrolling through Instagram and seeing complaint after complaint. What's this about a flood in one of my towers? You're making me look bad, Davis!"

I scowled at the phone, happy that Calhoun couldn't see me. MGMT Hospitality Management employed a social media coordinator to put on appearances and make the hotel look inviting and high-end. It was their job to address disparaging content online.

"It's hardly a flood, sir. More like an overflow. Maintenance was alerted and my supervisor is taking care of it. Those guests have been moved to a new room. The storms have put a damper on business," I said, using Tim's excuse. "Every shop on the island is feeling it."

"I'm not every shop on the island! The Pearl should be a place people are fighting to book, rain or shine. The Occupancy Register tells me those cheap hotels on the other end of the island are booked to their eyeballs. I don't give a good *gotdamn* about every business on the island. I give a damn about mine, and mine is failing."

I sifted through the stack of reports that showed up on my desk each morning until I got to the Occupancy Register, which tracked how many rooms each hotel had available at any given time and the nightly rates for those rooms. Smaller, older hotels on the other end of Black Diamond could steal guests by running a special, which bulked up their occupancy and left a hotel like The Pearl, with nightly rates an average of three times higher, in the dark.

"I'm gonna lay somethin' out to ya," Calhoun drawled. "You'd better pull something out of your ass to bring people to The Pearl. I want every floor so full there's a line to use the bathroom. Make it happen because if I come down there, it won't be a social call. You do not want to see my thousand-dollar boots cross that threshold."

A glance at my desk calendar made my heartbeat pound a dull thud in my ears. Maybe I could manage Calhoun's demands in a bustling, metropolitan city but Black Diamond was a laid-back twenty-three-mile man-made island. Calhoun had tropical getaway dreams with a Texas town tourism budget, and as much as I wanted to save the day, I was doing the best I could with what I was given. The Pearl was at sixty percent occupancy, which was doing pretty well in the offseason.

"I heard through the grapevine that MGMT has been collecting candidates to manage marketing and events for The Pearl. I'd really like to get that person hired. A property this size requires all of my attention just to keep the lights on, let alone the time needed to market this place and manage events and programming—"

"A luxury hotel on an island coast should be a quick sell. I built the damn thing; I know it's a nice place. No reason you can't sell event space."

"The hotel isn't *exactly* a bargain," I argued. "With what it costs to run this place, finance won't give me clearance to drop rates—"

"Because it's bullshit! We both know the people who can afford nice hotels aren't worried about rates. But I hear you when you say you don't have time to promote, so your new marketing and events manager will be by this afternoon. The hell is that gal's name…"

I sat in stunned silence because I thought I'd just heard Harlan Calhoun tell me I had a new employee. Not a group of employees to interview and consider. An employee had *already* been hired. My chest grew tight at the revelation.

"Yeah…Kari Savoy. Her salary ain't much to sneeze at, but we got her to agree to some nice benefits to make up for it. Put her in one of my condos, a nice one with a good view, a parking spot, all the perks. She's the best candidate for what I want to pay, so when I say red carpet, I mean it. Roll it out, put her to work. And remember what I told you when I hired you, Davis. I brought you in, and I can take you out. Fill up that hotel."

The implied *or else* was crystal clear as a sharp click cut off any response I might have had. My future at The Pearl, and consequently any hotel of its caliber, was at stake.

"So…that was Calhoun," said Vance.

"The man, the myth, the legend."

"The loudmouth. Did he just say he hired someone for you?"

I pushed out a frustrated sigh and rubbed my temples. "Ten dollars says she's a leggy blonde with a marketing degree so new, the ink is still wet. A friend of a friend, if I'm lucky, so I can't fire her without making waves. Who else would he get to work here for cheap?"

Vance chuckled at my description and shook his head. "At least you get a little help, right?"

"Help I have to train is not help. And who knows if she even has any experience in hotel marketing?"

"To be fair, you've long needed someone to take over events."

"Remind me to be careful what I ask for."

Vance sat forward in his chair, indicating a change in subject. "You should come by our mixer tonight and let off some steam. We're all set?"

I quickly flipped through the roster of events scheduled

for the day, nodding when I saw Wanderlust Travel booked in the entertainment complex. Vance was an extrovert and very much a people person. He served drinks and snacks, encouraged games and karaoke, and helped the guests mingle with each other. Though it wasn't his job, his mixers brought people to the hotel and were already legendary on the island, drawing in locals and tourists alike.

"I'll just bring the room down, and I've got a lot of work to do. Justin is your lead, so let him know if you need anything."

"You can knock off early some nights, Davis. The work will still be here tomorrow."

"Unfortunately, that's true. The work will still be here tomorrow, and it'll be joined by even more work."

I stood, ambling across the room to the glass cabinet showcasing my collection of meticulously built Harley model motorcycles. I opened the door and pulled one out, turning it in my hands and admiring it, as was my habit. Building motorcycle models had been a hobby since my youth, something that always brought me peace.

"Don't let a guy in ugly cowboy boots tell you who you are. You've got this."

I hummed noncommittally, grateful for the concern but not entirely convinced. "I'm fine. Just...*hungry*. Where the hell is my breakfast?"

The door to my office flew open as two residents that I'd seen entirely too much of lately rushed inside, each trying to talk over the other. Vance, like a sucker, held up both hands and ducked out, leaving me alone to referee the cage match that was bound to throw down in my office.

"I'm tired of you following Carl around, and I'm going to make sure Mr. Scott puts an end to it!"

"You can't stop me from going where I want to go when I want to go there!"

"Ladies!" I stepped between them, creating distance and

preventing them from going at each other. "This office is a place of business. Lower your voices."

Lillian Roberts, a well-dressed, mature, heavy-set woman with a short, spiky hairdo, and Patrice Phillips, a younger honey blonde with a curvaceous shape, stood in the middle of my office. Both fumed so hard they were out of breath.

Lillian and Patrice were the best of friends when they moved into The Pearl. They lived on the same floor and Patrice was a single recent retiree, so Lillian and her husband, Carl, often invited her to dine and do activities with them.

Until Carl started paying too much attention to Patrice, and she did more to encourage than dissuade him. They'd been at each other's throats and in my office, often with one grievance or another.

"I'm tired of looking at her face, and I will not tell her again."

"Mrs. Roberts, I'm not sure what you want me to do. I can't stop Ms. Phillips from—"

"And I already told Lillian that I don't care what she's tired of looking at!" Patrice spat, a hand on her hip. "I pay to live here like she does. I can go anywhere I please."

"Like I can't see right through that cheap ass lace front. She comes to The Bistro at the exact time Carl and I have breakfast every morning, made up like a *hussy*. We go out to walk the golf course, and there she is, prancing those thighs around the grounds. We go out for our regular activities and wouldn't you know it, this heifer—"

"I've asked you not to call Ms. Phillips names. I really have to insist."

Lillian's thick lips pressed together as she emitted a loud grunt. "There are other words I could use, but I'm a lady. Unlike that heifer."

"Call me a heifer again and I'll beat you with your own cane, Lillian."

Lillian set her quad cane a few inches away and opened

her arms wide. "Nothing between us but space and opportunity! Come on! I'll clean your clock."

"Please! You can't stand longer than a minute without that damn cane." Patrice whirled around, the full skirt on her short fuchsia dress flaring out as she turned to face me. "Tell her to leave me alone, Mr. Scott. I'm not changing my schedule or how I live just because her husband likes to look at my backside."

"There's enough of it back there. He can't miss it!"

"You wish you had something to look at!"

At the sound of an amused chuckle, all three heads turned toward the door.

Two

KARI

Whatever last-minute jitters and unease I'd been entertaining when I arrived at The Pearl Hotel and Residences quickly dissipated.

Justin, the assistant property manager at The Pearl, had introduced himself as soon as I stepped through the doors and led me to my appointment to meet Davis Scott. He and I stood in an open doorway and watched a loud, hilarious argument terribly refereed by a tall gentleman whose head bobbed from one middle-aged woman to the other.

I had almost declined the disappointing, near criminal offer from MGMT, the hospitality management company I'd interviewed with, and resigned myself to becoming one with the couch after my role at my previous employer was elimi-nated. Sensing that I was about to walk away from an oppor-tunity disguised as a challenge, my best friend since college, Dionne, convinced me to at least drive down to the island.

"Take a tour, meet Davis, hang out with me and Jason, and then make your decision." She knew Davis Scott, The Pearl's

GM, through her husband's recreation business, and while she didn't exactly vouch for him, she also had nothing negative to say.

The man I assumed was Davis seemed relieved by the interruption and regained control of the situation. "Ladies, I'm afraid I have a meeting and can't resolve this for you. Justin, please escort them back to the Paradise tower."

"Not until you tell her to leave me alone!"

"I'll leave you alone when you leave Carl alone!"

"Why don't you both leave each other alone?" Mr. Scott suggested, rubbing his temples.

"Are you ladies guests?" I smiled at the pair.

"Owners," replied both, staring hard at me.

I detected a note of frustration and a tight pinch to Mr. Scott's voice. "Mrs. Lillian Roberts and Ms. Patrice Phillips own condos on the property. They have communication issues that they often come to me to resolve, though it's not my job to manage personal squabbles."

"We don't have communication issues," the older, shorter one of them snapped. "She has comprehension issues. I tell her to stay out of my business, and here she comes, prancing her wide ass into it."

"This land doesn't belong to you, Lillian. I can go anywhere I please, and there's nothing you can do, so get over it." The more buxom of the two cleared the curl from her lip and smiled in my direction. "Now, who are you, and why are you in our business?"

"Oh, I'm—"

"You'll officially meet her in due time," Mr. Scott interrupted, herding them toward the door. "Justin will see you out."

They caught the hint, following Justin and bickering as they did so. Davis waved me to the empty seat in front of his desk. I felt his deep, loud sigh as he sat.

"Ms. Savoy, I presume?" he asked, consulting his

computer screen. When he looked up, his countenance was not warm or welcoming.

I slid the chair back a little and sank into it, crossing one leg over the other. "I was supposed to come in later, but I thought it would take me longer to get across the bridge, and—"

"Well, you're here now." He tugged at his jacket, fussing with the buttons to open both sides before relaxing in his seat. "I apologize for the…show. I'd like to promise that isn't a regular occurrence, but I can't. Condo owners think they run the place."

He wore tight curls atop his head, cut close around the sides with a razor-sharp edge, had a smooth café au lait complexion, and intensely dark brown eyes framed by bushy but manicured brows. His suit jacket fit him like it was sewn around his solid arms and chest, and there wasn't a thread out of place on his crisp white shirt nor his multi-colored tie. I was alone with a man whose brooding, rugged good looks might have taken my breath away had I not made Dionne send me a photo.

Davis Scott was a sight for any kind of eye, sore or not. *Maybe this won't be so bad…*

"So, Ms. Savoy—"

"Oh, please, call me Kari. I'm not into formality. We're on the same team, right?"

"Mr. Calhoun tells me you're our new director of marketing and events. You'll have your work cut out for you."

I tipped my head in confusion. "Are you hazing me, Mr. Scott? Is this how we begin our relationship?"

"We don't have a *relationship*, Ms. Savoy. MGMT hired you to do a job, as I understand it. I'll make sure it gets done for however long you remain here."

"For however…" I sat up straight, biting down on my

bottom lip before I finished that sentence. "You assume I'm a short-timer?"

"I make no assumptions, Ms. Savoy. Since I was informed not even one hour ago that I have a new employee, you'll forgive me for not throwing you a welcome party."

I was beginning to understand the situation, his terse tone and attitude. I even commiserated a little. I sat forward, resting my elbows on the desk. "I imagine that would be difficult to hear, Mr. Scott. I was an excellent choice for this position, though. I'm eager to prove that to you."

"The only thing you need to prove to me is that you're aware that this isn't a working vacation. The Pearl isn't some tiny, fly-by-night roach motel where you can work a few hours and then sunbathe your afternoon way. I don't know what your experience is, but—"

"Oh? Well, allow me to share," I interrupted, sitting up to unzip my portfolio, and laying my impressive CV on his desk. I paid enough to have it done; it better be impressive. "I come to you by way of The Fairmont Golf Resort in Austin, where I managed events and marketing. The Fairmont is an award-winning property that enjoys nearly full occupancy year-round, mostly thanks to programs I developed."

"Ms. Savoy..."

"*Kari*...please."

Impatient, but clearly trying hard to be amicable, he cleared his throat and began again. "This resort is larger than the Fairmont. We also have owners, which, as you've seen, adds a layer of complexity. I need someone who can bring people to this island and through the hotel's front doors. I need a full-time, experienced marketer cycling an ever-changing offering for those who choose to purchase a home or book a stay here. I don't have time for hand-holding someone who needs guidance every step of the way."

I was taken aback by the blunt assessment of my qualifications. My time at The Fairmont and my degrees were enough to impress his boss but were not good enough for him?

Who the fuck is this dude?

"I assure you, Mr. Scott," I replied, sounding more calm than I actually felt, "I have coordinated hundreds of events in a five-star resort environment. As for marketing strategy, I have a few ideas to bring in guests and homeowners to The Pearl."

I shifted to dig into my portfolio case, waving away tendrils of hair that had loosened from my bun to hand him several glossy publications.

"During my tenure, The Fairmont underwent an expansion. For my master's thesis, I conducted a deep study on the resort industry and how a property grows patronage. I crafted a survey to send to every guest that had ever stayed at the resort, and based on the survey results, I designed an extensive campaign across multiple platforms to bring people in to tour the updated property. That campaign alone drove up bookings by fifty percent."

"I can see how that campaign could be effective at a small golf resort in Austin, Texas." His pause was pointed and did not go unnoticed. "The Pearl is a larger property at a higher price point. It's chess, not checkers."

I chuckled lightly, rolling my tongue across my teeth. "Mr. Scott, I have access to the Occupancy Register just like you do, not to mention the market and earnings reports. We can compare The Fairmont and The Pearl if you like. One of those resorts is nearly full. The other is The Pearl."

I pulled a bound report with a clear cover from a pocket inside the portfolio and slid it across the desk. "My research and the strategies I put in place were based on a variety of properties, stateside and worldwide. Occupancy is only half the target—what good does it do to have a full hotel if you have to sell rooms at a discount that eats into profits? And if I were being petty, I might mention that The Pearl can't even sell their extra rooms. The Fairmont achieved near-complete occupancy without adjusting rates by showing guests how far their dollar spends, especially for amenities that other hotels roll into a resort fee."

Mr. Scott sat back, hands clasped. Visibly seething... but quiet.

"Working with The Pearl is ambitious, but I've proven that I have education *and* experience, Mr. Scott. I also have the drive and energy to learn how to bridge the gap of a boutique beachside hotel and residence property. Not only that, but the benefits of a fresh perspective could—"

"Ms. Savoy." The rich tenor of his voice interrupted my stream-of-consciousness ramble, which was a good thing because I was moments from an impassioned speech.

I wanted this job.

Hell, I needed this job.

The pay sucked, but sitting across from this man that acted like he knew me and would summarily dismiss me, were it his choice to, made me want to fight. This was the challenge, the change, the new direction I'd been seeking.

And my boss wouldn't be so bad to look at if he ever stopped scowling.

"May I speak frankly?"

"Please do," I replied.

After a pause, Mr. Scott unclasped his fingers. "This is Calhoun's first resort property. It's more a mogul's wet dream than a business that makes sense. It was expensive to build, which puts pressure on his bottom line. It's a bear to run, which puts pressure on me, and as a result, my staff. Today alone, I haven't even had time for breakfast. Most new hotels don't turn a profit for years down the line, but unless I get ahead of this downturn, I will run this one into the ground prematurely."

He paused, meeting my gaze before looking down at the stacks on his desk.

"Calhoun wants Caribbean island miracles on a stateside resort budget. By *summer*."

He turned his head to glance at the calendar. We both blanched, mentally counting the paltry number of months until the end of May, which marked the unofficial start of the summer season.

"I don't have the time or concern for this tap dance." He waved his hands in the air and frowned. "I'm not convinced that you have the experience that I need to fill The Pearl, but I don't see how I have much of a choice, given that MGMT has already hired you. I need you to get to work."

A light *buzz-buzz* stole his attention, and he rolled his wrist to check his watch. "I meet with my team weekly. You'll be expected to gather issues in your department that need to be discussed at the management meetings, which, by the way, are non-negotiable. Don't miss my meetings."

"Sounds like a real good time," I muttered. "But before you start doling out orders, I need to get something straight with you, *Mr. Scott*. I haven't signed my paperwork yet. I was skeptical when I got the offer. I decided to wait until I could see the property, tour the hotel in person. We also have friends in common— Dionne and Jason Woods?"

I waited for him to acknowledge the familiar names before I continued.

"Dionne begged me to meet you first, get a vibe for the place. Now, I could be burning a bridge, but the chances that I'll be back unless I work here are low, so I'm going to speak frankly as well. This job is a lot of work for not enough money. I'm educated and experienced, so you know what my salary *should* be."

I paused, eyeing Davis, reading his expression as he picked up my meaning.

"You didn't pick me, but you need me. I'm ready to move to Black Diamond, but—and I said I was going to be honest— I will not move my life and use my experience, education and youthful vigor to bail you, MGMT, and Calhoun out. Not while working for an asshole for pennies."

Mr. Scott sat still, a grim seriousness lining the angles of his jaw as if he had turned to stone. I was determined not to say another word until he kicked me out on my ass.

Or…showed me to my office.

His watch buzzed again. He snapped to attention and tapped a button to silence it.

"My meetings are held in the main conference room. I'll show you there, after which Justin will take you to human resources. Calhoun tells me you'll be staying in one of the condos that his firm owns."

He exhaled, then stood, pulling both sides of his jacket together and fastening the buttons in a sexy, fluid motion. "Your housing can be ready for you by Sunday morning. I need someone to begin right away, so if you're staying, I hope we'll see you Monday morning."

"Do you want me to stay?" I smiled, tilting my head in a way that seemed to taunt him.

"What I want is irrelevant. That decision is solely up to you."

I chuckled, standing to face him. "That's not what I asked you, Mr. Scott."

The discomfort in his expression was palpable. *You don't have to play with the man's feelings, Kari. You know good and well you're not going anywhere.* I extended a hand to him. "I'm looking forward to working with you."

He gripped my hand, giving it a polite squeeze, then released it. "Welcome to The Pearl, Ms. Savoy. And good luck."

"Any way I could get you to call me Kari?"

I swear I heard him chuckle, but the laugh didn't reach his face. He picked up a leather folio and pulled his office door open. A soft beep emitted from a robotic rolling cart. Davis opened the lid and pulled out a plate covered with a silver dome, then closed the lid and pressed a button marked *complete*.

The cart beeped and reversed course. Wide-eyed, I watched the machine roll down the hall.

"Delivery robots," said Davis, lifting the dome to reveal a beautifully plated breakfast and a paper cup bearing the hotel's logo. "We can't keep flour in stock, but we have robots."

Three

KARI

"You cannot be mad at me, Kar."

Fresh from leading a beach yoga session, Dionne still wore a racerback tank top and high-waist leggings in blue and grey print. She shrugged on an athletic jacket, probably Jason's since it seemed several sizes too big.

"Can't I?" I sucked down another mouthful of chocolate, vanilla, and caramel swirl king-sized milkshake we were supposed to be sharing. "You trapped me," I said, dunking the straw deeper into the glass.

"I did not."

"You said Davis Scott was handsome, that he was an impeccable dresser, that he was dedicated to the success of his hotel—"

"Did I lie?" Dionne interrupted.

"You didn't even hint that he'd have a rod up his ass and be rude as every fuck."

"You're right," she replied. "Because Davis isn't always

like that, and I didn't want to discourage you before you saw the island. Does it matter? You're still taking the job, right?"

"Like I have a choice. I need a job."

"Davis is bad at first impressions. I promise he gets better. And wait until you see him in his riding gear."

I pursed my lips, sending a glare across the table. "You should have mentioned that he was a grumpy, frowny…*puckered* man."

"Puckered?" Dionne cackled. "Are you picking up lingo from the kids?"

I laughed. "Moses says that about half of his professors. Davis Scott is a tight. ass. He won't even call me Kari. He about *Ms. Savoy*'d me to death today."

Dionne giggled. "He just needs to relax around you. He takes his job seriously."

"Way seriously," I agreed with an emphatic nod. "His assistant was pretty funny. I get the feeling the staff don't really like him."

"He's not there to be liked. For that matter, neither are you."

"I'd prefer it, though. You like *your* boss," I shot back. Dionne's boss owned Tikis & Cream, a smoothie shop on the boardwalk. When Ameenah was in New York helping her parents run their restaurant group and living with her record producer boyfriend, Wade Marshall, Dionne ran the shop. They'd met a few years prior on Black Diamond and had been inseparable ever since.

"My boss isn't puckered," Dionne replied, then snorted. "How are the kids? Do they know about your new job yet?"

I wilted against the worn brown leather seat at Adele's, an adorable eatery a few blocks from Dionne and Jason's house. After the management meeting, then a long afternoon with human resources, I'd been looking forward to a few hours with my best friend. Tonight, I'd sleep, then drive home to finish packing since I was due to be back on the island on Sunday. I ached to show Davis what I was made of.

I didn't know why, though. Something told me he wouldn't be impressed if I could bring thousands of people through the doors by the weekend.

"Mo is great. Acing his courses this semester and volunteering with Black MDs, that organization he started with a few of his frat brothers to encourage high school kids to go into a career in medicine. All while still playing lacrosse. I'm proud of that kid."

"And Reyna?" Dionne prodded.

My smile faded a little. "Reyna is...headstrong. A tough cookie. And failing her classes. I'll be surprised if she makes it back to SMU next year."

Dionne frowned. "Oh, no. She's not doing well, then?"

"Nope," I answered, pressing my lips into a tight line. "I'm not sure she's been to class all semester, which is a great way to waste the tuition money our parents saved for her. She could skip class and get shitty grades in Austin instead of expensive ass Southern Methodist University, but bringing her home means she's in my face all day and..."

I shook my head. "Neither of us wants that. And I don't think she'd come. As far as I know, she spends every night at her boyfriend's place instead of the apartment I pay for."

Dionne winced. "She was such a sweet kid when I met her, but I guess grief changes people. I know Reyna is a challenge, but—"

"A challenge?" My brows shot up as I tossed a caustic, sarcastic laugh into the air. "That girl is sending me prematurely gray."

Dionne shot me a sympathetic smile, then sucked down the last of the milkshake. "Want another one?"

"Ugh, no." I shook my head, wiping my fingers on a napkin. "It was delicious, though. This is a cute place." I glanced up at the ceiling of the cafe, admiring the exposed wood beams and the fans gently circulating salty sea air throughout the room.

"Isn't it? When Jason works nights, I practically live between here and the bookstore next door. It's my favorite place on the island. Ameenah brought me here one day after we closed the shop and I fell in love with it."

"How is Ameenah?" I picked up the plastic-coated menu and read over the items offered. I had a feeling I'd be spending a lot of time at Adele's. "Is she back for the summer or still pulling double duty between here and New York?"

"She's on the island for a few weeks, then back to New York when her parents leave on their next scouting trip for Porter Restaurants franchise locations. She doesn't mind it too much since Wade is based there."

My brows rose, sensing hot goss incoming. "Sounds like things are serious."

"I told her it was serious from jump, but she didn't believe me. Now look at her—ridiculously in love and living her dream, flying from New York to Black Diamond every few months. I'm running the shop full-time, mostly."

"So…is she expecting something shiny soon? It's been a few years, right?"

"She won't say if she thinks he'll propose soon. I can't believe it hasn't happened already, but Wade and Gage have been preoccupied with getting Tuneage Collective up and running."

"I guess Wade has been too busy trying to be a music mogul, creating a label, and developing artists to get engaged."

"You'd think, but he sure likes having her up there. And when she's here, his ass is not far behind."

I smiled, making cooing sounds. "They sound sweet."

Dionne rolled her eyes. "They make Jason and me sound like an old married couple, and we're still newlyweds." She glanced at the glittering stones on her left hand like she still wasn't used to them being there.

"Anyway…" Dionne continued, "what do you think the kids will say about you leaving Austin?"

"They're probably happy to be rid of me."

"Nonsense. Where would Reyna and Moses be without you? Literally, where?"

I rolled my answer around my head before giving it air and sounds.

"They don't see the sacrifice it took to keep them together. Moses gets some of it, but Reyna has blinders on. They don't know what parts of my life I put on hold to make sure they finished school and became productive members of society. They're used to me being there, taking care of everything, being the authority figure. I'm afraid they'll see me moving away as abandonment. And after losing their parents, I don't want to make them feel that."

"You're four hours from Austin. Phones and FaceTime and planes exist. And they're both away at school. They hardly come home, anyway. It's time to make a move for yourself, Kari."

"True." I sent a sad smile across the table. It was time, but I knew leaving my siblings would be harder than I told myself it would be. "I hope they see it as me making a move for myself and not me running away from them the first chance I get."

Dionne peeled away a layer of the cinnamon roll we were supposed to be sharing, but I was full from the milkshake, and talking about the difficulties of raising my siblings always sapped my appetite. "Let's not talk about how you had to choose between staying in Houston or moving back home so they wouldn't be split up in foster care. As for Reyna, she's a…what are they called? Millennial? That age group that people say are self-absorbed and need to be winning all the time or the earth will tilt off its axis?"

I giggled. "No, Dionne, you and I are millennials. And thank you for that unflattering description of our generation, by the way. Rey and Mo don't like to be put in boxes."

"Of course. They want to be individuals, just like everyone else."

Dionne smiled up at the server, who left our bill at the corner of the table. I snatched it up and dropped it into my lap. Dionne reached over and placed her hand on top of mine, giving it a reassuring squeeze.

"I'm glad you're moving here," she said softly. "You need a fresh start and new opportunities. Speaking of…"

She rolled her eyes up so they met mine. I already knew what she was about to ask. "Noah is still in the past, right?"

I sucked my teeth, rolling my eyes. "Girl, yes. Noah has *been* history."

"Does he know you're leaving Austin?"

"Not from me. We haven't spoken in months."

"He just stopped calling one day and…" Her hands whipped around in a flurry of movement. "Nothing?"

"Not shit. Five years of on, then off, then on again because he was bored and between girlfriends, then he dissolved into thin air. Then I heard he was parading a woman around; she's hanging all over him at lacrosse matches."

"*Girl.* I guess he was trying to tell you something without telling you something."

"Say less." I twisted my lips into a surly frown. "I can take a hint."

Noah Grayson was handsome, smooth, funny. Seemed to really enjoy working with high schoolers. He taught Humanities and World Studies and coached Lacrosse—he even helped Moses walk onto a team in Louisiana.

Unfortunately, Noah was allergic to commitment, and whenever we got close to being serious, his habit was to back away. Most men my age didn't want an instant family, let alone a young woman raising her siblings, one of which required more attention than the other.

Noah was not a father figure, more the fun uncle type.

During a rough period with Reyna, I looked up and realized Noah had disappeared. I hadn't heard from him in weeks—no texts, emails, or chats. I was unfriended on most social media platforms and one day, I figured out why. He had a new girlfriend.

"Mmmmph," Dionne grunted. "Onward and upward. Was the dick worth your time, at least?"

I lifted and lowered my shoulder in a non-committal shrug. "If you like the occasional fuck with his socks and shoes still on. Not good enough to act like a jealous ex from a Tubi movie. Noah was like...spaghetti. It's good in the moment, especially if you're hungry, but who's really going wild for *spaghetti*?"

Dionne laughed. I yawned.

"Oooh, if I didn't know you better, I'd say you were telling me I was boring." Dionne smirked but stuffed the rest of her half of the cinnamon roll into her mouth.

"But you know me." Suddenly, I ached to give in to the weary feeling settling into my bones.

"Yep, so I know you are dead on your feet. Let's head to the house so you can get comfortable. You want some coffee to go?"

I shook my head, reaching for my satchel. "I'd better not. I need rest tonight so I can drive back to Austin in the morning. It's going to be so exciting living close to you again. I missed you."

"I missed you too! And honey, I'm so proud of you. This is the chance you've been waiting for— a dream job on an island, close to me..."

My eyes involuntarily rolled, though I was touched by the sentiment. "Let's go, before you get sappy."

I pulled out my wallet, counted out enough cash to pay

THE PEARL AT BLACK DIAMOND BAY   29

our bill and leave a healthy tip, then slid the money under the check and scooted out of the booth. I waved to the server as we headed toward the door.

"By the way," she said, catching the door as I held it open, "my new beach yoga class starts in a few weeks. It's a flow class, which is great for stretching and relaxation. And I know you'll love this cycle class Jason started taking. Wade goes when he's in town. I'll introduce you to the instructor. He's *single*," she added in a sing-song voice.

I groaned, sliding into Dionne's car. "My penance for letting you help me get this job is that I have to avoid you folding me up like a pretzel. Or setting me up with island dick that promises to fold me up like a pretzel."

"One way or another, I'm gonna get you folded. Don't act like you don't need it. We just discussed how Noah has been out of the picture for a minute."

"I will not deny it." I pulled the seat belt across my body and snapped it into place as Dionne's car bubbled to life. "I just don't know if I want *you* hooking me up."

Four

DAVIS

Vance slid out of the booth, gesturing toward Whiskey Blue's makeshift tiki bar. "I need to make a pit stop. Either of you want another beer?"

The gathering of people around the bar made me groan. The long line and mediocre drinks were hardly worth the wait. I shook my head and picked up my bottle. "Thanks. I've got enough to work with right here."

"I'll take a refill," Jason replied.

"Back in a minute."

I sucked down a swallow of the almost warm and nearly flat pilsner that I'd been nursing most of the evening. Most nights, or at least the nights that Jason worked at The Play-house, an indoor gaming center, Vance and I would take a ride out to meet him for a beer or two.

While Vance and I had known each other since college, I met Jason through the bowling league he'd started up almost as soon as he hit the island. He and his wife, Dionne, visited island hotels and restaurants to promote their beach recreation company, offering lessons on canoeing, kayaking, and paddleboarding, as well as fishing charters and activities like beach yoga, volleyball, and bowling. Jason co-owned The Playhouse and spent his nights running back and forth between indoor mini golf courses, batting cages, and the go-kart track.

I hadn't bowled in years, but I jumped at the chance to get out of the hotel a few nights a week. The next season wasn't set to begin for a few weeks, but we'd kept up our habit of meeting up for a drink, especially as calls from Calhoun became more frequent. I could drink for free at any of the hotel bars, but the drinking that I wanted to do wasn't a good look on property. Besides, it was nice to walk out the front doors and occasionally dream of never walking back in.

It wasn't all bad. Running a premier hotel and residence on an island was nice work. I had access to a luxurious community with stunning ocean views, rooftop pools, ultra-modern gyms, private beaches, and exclusive restaurants. The perks outweighed the challenges, which was why I stumbled back through the doors of The Pearl every night after letting off steam over a flight of microbrews.

"Your face is depressing me, Davis," said Jason.

Vance slid back into the booth with three bottles of a local IPA, uncapped and frosty with condensation. He slid one over to me. "No way that shit still tastes good. Probably warm and flat."

I gripped the bottle by the neck and poured a few swallows of amber ale down my throat. It was good going down, refreshing. Took my mind off my troubles, if only for a moment. Perhaps that was why people drank. And kept drinking.

"Apologies for my face," I got out before a beer-flavored belch escaped my lips. "Today was challenging."

"Poor guy didn't get his breakfast on time and had to take a difficult phone call," Vance teased. "He also got a new employee who will, we hope, take a load off. Tell this guy to cheer up."

"D's friend, right?" Jason asked. "She's sharp. She's excited and ready to work. What's the problem?"

"She's only a benefit to me if she actually brings in business," I replied. "Calhoun has me over a barrel, and I don't have time or money to spare."

"That cheap ass is always threatening to shut shit down," Jason said, picking at the remnants of the barbecue chicken nachos we'd shared. "Look who's still here."

"This time feels different. I didn't expect us to turn a profit so early out, but we shouldn't hemorrhage money, either. I'm busting my ass and Calhoun—" I cut off my statement, what I really wanted to say. It wasn't for Jason's ears, but he knew me well enough to read my mind. "I don't know the answer, J."

"Seems obvious to me," said Vance, helping Jason pick through the nachos. "You have fresh blood in the office. A fresh, young, educated perspective."

"Who went to the University of Houston."

"So did you," argued Vance. "So did I."

"And *then* I went to Cornell."

Jason laughed. "The Cornell School of Hospitality grad looks down his nose at others. Come on with that shit, Davis."

"I've been working in hospitality since I was a teenager. She doesn't know it, but she's green. I don't have time for green."

"Green?" Jason's voice rose to a shrieking pitch. "She has a master's in hospitality management. She ran an entire department, Davis. She's got a portfolio full of professional success, if you could stop being mad that you didn't get to choose her. Her old spot loved her, they just loved someone else for a lot less money. When the Fairmont cut her, D got the idea to tell her about the job."

"Yeah, thank Dionne for me. Nobody thought to consult me about the talent I want in that role? She's earnest and semi-experienced, but not when it comes to working in high-value property management. She's worked for one resort, and she did well there, but The Pearl is a different animal. She's not who I'd have hired."

Jason stared at me, his dark eyes laser-focused. A crease spread across his forehead as his brows lifted in question. "But she's *hired*. So Kari is there for what? Something pretty to look at?"

"She's attractive. And she has a smart mouth to go with that pretty face."

"Attractive?" Jason laughed. "My aunt is *attractive*. She's fucking gorgeous, Davis. And you get to work with her. All day."

Jason had a point, and I didn't miss it. Attraction to her would be typical and expected. Kari's legs were long and muscled, from what I saw in the skirt she wore in her interview. Her eyes were a warm and inviting brown. Her features added up to a desirable ratio, and Kari's lively and upbeat outlook would be a welcome change to the atmosphere. She was confident in her abilities and convincingly determined to make a difference at The Pearl.

Those traits would get her past her probationary period. After that, when she became accustomed to working at The Pearl, being beat down by Calhoun, MGMT Hospitality, and condo owners and staff, I expected her attitude to match mine —paying the bills, doing the best I can, watching the Titanic sink and not being able to plug the hole made by the latest iceberg.

"She's my employee, so it would be inappropriate to consider how Kari being *fucking gorgeous* benefits me." I tipped the bottle into my mouth, swallowed, then muttered, "But I was relieved when she decided to stay after threatening to leave."

"See? There, and when you're off the clock, and she's not your employee—"

"She's always my employee, Vance."

Vance playfully sighed, tossing up his hands. "Fine. Play by the rules, but you have help now. Much-needed help, so find a positive thought and hang onto it like a life raft. You're always worried about something."

"I'm always worried about everything," I said quietly. "Are you two going to keep picking at the crumbs, or do you want another pan of nachos?"

"I shouldn't," said Vance. "I've been eating junk all night."

"Yeah, I'm out too," Jason said. "I need a workout in the morning. You game?"

"Not unless you're coming to work out at The Pearl."

Jason exploded in laughter. "It looks like Nautilus threw up in there. The weights are probably gold-plated. I was thinking of doing a couple miles on the beach and the 7 a.m. Soul Cycle class. Vance, are you in?"

He shook his head with a smug grin. "Athena and I always have a date in the morning. Can't miss it."

I let out a grunt, curling one side of my top lip. "You two make me sick. I'm already sorry I got you to buy a condo here. Now I gotta look at this bliss all the damn time." Vance laughed as I leaned to one side so I could pull out my wallet. "Jason, how much do I owe you for tonight?"

Jason waved me off before sliding out of the booth, grabbing his helmet from the other end of the table. "Your face doesn't depress me anymore. That's payment enough. I've gotta head home. D is probably about to call and see where I—"

Just then, his cell phone chimed a familiar tune, as if to say, *see, what did I tell you?* He smirked, pulled his phone from his pocket, and slid his finger across the face. "Hey, babe. I'm leaving right now." He flashed two fingers at me and headed toward the door, fishing for his keys in his pocket.

"I'm heading out, too," Vance said. "Athena and I do our nightly reading at ten o'clock. You want to ride together?"

"Nah," I said, waving him off. "I need a few minutes. Say hey to Thena for me."

I lingered a while longer, watching late-night patrons arrive and depart Whiskey Blue. A few were in groups, but most were couples, dressed to impress one another in their best skin-revealing island attire. Sitting close, smiling into each other's faces or out on the dance floor, taking advantage of a slow night to cling to each other and sway to the beat coming from the speakers overhead.

A salty wind blowing up from the Bay, the aroma of burning wood from a bonfire on the beach, and the buttery scent of lobster tail cooked over hot coals all brought back memories of spending evenings with Charlotte. I longed for those peaceful nights when words were unnecessary. The memory of Charli's body pressed against mine, her scent enveloping me lingered in my dreams.

As soon as she entered my mind, I pushed her back out. Thinking about her wouldn't bring her back to me, wouldn't bring her feelings where I'd needed them to be. She took what she wanted and left me high and dry. It was a wonder I even missed her, but my breath caught in my throat at the thought of her.

Or perhaps what I wanted from her but could have never had.

If I could manage it, I'd never think of her again. It hurt to miss her. It hurt to wish for what she threw away, what I escaped when I ran from New Orleans and buried myself in work.

The idea of repeating the mistake I'd made with Charlotte —falling in love with a person I worked with—was the most glaring reason to never consider Kari Savoy as an option. Long legs, a bubbly personality, and a face card that would never decline notwithstanding, she had signed her paperwork and would not only be an island resident as of this coming Sunday but the newest member of my management staff, whether or not I liked it.

I downed the last of my beer and slid out of the booth, fished my keys from my pocket, and headed for the front door. Jason, who had parked his sport bike next to my less sporty but more powerful Harley, had already left, as had Vance on his Ducati. I secured the chin strap on my helmet and tightened it, then inserted the key and turned the ignition to the ON position, pressing the button to fire up the engine.

Few things gave me more pleasure, or calmed and soothed my nerves better than the symphony of irregular, lumpy rumbles from a Harley engine. I basked in the vibrations for a few moments before I popped the bike into gear, gave it some gas, and rolled through the parking lot. Once I hit the intersection that led me onto the street, I opened the throttle and shot into traffic, speeding toward the end of the island.

Five

KARI

I rolled over, my body heavy with sleep and my mind foggy. My limbs ached from the long drive the day before, but the warmth of the room and the cozy familiarity of Dionne and Jason's duplex a few blocks from the beach eased the discomfort. As I yawned and stretched my arms above my head, I heard footsteps on the tile floor.

"Well, look who's finally awake."

"Ugh," I groaned, arching my back in a delicious stretch. "I guess yesterday took a lot out of me."

The scent of coffee and something delicious filled my nostrils, making my stomach rumble.

"I started to wake you, but I'm pretty sure you snarled at me in your sleep. I figured your drive would go better if you were well-rested."

I pushed myself so I was sitting all the way up, still wrapped in the blanket. "Is Jason here? I'm just wearing a t-shirt and boy shorts."

Dionne shook her head, concentrating on her muffins. She

was poking the golden-brown tops with a toothpick to make sure each one was fully cooked. "He went to work out, then he has a fishing charter today, so he'll probably head straight to the pier."

Whipping the blanket off of my body, I reached for the overnight bag I'd tucked between the couch and the futon and started pulling out items—my toiletry case, a change of clothes, an exfoliating bath puff, and a towel.

"Okay if I hog the bathroom? I need to get on the road."

"Make yourself at home. You want a couple of these muffins to go? I have lemon zinger and apple spice. I'm testing flavors for our new promotion at the shop, and I always make a few extra."

"Sure, they smell great."

A half-hour later, I emerged dressed comfortably in my favorite leggings, an off-the-shoulder graphic tee, and ballet flats. The humidity made my hair voluminous, but I'd wrestled it into a ponytail and wore my signature gold hoop earrings. Aside from shaping my brows and applying a layer of lip balm and sunscreen, I would make the drive bare-faced to let my skin soak up the sunshine.

Dionne poured coffee into a travel mug, placed the cap on, and twisted it closed. Then she placed the mug next to a thermal lunch sack and pushed both to the edge of the counter.

"I made a little care package for you. Bring my mug and lunch sack back here."

"Thanks, D. I'm sure I'll appreciate this around the halfway mark."

I repacked my overnight bag and slung the strap over my shoulder before making my way to the kitchen counter. Flipping the top of the canvas sack open, I smiled at the assortment of muffins, carrots, graham crackers, and a sliced apple.

"I feel like you're sending me off for my first day of school." I held out an arm and waited for her to move around the counter to step into a hug. "I'll let you know when I'm back on the island. I want to settle in before I start work on Monday."

"I can't wait until you're local. Are the kids home this weekend?"

I shook my head. "Both said they were staying at school, so it should be a quick in and out."

After promising to drive safely, I rolled out of the drive-way, heading to the main drag that would take me to the bridge separating Black Diamond from the rest of the world.

It was sunny and warm, with no hint of the storms that had been plaguing the island for the past few months. Light traffic and my playlist made the drive fast and easy. I sipped coffee, ate the muffins Dionne packed for me, and snacked on fruit and crackers as I zipped up the highway. In no time at all, I was turning onto a tree-lined street of houses all in a row with lush green lawns and sedans in the driveways.

It felt like a lifetime, but it wasn't really that long ago that Moses and Reyna were carefree kids in a loving two-parent, two-income home in a safe neighborhood. They were the average suburban upper middle-class family, living in a split-level house with a big backyard and plenty of space for Moses to practice lacrosse moves. Reyna's typical pre-teen bedroom was full of books, dolls, and posters of her favorite groups. They had everything they needed and more.

I had been living in Houston for four years, having worked my way up to an executive position at a boutique downtown hotel. The opportunities for career growth and social event planning were endless. My biggest concern at the time was planning my twenty-fifth birthday celebration, something I had been saving up for and working with my father for months to mark the milestone age.

A driver distracted by a mobile phone crossed the center line on a highway and tore our worlds apart.

The following weeks were a chaotic nightmare. I was

suddenly responsible for decisions I never thought I'd have to make when my father nonchalantly informed me of the clause in his will that I would serve as guardian and executor of the estate if something happened to both him and his second wife. Though Reyna and Moses were technically my stepsiblings, my father wanted me to ensure their stability and keep them together.

What would be the chances of losing them both? Apparently, one hundred percent.

In a matter of days, I was tasked with making a difficult choice: disrupt my siblings' lives by moving them to a new city and forcing them to adapt to more changes or put my life on hold to return home to raise them. Either way, life would be drastically altered.

The decision was obvious, but not without its challenges. While my siblings were taken care of financially, the emotional toll was heavy. But we'd made it—mostly together.

I smiled and waved at the familiar faces along my route—Mrs. Robinson tending to her flowerbed, Mr. Pekoe unloading groceries from his car, and Mr. Rafa and his wife relaxing on their porch swing while their daughters played outside.

Moses had finally moved the last of his things into the off-campus apartment he shared with two other students at Xavier University. Reyna spent most of her time near the SMU campus in Dallas. She shared an apartment, which only worked because Reyna spent a lot of time at her boyfriend's place.

And I was leaving to live and work on Black Diamond. It had never been in my plans to sell the house, but maybe we had outgrown the sprawling five-bedroom home.

As I pulled into the driveway, I narrowly avoided hitting a dusty black sedan. I didn't recognize the car, but I suspected Reyna was involved.

I entered the house through the garage and stepped into the kitchen. My nose wrinkled at the sour smell that permeated the air. A pile of dishes sat in the sink with not enough murky water to soak off the dried, crusted red sauce. On the stove, which was filthy, a few bloated spaghetti strands sat at the bottom of a pot. Next to it was a saucepan of what looked like straight-from-the-jar pasta sauce.

"Well, somebody went wild for spaghetti," I mumbled to myself. I turned to find the kitchen garbage can overflowing. It had been empty when I'd left the morning before, so whoever Reyna brought home had been well-fed, apparently.

Articles of clothing littered the living room—leggings, a t-shirt, a bra, and a pair of men's jeans were haphazardly tossed over the couch and loveseat. I started to pick them up, then decided against it. Reyna's favorite Converse and a pair of men's sneakers were visible under the coffee table.

A pungent aroma filled the room—a mix of herbs, smoke, and an unmistakable skunky scent.

I tilted my head, tuning in to the sounds coming from upstairs. Beneath the bass, I could make out the distinct sound of feminine moans, accompanied by a man's voice and a steady thump. My sister and I had never seen eye to eye, but this… I shook my head and rolled my eyes upward in exasperation. This was a whole new level.

Reyna and her boyfriend had been together since their junior year of high school. They applied to SMU together, and I wasn't surprised when they were both accepted. I drew the line at her living with him, at least not as long as I was controlling the trust that the insurance policies, savings, and any proceeds from the accident settlement poured into. Reyna threw a screaming, crying fit, but I stood my ground.

Fat lot of good it did. They were together all the time anyway, and now they were here. In this house. Having sex. I paced, not knowing if I should go upstairs and bust up their little tryst or let them finish. How long could a couple of nine-teen-year-olds last?

My patience grew thinner by the minute, but after a few

irregularly paced thumps and what sounded like bored moans, I made my move.

Heavy drum beats and lewd lyrics thumped from the other side of the door. I froze, recognizing the song—it was a raunchy rap tune with lyrics that made me blush. She insisted on playing it nonstop as loudly as possible. My jaw clenched as I used the heel of my fist to pound on the door.

"Reyna!"

I gripped the knob and turned it, throwing the door open. My sister straddled the body of a man I didn't recognize, blonde box braids flowing down her back. Her beau sat up, his eyelids droopy and mouth half-open.

Reyna whipped around at the sound of the door opening. "Do you mind?!" she screeched but made no move to cover herself.

"Yes, I mind. Turn that shit off!"

She picked up a slim remote, pointing it at the screen in the corner of the room, muting the TV.

"Happy now?" she spat, tossing the remote onto the cluttered nightstand, then pulled a joint from her companion's fingers and closed her lips around it. The tip glowed, then plumed furiously as she handed it back to him. Her eyes were rimmed red and glassy, and seeing her nude made me realize how thin she had become. She was always petite, like her mother, but she seemed to have dropped some pounds since she'd gone away to school.

Reyna dismounted, landing next to her companion. He scrambled for the blanket to cover himself, scooting back against the headboard.

"You're supposed to be gone all weekend," she said, her voice squeaky with the effort to hold the smoke in her lungs as long as possible. "I thought I'd finally get some fucking peace in this house."

"*You're* supposed to be at school. And who is this guy? What happened to Erwin?"

"Erwin," she said, half-coughing, half-laughing, "is a fuckin' nerd. His parents gave him the lecture about grades and shit. He couldn't come back this semester unless he buckled down. He just wants to study all the time."

She exhaled a column of grey smoke into the air. "Why you askin'? You tryna be a cougar now, Kar? He's about your speed if you're done running through Mose's teachers."

I marched into the room, grabbed the half-smoked joint from her companion, and ground it out in the makeshift ashtray. It was full of evidence that they'd probably been high since they came in the door.

"You can't just bust in here and take my shit, Kari!"

"Get up, get dressed, get downstairs. You," I said, directing my words to the young man clutching a sheet over his body, "need to be up and out of here."

"He's with me. Where's he supposed to go?"

"Back where he came from. I'll drive you to school if I need to, but he is leaving."

Reyna bounded out of bed, standing nude in the middle of her bedroom. "I am so *sick* of your *shit!* You don't get to play Queen Bee anymore, Kari. I'm grown and I can do who and *what* I want."

"Au contraire, little sister. You depend on me for room and board and college tuition. And money, which it appears you're spending on weed, so guess who just lost her monthly allowance until further notice?"

Reyna's face turned red, her eyes twin orbs of fire. Her jaw dropped as she emitted her signature screech. "I *hate* you!"

"Imagine how I feel about you. You left a mess downstairs that I'm not cleaning up, so you and your dick appointment need to get moving."

I stormed out of the room and headed downstairs, pacing until I heard two sets of feet stomping down the steps. Reyna was dressed, her braids pulled into a ponytail and a backpack slung over her shoulder.

"Don't worry about driving me to school. I'll head back with Ronelle." Her date seemed embarrassed as he picked up his jeans and slipped one leg and then the other into them, then sat on the couch to tie his shoes.

"College is supposed to make you smarter, Reyna. If you think you're going anywhere with him with this house a mess—"

"Look, I was planning to clean up before we left. Mo said you'd be gone all weekend." She snatched up her bra and other clothes and stuffed them inside her bag. "But you're kicking Ronelle out, and he's my ride."

"I told you I would—"

"And no thanks to you lecturing me all the way to Dallas. You're the queen of the fucking house. *You* clean it."

"So you come home, feed some guy everything in my refrigerator, leave a mess in the sink, on the stove, the garbage is full—"

"I don't have to do shit you tell me to do. You said we had to go, so we're leaving." She tossed her head toward the young man sitting on the couch, watching our argument. "Get the fuck up, Ronnie," she snapped.

I wanted to grab her by the shoulders and shake the ever-loving mess out of her. Instead, I watched them walk out the door. A few moments later, the engine whined as the car pulled away from the house.

An hour later, I had loaded the dishwasher, mopped the floor, emptied the garbage, and worked out most of my frustrations by scrubbing caked-on pasta sauce off the stove's ceramic cooktop when my cell phone buzzed.

I checked the caller ID and my shoulders sagged. Whether it was from relief or exhaustion would remain to be seen. I picked up the call, pulled out a chair from around the kitchen table, and sat down.

"Let me guess, you just talked to your sister."

"Uh-oh," Moses groaned on the other end of the line. "What she do now?"

I sighed, rubbing the pads of my fingers over my eyes. "Just, you know, brought home some guy, fed him the entirety of my refrigerator, stripped him in my living room, had sex with him in her bedroom, and smoked copious amounts of chronic while doing so. This house stinks like a… whatever a house that stinks like weed smells like."

I couldn't get used to how manly my baby brother sounded lately, but his chesty laugh soothed my soul. Reyna put me through my paces. Moses was the glue that held us together…and kept me from kicking her out of the house.

"Kari, they're freshmen in college," he said around residual chuckles. "They can't afford *actual* chronic. It was probably half dandelion stems."

"How are you so knowledgeable about weed, young man?"

"I'm pre-med. We study stuff like that."

"Sure, Mose. Tell me another lie."

"Well, I'm not into it, but my friends are, uh…experienced," he said after clearing his throat. "So, what did you tell her?"

"That her dick appointment had to leave, and she needed to get downstairs and clean up her mess."

Moses groaned. "Did my big sister say the words *dick appointment*?"

"She did."

He howled, then added, "One night with Dionne on the beach and you're using terms like 'dick appointment.' So, how did '*I'm the boss, do what I say!*' work this time?"

After a pause—because I knew he was waiting to hear my response—I answered. "About as well as you think it did. She told me to go fuck myself and they left."

"Mmmhmm," he hummed, all-knowing and smug.

"You're trying to run her and she ain't hearing none of that noise. She's never been here for that."

"At some point, she has to acknowledge that I'm an authority figure in her life."

"Reyna ain't acknowledging shit about an authority figure," said Moses, laughing as he did so. "I keep telling you what you're doing isn't working. You got to come at it another way."

I smirked. "What are your suggestions, Mr. Xavier University of Louisiana, pre-med?"

"*Shiiiit*," he said, dragging out the word. "I'ma let you and Rey work that out."

"What good are you?"

"I'm Moses Savoy. I'm everything good. So...you got the job, right? You're moving to an island or what?"

I filled him in on the excitement of the day before, including a thorough description of my new boss, Mr. Scott. "You remember you told me your anatomy professor was puckered? Well, this guy is the very definition. Fine as hell, but you could find a picture of him in the dictionary under uptight."

"You would know."

I sucked my teeth and slouched in my chair. "Shut up, Moses. I'm not uptight."

"Yeah, okay. Listen, I'm about to head to a lacrosse scrimmage. I wanted to check in, see how yesterday went. Don't let Reyna get under your skin. She'll fight as long as you do. And she's younger, with more energy and snappier comebacks."

"Yep," I answered, resigning myself to our usual conclusion about our sister. "I wish she could be a little less Reyna."

"At least we know she don't let people give her shit. I'll call her, a'ight, big sis?"

"What did I tell you about dropping consonants like you're not educated at a very expensive university?"

"What did I tell *you* about that respectability politics bullshit? How I talk don't got nothin' to do with how much I done learned."

I shuddered at his purposely poor grammar but laughed. "What you just said bugged the shit out of me. I am indeed uptight. Love you, Mose. Have a good game."

"Scrimmage," he corrected, then added, "Love you, Kar. Be easy."

I ended the call and tucked the phone away, then pulled it back out and tapped out a text.

> Kari Savoy: I love you and I want you to be safe. Let me know you made it back to school.

I wouldn't get a response from her soon, so I headed upstairs to pack up my things to take to Black Diamond. As soon as I entered my bedroom, I called up the episodes of Real Housewives that I'd missed. I wandered around the room, piling the items that I wanted to take with me into two suitcases and a stack of boxes.

And entertaining second and third thoughts about accepting a job four hours away.

I'd thought I was ready. I'd thought we were *all* ready. I wasn't supposed to have to worry about them anymore, but I feared setting Reyna up for a situation where she would be in over her head or put herself in danger.

I had finished packing and my suitcases, stuffed to the gills, stood next to each other just outside my bedroom door. A text interrupted the Nick at Nite lineup as I lounged in bed. I glanced over at it, perched on the charging dock, snatching it up when I realized it was Reyna.

> Lil Sis: I see you tattled on me. Here's your damn text. I'm back on campus.

A chuckle escaped me as I read her message, unexpected

but not entirely surprising given Moses' usual role as referee between us. I carefully crafted a response, fully expecting a snarky comeback in return.

> Kari Savoy: Thanks for letting me know. I'm sure Mo told you I'll be gone for a bit. I'm closing up the house while I am away. Please let me know if you're planning to come home. I can send you some money to get groceries.

> Kari Savoy: And I like to know where you are in case you need me.

> Lil Sis: K. Whatever.

I chuckled to myself, knowing exactly what she was going to say. To my surprise, three dots appeared on my screen, showing that she was typing another response.

> Lil Sis: Mo said you got a job on the beach. Have fun now that you're free.

I grinned, then replied,

> Kari Savoy: We have lost enough of our family. I hope to never be free of you. I'm a phone call away, like always.

A few moments passed, and just when I thought the conversation had ended, the three dots danced again.

> Lil Sis: K. Like I said, whatever.

Rather than bait her and try to get the last word in like always, I locked the phone and put it back on the charging dock.

You got to come at it another way.

Six

DAVIS

A salty ocean breeze drifted through the stone patio at Breakers. Across from me, Vance and Athena were side by side, their tanned faces bathed in sunlight filtering through the white umbrellas shading our table. Both had demolished their breakfasts, leaving nothing but crumbs and smudges of syrup on their plates. Meanwhile, I pushed the remains of pancakes around my plate.

"It's so rude of you to ask us to breakfast, then stare at your food the entire time." Vance stirred a packet of stevia into his mug of green tea while Athena poured cream and sugar into a cup of dark roast coffee. "You've barely said two words since we sat down, and you were quiet during our workout."

"Don't know how you two noticed, the way you were making eyes across the gym and carrying on."

Athena snorted, then drew her lips in to avoid laughing, pulling her attention back to doctoring her coffee refill. It was a local favorite, but it was much too bold for me. I preferred a blonde, lightly roasted blend.

I set my fork down, forcing my gaze up at my breakfast companions. "Sorry. I'm…frustrated and I'm taking it out on you two. You do make me sick, though. Is this mushy phase going to end soon?"

"Nope," Vance answered, dropping an arm behind Athena to rest on the back of her chair. "I'm hoping you find somebody to cake and be mushy with. I thought you'd have that on lock, out here with these beautiful island ladies."

I snickered. "Let's not pretend I live on Barbados, my man. It's literally Texas."

"Are you still mad about your new hire?" Athena asked. "As much as you've been complaining about needing help, even with Vance doing some of the work, I'd think you would be happy."

"She isn't who I would have hired, and I feel *a way* about someone being assigned to my resort without consulting me. What if I don't like her work ethic? What if we don't get along? What if—"

"Bro," Vance interrupted. "She's here. You didn't hire her and can't fire her, but it's not like Calhoun brought her in off the street."

"Sounds like she knows what she's doing." Athena gave me a sympathetic smile. "Aren't you just throwing a tantrum because you didn't get your way?"

"Yes." I scowled, then relaxed and picked up my coffee mug, scowling again to find it empty. "It doesn't matter how I feel anyway. She moves into her condo today. I have to play nice and pretend I'm happy to have her here."

I flagged down a member of the restaurant staff and signaled for a refill on my coffee. They nodded and rushed back into the restaurant.

A playful grin spread across Vance's face. "Oh, *no*. Let her take some work off of your plate— and mine? Poor Davis." A chesty laugh spilled from him. "Make sure you bring her by the Wanderlust suite. She and I are going to be great friends. What was her name? Kerri?"

"Kari," I corrected. "This shit is not funny. I have no time to rework my flow to account for another person."

"Oooh, he's cursing," Athena whisper-yelled to Vance.

Vance leaned forward, steepling his fingers together. "You need to defuse this situation right away. Get on equal footing. You should take her out, tour the island—"

"She's my employee! On what planet would that be appropriate?"

"I didn't say date her, Davis. If you two are going to work together this closely, you need to know more about her than her work habits. This needs to be a partnership. Calhoun is counting on the both of you to pack the place out this summer."

Vance paused, then after a brief hesitation, went exactly where I knew he'd go. "And if things ever have the chance to turn into more, you'll have a foundation of respect and friendship."

I rolled my eyes. "You and I both know it's not a good idea for things between me and an employee to turn into more."

Athena leaned in, brows hiked. "Is there tea? What am I missing?"

"Uhhh…you wanna tell her?" Vance asked me.

I shrugged, flipping a hand in his direction, and went back to sulking. "Go ahead. You're chomping at the bit to tell my business."

"It wouldn't be the first time Davis has fallen for a woman he works with. His last relationship imploded when his coworker at the Maison New Orleans threw him under the bus. Both were in the running for management positions. She got close, expected him to step aside and let her take the promotion. When he didn't, she got mad and reported the relationship. She was promoted to General Manager—"

"The hotel didn't want to be in a position where she could hold anything against them," I added for context.

"Right. Davis then had to work under her. She started holding things over his head, dangling special projects and even a promotion. Davis felt he couldn't get ahead with her at the helm, so he put his degree and years of experience to work turning several nearly failing properties into profitable ventures before answering Calhoun's call to manage The Pearl."

"So...what does that have to do with Kari?"

Vance grinned. "She's his type. Brown-skinned, long legs, big doe eyes, natural hair. Hips...and...*body*. Know what I'm saying?"

Athena nodded, catching Vance's meaning.

"Plus, she has that tenacious Big Dick Energy that's kryptonite to Davis. Didn't you say she told you she wasn't moving here to save your ass?"

"I believe her words were that she wasn't moving to work for an asshole."

I looked up to see our waiter with a mug of fresh coffee. Handing them the empty cup, I waited for them to leave the table before I continued.

"I'm not one of those tragic heroes in those romance novels Athena makes you read. The situation with Charlotte wasn't that dramatic or noble. She made a power play. I knew she wouldn't treat me fairly, and I needed a change of scenery. It was ugly, but I survived. I've dated since, but never someone I worked with."

"First, I don't make Vance do a damn thing," Athena replied. "Second, maybe Kari will be a different experience for you."

"Can we talk about something else, please?"

Vance held his hands up in mock surrender. "Alright, *Mr. Sensitivityyyy*," he sang. "Thena has a few afternoon appointments. You want to ride? Nothing like some wind therapy to clear your head."

I perked at that. "I have never heard a better idea. I'd actually like to avoid being here when Kari shows up. I wish I had more time to settle into the idea."

"She probably does too. Just remember, it's not about you, Davis," Athena said. "It's about the success of The Pearl, and if Kari is the key to making that happen, you need to be ready to work with her."

Laughter erupted from the pool, where a lively game of water volleyball was underway, adding to the idyllic atmosphere of the resort. Their carefree joy was as a reminder of my goals for the place. I wanted to see more scenes like this, guests and residents enjoying themselves without a care in the world. I needed Kari to achieve that.

Athena rolled her wrist to check the time on her smartwatch. "I need to head out. I have some prep for my appointments, and I have to drive in to Corpus Christi."

She smoothed out her colorful strapless sundress as she stood.

Vance rose as well, bending over her to drop a kiss on her lips. "Have a good day. We're going to ride, but you can call me if you need to."

"Ride like you have some sense, Vance Griffin."

"Yes, ma'am...*Athena* Griffin."

"Not yet," she said, winking. "But soon. Love you."

"Love you too, gorgeous."

She waved as she hurried to the gate that led away from the patio to the Paradise tower. Vance resumed his seat, but not before he watched her figure fade in the distance.

"Seriously," I commented with a slow shake of my head. "You're so different. You drink green tea. You read romance novels. You..." I nodded my head toward Athena's retreating figure.

"I...bagged that woman right there. Sight unseen, practically. We make each other happy. You can have that too."

"I'm not likely to have that with an employee."

"Not with that attitude. Unshackle the chains from around your heart, man. It starts with mutual respect. She *wants* to impress you. Let her."

I wanted Vance to be right, but it was hard to trust his optimistic, deeply-in-love point of view. Kari could be a great addition to the team at The Pearl.

Or she could be some corporate lackey, transferred in by Calhoun or MGMT to spy on me. I had to remain professional and keep her at a distance.

No matter how pretty her smile might be.

Seven

KARI

The drive to Black Diamond was easier this time around, knowing I'd be staying for a while and anticipating the excitement of a new job, new surroundings, and a whole new life. Two days before, I'd been nervously rehearsing questions and reciting my confident, practiced responses, telling myself that Davis would be a fool not to welcome me with open arms.

And...he didn't exactly. He acquiesced, which was as much victory as I could claim at the moment. I needed to develop a plan to get on his good side, and that plan had to involve getting started on the actual work I'd been hired to do.

Davis' obvious skepticism gave me pause. I wondered, once again, what I was getting myself into, knowing that I was leaving an empty house behind and a rebellious little sister who knew that I wouldn't be home to moderate her activities. I probably wouldn't know until I was in the thick of it. In the meantime, I could enjoy living in a luxury hotel on an island with access to the beach and multiple pools whenever I needed to soak up some sun.

As the afternoon blazed through the windshield, I pulled into the underground parking deck at The Pearl, followed the directions toward resident and employee parking, and found a spot. I slung a bag over each shoulder, lugged two rolling suitcases toward the elevator, and pressed the button to call it.

A few moments later, the doors slid open. Expecting it to be empty, I lunged forward—into the broad, molded chest of Davis Scott.

His arm shot out, a large hand firmly gripping my shoulder. I steadied myself and backed up, releasing the suitcases I'd rolled across the parking deck.

"Ms. Savoy," he greeted me, in the same crisp tone from our conversation the day before.

"I am *so* sorry. I expected the elevator to be empty."

I moved back a few steps and took in the view of him. He wasn't in his finely tailored, well-fitting suit. Instead, he wore a skintight neon green and black racing shirt and pants, with molded black boots.

"Dionne mentioned you had a bike. I guess I assumed she meant a ten-speed."

He nodded. "I'm headed out for a ride with Jason. Do you ride?" An eyebrow rose as he asked. He shifted the helmet he'd propped against his hip.

"No," I offered quickly. "My brother does. I recognize the gear."

"Ah. Well." He turned and pointed. I followed his gloved finger to a Harley parked a few spots away. It was simple and understated, jet black and shiny chrome. "That's mine," he said quietly.

"A Harley. You're a *serious* biker, then," I commented, smiling. "Moses rides one of those sportbike things."

Davis chuckled deep in his throat, then gripped the helmet in both of his hands. "The younger generation prefer the newer , lighter bikes. Shiny, push button, plastic molding, electric components. This bike is special to me, so I've taken care of it."

"I see." I grabbed the handles of my suitcases. "Well, these won't get themselves upstairs." I waited for him to step out of my way to the elevator.

"Do you need assistance?" And just as I was about to think it was sweet of him to offer to help me, he added, "Justin is in. I'm sure he'd be happy to help." He unzipped a pocket and pulled out his phone.

"No! Don't do that." I maneuvered around him to the elevator with two bags on each limb and pressed the call button again. "I can manage. Thank you."

"No problem." He slipped the helmet onto his head and snapped it into place. In a voice now muffled, he said, "Have a nice day, Ms. Savoy. See you in the morning."

He turned on a heel and made long, purposed strides toward his bike.

What a waste of a nice ass.

Despite telling Davis I didn't need help, I pulled out my phone as soon as he was out of sight and earshot. With more bags and boxes in the car, I would get more use out of a luggage rack. I dialed the number that Justin had slipped me the day before, should I need help.

"Yo," came the light, friendly greeting.

"Hi, Justin. It's Kari Savoy. The new...uh...Director of Marketing."

"Oh, hey. Davis had housekeeping clean your condo and guest services has your keys. When do you think you'll make it in?"

"Right now, actually. Any chance I could get a luggage cart?" I glanced over the grouping of items surrounding me. "I've got a lot of stuff, and I'd rather not drag my belongings through the lobby."

"I feel you on that. I'll be right down."

"You don't have to come down. I don't want to get you in trouble with Davis. I just need—"

"Don't worry about it. I move around a lot. I'll grab your keys and be right there."

While he was on his way down, I went back to my car and lugged the rest of the bags and boxes from the trunk. When the elevator chimed and the doors slid open to reveal Justin in dark slacks and a short-sleeved white hotel polo pulling a wheeled cart, I was more than ready for him to load all of my things onto it.

He handed me a sealed manila envelope with a key fob inside.

"We call these keys. You need a fob to get in and out of the hotel and the parking garage after 10 p.m. You also need a fob to get to the residence tower. This stops hotel guests from wandering around on owner floors."

The elevator doors opened to the main level of the Paradise tower. I heard the bustle of the reception area as we passed the owner services office, the bank of mailboxes, and the busy cafe, then crossed the hall to a second bank of elevators. When it arrived, he glided the luggage cart inside.

"Swipe your fob. Make sure it's working."

I pulled out the device and ran it across the infrared reader. "What floor am I on?"

"Nine," he answered. I pressed the button, and the cube glided up soundlessly, then chimed as the doors slid open. Justin nodded to me to step out. He followed with the cart and tilted his head to the left, and we started walking.

"So you came down from Austin, huh? Never been."

"It's hot. Not bad for the arts or tech, though."

"Yeah, I've been meaning to hit that South by Southwest joint for a while. Just haven't had the chance. Getting a job was more important, and when this position popped up…" Justin chatted while ambling down the hallway. "Jumped on it."

"How old are you, Justin?"

He grinned, showing off a set of dimples. "Twenty-six."

"And how long have you worked for The Pearl?"

"*Psssh*," he hissed, making a whoosh sound with his teeth. "Practically since before it opened. I hounded the management company, and they eventually hired me to work guest services. Worked my way up to Davis' assistant. He needs a buffer between him and the staff. I figure I'll do this a while, stack some cash, figure out my life."

"Not a bad plan. A resort hotel is a nice place for a kid to work."

"Yes, ma'am."

My eyes narrowed. "I don't think I'm old enough for you to be calling me ma'am."

Justin laughed, those dimples making an appearance. "Sign of respect, ma'am."

"Boy, if you don't stop…"

Justin cackled louder. "Ay, if you're gonna call me shit like *kid* and *boy*, I'm gonna call you *ma'am*. I'm grown." He stopped in front of a door at the end of the hallway. "Home, sweet home. This is you."

I noticed the long sunlit path from the elevator, thick wood doors, golden wall sconces every few feet, and enormous picture windows. When I opened my door each morning, I would be greeted by views of the hotel pool and sauna, the outdoor entertainment venue, and beyond that, white sand and blue-green waters.

If there was any lingering doubt that I'd done the right thing, they were gone, washed away as I took in the view outside my home. And that was just the outside of the suite.

I swiped the fob across the reader. It flashed green and the locks disengaged.

The suite smelled…not just clean but scrubbed. It was bright and airy, ceiling fans turning slowly, our feet echoing on stone tile. The walls were a muted taupe with hotel-style art hanging along the walls—architecture, abstract paintings, photographs in distressed wood frames.

The condo was immaculately organized, from the large kitchen island, perfect for seating four people at a bar height table, to the cozy living room furnished with a comfortable couch and matching armchair and ottoman. The flat screen TV was mounted on a wall that divided the living room and bedroom. On the other side of the divider, a king-sized bed was bathed in sunlight streaming in from the patio. A set of pocket doors led to the closet and the bathroom.

"Not bad, not bad," I mused, wandering through the suite while Justin rolled the luggage rack inside. After living in a five-bedroom home with two young adults, downsizing to a condo and living alone would take some getting used to.

"A'ight, so…" Justin huffed while sliding the last box against the wall in the entryway, then stood, stuffing his polo shirt into the back of his pants. "The corner units are smaller, but the view is better than the bigger units, so we set you up in this one."

He gestured toward the wall of windows, but I'd already taken notice. Nine floors below, guests sunbathed at the pool. A few were at the swim-up bar, and the patio bar was bustling, but my view, mostly, was Black Diamond Bay.

"Is this what all the condos look like?"

"Pretty much. The condos with two or more bedrooms have wrap-around balconies. Then there two penthouses. One is owned, the other is for sale. They have their own elevator lobby."

"I'd love to see one of them."

"You'll make your way around, I'm sure. I wish I lived on property."

I turned, frowning in surprise. "You don't?"

He pulled out a chair from where it was neatly tucked at the kitchen island and slid into it. He swung one leg back and forth, a shiny black Oxford keeping time with his rhythm.

"Nah. Only management gets the option, and only Davis and now you—actually do."

"Oh." I sat in the chair next to him. "Why is that? Is it not a good thing to live on property?"

Justin smirked. "I heard you know the industry. What's the spot you worked at?"

"The Fairmont Golf Resort at Austin."

"Would you live there?"

"No," I answered quickly, laughing. "The Fairmont is for people who think they're semi-pro golfers in the middle of nowhere. It's not on a beach. It doesn't have this view. Don't tell me I'm going to regret being excited about living here."

"I ain't said all that. I'd love to live on property and have access to the pools and restaurants all day and all night. The Pearl is a nice spot, but it's still going through some growing pains. Some of the management like to leave this place behind at the end of their shift."

"And is Davis one of those people? You can tell me. I told him he was uptight to his face."

Justin laughed, tossing his head back and putting every tooth on display. "Okay, Kari...you kinda wild. We're gonna get along. Davis is a cool dude once you get to know him."

"Is getting to know him the problem?"

He bounced his head back and forth. I took that as a yes. "He keeps to himself. Some drama at a hotel he worked before keeps him quiet, head down. He's serious about this place, takes everything that happens here personally."

"I hear the owner puts a lot on his shoulders."

He confirmed, his head bobbing. "Between him and MGMT, he doesn't get a moment's peace. Davis feels like it's his job to dig the hotel out of this hole the owner dug. Which is why it's a good thing he hired you."

"He didn't really hire me," I muttered. "Unfortunately, I'm a pawn in some game between Davis and the owner. And I'm nervous about being in the middle."

Justin winked, then hopped down from the chair. "Don't trip. Davis is some bark, but very little bite. He's trying to make guests and owners happy while keeping Calhoun in Houston where he belongs. And it's our job to help him do that."

He glanced around, pointing at the neat pile of my belongings stacked against the wall. "You need help with any of this?"

I shook my head. "I've kept you from your post long enough. I hope you get to enjoy some of your weekend."

He grinned. "No doubt. I've got my riding gear in my backpack. Ready to hit the streets as soon as I'm off."

"Riding gear? Like...motorcycle riding?"

"Yeah." He stood, pushing his chair in. "Why?"

"I've never met so many people that ride before. I ran into Davis in his gear when I arrived."

"Oh, yeah. Davis, his friend Vance, Jason—we ride together sometimes. His bike is bigger, better. A classic. I'm building a bike, so he helped me design it, dig around for parts."

I pondered that morsel of intel for a long moment. On the surface, Davis didn't strike me as a man that would take time to help someone build a bike from scratch, down to helping him scavenge for parts. Maybe Justin was right. Maybe Davis wasn't as uptight as he'd come across.

Justin laughed at my thoughtful expression, then headed for the door. "Lots of surprises around this place."

I nodded my understanding and locked the door behind him when he left, then turned to view my new home for the foreseeable future.

Here goes everything, Kari.

I squealed, then headed to find my phone and call Dionne.

Eight

DAVIS

Before I could remind myself that Kari was a member of my team whose help I desperately needed, I fell victim.

"Good morning!" she chirped, setting an overfull tote bag next to my desk. "I wasn't sure what time to come in. Or where I'd be working, so I'm dragging my desk around with me."

I'd unlocked my office and, after a few minutes, Kari entered, commanding attention. My eyes followed the contours of her body, lingering on the curve of her hips and the crisp cotton blouse tucked in at her waist. The top two buttons were undone, revealing a pearl pendant that gleamed against her skin. A mass of voluminous curls were tamed into a low ponytail at her nape.

"Ms. Savoy." I cleared my throat, bringing my eyes to hers. "Good morning."

She took a turn in the center of my office. Like most people, she was drawn to the cabinet that held my model bike collection. She paused in front of it, then bent over to peer more closely. Long, shapely legs, accentuated by a high-waist skirt, drew my attention and held it hostage.

"Wow! Did you build these?"

I blinked away the distraction—not to mention a growing, unneeded attraction. At least I'd had breakfast and began my day before she brought the scent of something floral with vanilla and musk highlights to my consciousness. "Ms. Sav—"

"They're Harley models, right?" She pulled one of the glass doors open and reached inside to pick up one of the models.

"Don't!" I stood, barking the word louder than I intended to.

Her shoulders jerked. She yanked her hand back, whipping her head around to glare at me, eyes wide.

"Please," I began again, but like a civilized person, with one hand raised and almost pleading with her. "They are meaningful to me. A few are quite old, and I don't like people touching them. If…if you wouldn't mind?" I directed her to the chairs in front of my desk. "Please have a seat."

"Well, damn," she muttered, pushing the door closed. My heartbeat slowed to a steady thump the further away from the cabinet she moved. She took a seat in one of the chairs in front of my desk. "You can call me Kari."

I sat again, then exhaled, rolling my eyes up to hers. "Actually, I cannot."

"Cannot? Like, physically cannot? You scared of me?" She tipped her head, a smile on thick, glossy lips. "You call Justin by his first name."

"Until we become more acquainted, it's more appropriate. And professional. How was your first night on the property?" I asked, swiftly changing the subject.

"Nice," she answered easily, crossing one leg over the other. One of her feet, clad in heels, swung to the beat of the muted music that was always playing overhead. At some point, I tuned it out, but watching her body fall in line with the rhythm, I noticed it again.

She looked well-rested and energetic, a good sign.

"I took a long walk around to acclimate myself. The grounds are beautiful, and there's so much to offer. I am going to love living nine floors above work. Back home, my commute was at least forty-five minutes. I have questions about the condo I'm staying in, though."

"Is there an issue?" I asked, sorting through the reports that Justin had left on my desk. "I thought you would like the corner, but I can move you if—"

"I love the corner, actually. I wanted to know if I could... you know, personalize the place."

"Personalize it?" I stopped sorting and peered up at her.

"Yeah. Take down that stuffy hotel wall art and put up my own. Just a few light touches."

My head tilted slightly, betraying my confusion. "Is the condo not sufficiently decorated?"

"Sure, if I want it to look like I live in a hotel."

"You *do* live in a hotel."

She laughed, then sighed, glancing out of the window at the surf in the distance. "You take things so literally, Mr. Scott. I'll keep that in mind."

"Art and minor decorative improvements should not be an issue. Paint and any changes to flooring will require approval."

I went back to sorting the stacks of the usual reports, glancing at each of them before moving them aside. Justin provided notes on issues that needed attention, messages from the finance department...threats from Calhoun... and summarized them on the top sheet. So far, we were running well.

"Great. I'm excited to get started. So, from our conversation at my interview, you have a lofty goal and not enough time to achieve it."

"Correct," I confirmed. "Today, you'll meet your staff, and I'll run through the programming we've been able to launch. The team has been used to doing things without having a lead, so they are a small but mighty group. I don't have room in my budget to increase your headcount, so work with what you've got and fill in the gaps."

"How does Calhoun expect you to produce the targets he's trying to hit with so few people?"

"Simple. Calhoun thinks the hotel runs itself. He thinks all we have to do is write the contracts and everything else just happens. He doesn't understand that there are people behind everything that has to be done."

I met her furrowed brows with a shrug of my shoulders. "He made his money in gas stations and convenience stores. He heard hotels were an excellent investment that offer a high return. Unfortunately, this venture has taken more effort and money than he seems to think it should. I'd like to hear any ideas you might have to get him off my back."

"Of course." She nodded, folding her arms across her chest. I could already see the wheels in her mind turning. "Once I'm up to speed, I'll create a project plan to move quickly."

"Fine. I'll show you to your office so you can get started."

I led her down a hallway, pausing a few doors down. "You'll meet Vance, eventually. He and I are old friends. He owns Wanderlust Travel and rents this space. He and his fiancée, Athena, bought a condo here last year. They're just a few floors up from you. She's a concierge nurse if you find yourself in need of medical attention."

Further down the hall was an office outfitted with furniture, filing cabinets, a round table and chairs for small meetings and a view of the golf course. "This space should be sufficient, but please let me know if it isn't. I'll ask your team to come by to meet you. You can set up your work routines directly."

She stepped into the room, warmed by the morning sun, and slowly turned, her eyes drinking in every detail. The room wasn't luxurious; it was just big. But Kari smiled as if it was a corner office, moving toward the L-shaped oak desk and resting her palms on its surface reverently.

"Are the desk and credenza sufficient?" I asked, nodding toward the low, shallow cabinet for all the files she would need to store. "Do you need a bigger desk? A different desk? Another filing cabinet?"

She turned to me, a smile brightening her face.

"If you could see the closet I had to share with a woman that ate a tuna salad sandwich at her desk every day, you'd understand why this is special." She sighed, then finished with, "It's perfect. The office, the desk. The view, well…"

She bobbed her head side to side. "I had hoped for a beach view, but I suppose the gardens will do."

"I'm pleased you like it, Ms. Savoy."

"Well, I'll get set up straightaway," she said, moving across the office to open the blinds wider, allowing more of the sun's rays into the room. I turned to leave, but she called after me. "So, should I call you Mr. Scott?"

"That would be appropriate."

"I mean, if you're going to call me Ms. Savoy, I should call you Mr. Scott, right?"

"You may call me whatever you like, Ms. Savoy."

She smirked, then rolled her eyes and turned away.

"Is there an issue?"

"Nope. I'm fine. Mr. Scott."

I moved toward the door. "Come to my office when you're settled in. I'll share our current efforts and where you can pick up the reins."

"See you in a bit," she replied, already emptying her tote onto her desk.

On the short walk to my office, I watched Justin approach from the other direction.

Justin Lange was tall, thin, and wiry. His hair was styled in neat locs and tapered on the sides. A wide white smile often graced his long face, and his smooth ebony skin seemed to soak up the sun over the summer and fall.

He and I were cordial to each other until the day I saw him weaving in and out of traffic on a sporty Yamaha bike. Our conversations had evolved from stiff work chatter to bikes and motors since he was attempting to build a bike from parts pilfered from other machines.

"So…" Justin crossed one leg over the other, revealing a pair of black Coach loafers and no socks. "Have you seen her today?"

"Her?"

"Man, you know who I mean."

"I just showed Ms. Savoy to her office."

"Okay, so…" He paused, wiggling his brows.

"What are you referencing?"

Justin laughed. "Every once in a while, I throw out a test to see if you're better at picking up hints. That skirt? She's *wearing* it. Them legs are legging, bro!"

I cleared my throat. "Find your professionalism, Justin."

"A'ight., sorry. It's just…she's a *nice* addition to the staff. She's mad pretty."

"That's a good thing?"

"Can't hurt." Justin shrugged his slight shoulders. "Davis…"

"Justin—"

"I know how you are with new people. You can't afford to spend too much time in this stiff, standoffish thing you fall into. Help her feel welcome. It has to come from the top."

"How have I not made her feel welcome? I assigned her a nicer condo, gave her a prime parking spot, and I just showed her to an office that's probably the largest workspace she's ever had."

"I'm not accusing you of being unfriendly. Just…" Justin

paused, his head ticking to the right like it was an impulse he couldn't control. "You come off uptight."

I frowned. "Did Ms. Savoy speak to you about me?"

"Everybody speaks to me about you." He leaned forward, resting his elbows on the desk. "She's about to be your new best friend. She needs to feel like you trust her, that you value her opinion. She wouldn't be here if she couldn't do the job. You know talent when you see it. *I'm* killin' the game, right?"

He didn't wait for me to agree. At first glance, the skinny kid with an easy smile didn't seem to fit the idea of an assistant property manager, but—and I would never admit it aloud—Justin excelled at his job, and I had management plans for him.

"I helped her move in last night," he mentioned. I didn't react, but I paid attention. "She's cool people. Talkative. Energetic. The place could use some life, and I'm not talking about that geriatric fistfight that almost broke out last week."

I grimaced at the memory of two middle-aged residents about to come to blows over a man who, from my observation, didn't deserve the attention.

"She's interested in helping you put this hotel on its feet, so loosen up, Davis! And practice using her first name. You'll get nowhere with that *Ms. Savoy* stuff."

"My training—"

"—is good on paper, but bullshit in this building. This isn't the Ritz-Carlton. We play Bob Marley and the Beach Boys. We have a laid-back vibe, no matter how much Calhoun wants to charge for these rooms. She won't forget you're her boss if you call her by her first name. And if you want her help to get Calhoun off your back, you need her to be more than your employee. She needs to be a co-conspirator. An accomplice. An ally. Do you hear what I'm saying, Davis? You get me?"

Getting close to another woman that I'd spend nearly every waking hour with? I'd taken that risk before, and it didn't end well. It was the reason I was at an island hotel, away from everyone I knew.

Familiar and casual were difficult, but if I wanted to keep my job and make The Pearl the success it was built to be, I was going to have to do hard things.

———

"So…we have three weddings, a family reunion, a sorority event, and the monthly owners' mixer coming up. Those are all booked in event spaces, so I should be able to see…"

Kari tapped at the laptop keyboard, deftly moving through OPERA, the resort's hospitality management system. Though the Fairmont used a different system, most of them worked the same, highlighting booked and free areas of the resort.

"Good," she muttered, sitting back as the updated screen loaded. "We have plenty of space available to work with."

"I believe that was the point of hiring you," I said.

"Obviously. I needed to see it on paper, so to speak. Now we need to fill them."

"No problem," Justin quipped from the other side of the table. "Think about your staff, though. You'll be tapped if we take on another big event. We only have so many people and so much space with so much budget."

"Justin is right. We don't have the personnel to stretch ourselves too thin," I added.

"I'm aware," Kari said, mild irritation coming through. "This ain't my first rodeo, gentlemen. We also can't pass up opportunities for revenue. I think we should go hunting— seek out the kinds of events that would use the available space with minimal staff. What about corporate guests? They'd all be gone by Friday at noon."

"We offer corporate packages," I admitted. "And you're right about the weekday bookings. While corporate events require a certain level of attention, they're usually less demanding than weddings and reunions."

"Exactly!" Kari exclaimed, clapping her hands together in excitement. "Corporate retreats, team-building events, multi-day meetings—especially if they want to offer an afternoon of golf, a tour of the island, maybe bring a spouse and book the spa."

"I don't disagree. Corporate events have long been on the list, but I haven't had the time to implement them. This hunting idea you have—that sounds like hours on the phone selling the resort, and I've been too busy looking for flour for our flagship restaurant."

"That's exactly why I was hired, Davis," Kari said, singing the words while scribbling a note across a bright yellow legal pad. "Leave it to me. Get ready to see a lot more people here during the week."

"May I remind you that Calhoun expects a full hotel this summer? I'm much more worried about Memorial Day through Labor Day."

"Understood," said Kari, who did not seem nearly as worried as she should.

"Then you also understand that we are working on a tight deadline. We need to play our cards right, or it's the end of our jobs," I said, reminding her that this was as much her problem as it was mine.

"I hear you," Kari reassured me. "But if we panic, we'll make costly mistakes. Let's stick to the plan."

My brows rose. "There's a plan?"

Kari grinned at me, her eyes sparkling. "Of course. It's all coming together."

After our meeting concluded, I watched her from my office window as she strolled the grounds with a few members of the events staff. I had tasked them with reviewing every booking, top to bottom. Trailing them was Vance, his iPad and camera at the ready.

Kari was already a breath of fresh air. The staff, who were probably the happiest about her arrival, already gravitated to her instead of me. She was an infectious presence, someone who found magic in the mundane and wasn't afraid to share it.

With Kari already elbow-deep in her role, I now had time to focus on my actual job. A stack of reports sat waiting to be reviewed: revenue projections, resource allocation, customer feedback—the numbers wouldn't crunch themselves.

I only noticed the passing hours by the moving shadows in my office. I barely paused to refill my water bottle and blew through my usual dinner hour. A soft knock on the door broke my long, lingering gaze into the screen of my laptop. Vance leaned against the doorjamb in a t-shirt and jeans.

"You plan on working all night?"

I stretched, laughing at the popping of my joints. "I guess I got caught up. Kari took a huge boulder of work off of my desk, and now, I can focus."

"See? I told you she'd work out. Now you owe me, and I've come to collect."

"I'm afraid to ask how."

Vance laughed, then stepped into my office, leaning over to grip the back of a guest chair. "Athena and Kari met this afternoon and they haven't stopped chattering since. They're up there at our place, squawking about some dating show where people get married before they even meet in person. *Please* join us for dinner so I can have a man to talk to?"

I laughed, pushing my chair back from the desk. My stomach was at may back and had been rumbling for over an hour. Now I had an excuse to leave my office.

"For Athena's cooking, I can be convinced to help you out."

Every time I visited Vance and Athena's condo, the warm hues, framed photos on the wall depicting their adventures together, and the plush and comfortable furniture always made me feel at home. In comparison, my condo was sparse, outfitted with only the necessities. Kari's remark about wanting to decorate her condo and make it her own made me think, for the first time, about doing the same.

Calhoun made me feel as if I was temporary and could be replaced, so I didn't see the value in settling in. Lately, I'd realized that I'd had the longest tenure of the GMs he had hired, and as much as he complained, if he was going to replace me, he'd have done it by now. So long as Kari and I were successful in making it a good summer at The Pearl, Calhoun was stuck with me.

Us. He was stuck with *us*.

Athena turned from the stove as Vance and I came through the door. Her hair was pulled into a headwrap, and she wore a black ankle-length caftan. Kari sat at the counter, a glass of wine in one hand as she animatedly described something with the other. I salivated at the scent of fried chicken, vegetables, rice, and cornbread muffins that filled the air.

"You found him!" Athena said, her face lighting up. "Dinner will be ready in ten. Hope you're hungry."

"Starving," I admitted, stealing a glance at Vance, who was pouring himself a glass of scotch. "Vance found me just in time."

"Hello, Mr. Scott. I did not expect to see you after hours," Kari said, her face flushing slightly as I took a seat next to her.

"I can step out if you need to continue the Davis-bashing session."

"You sit right there," said Athena. "We finished bashing you hours ago. We've moved on to bashing strangers on dating game shows."

"Help me, Davis," Vance groaned. "How do you have six seasons of people marrying someone sight unseen—"

"Vance acts like proposing that we buy a condo on an island together after we met for the first time is any better."

"I waited until day four to ask you to move here with me."

Athena served dinner, and the conversation picked up, flowing from work to TV shows and books. I relaxed, feeling like I could breathe for the first time in a long time.

Kari's responses to comments and questions gave me new insight. I was so surprised at her being thrust upon me that I had not tried to get to know her. I hadn't even read the résumé she left on my desk. The mention of a brother and sister, a sad reference to the loss of her parents, her six years at The Fairmont—I had so much to learn about my employee. My *partner*.

Eventually I had to force myself from the clutches of the deep, comfortable couch.

"This has been a great time," I declared. The room was warm, made more cozy by a few glasses of alcohol, the company of good friends, and a woman I was gaining more respect for by the second. "I appreciate the invite as always, but my days begin early, so I will take my leave—before Vance begins another embarrassing story about our college days."

"I'll tell them all eventually." Vance and Athena stood to see me out.

Kari followed me to the door, slinging a crossbody bag over her head. "I'm going, too. I'm not fully unpacked, and I have a few hours of work waiting for me in the morning." She winked at me, then threaded an arm through mine. "Shall we?"

As we left the warm, laughter-filled condo, the cool night air felt like a sobering balm to my flushed skin. The stars seemed especially bright, casting a glow over the building. I was ever so aware of the proximity of Kari's body as we walked to the elevator in comfortable silence.

Living on an island resort had its perks; one of them was being able to hear the rush of waves on quiet nights. I stopped at a viewpoint overlooking the beach and Kari stopped with me. We stood there for a moment, taking in the serene view. The moon reflected off the water, casting a silvery path across the surface of the sea.

"I hope I never tire of this view," Kari murmured, her voice soft.

"I haven't yet," I admitted. "It's one of the few constants that keep me sane, that brings me back when I go off property, that makes me pick up the phone when Calhoun calls."

We stood in comfortable silence for a few seconds before she squeezed my arm gently. "Athena wasn't sure you'd come to dinner."

"Are you disappointed that she was wrong?"

"Not at all, Mr. Scott. I'm glad you came."

"As am I. I hope you'll enjoy your time at The Pearl, however long it lasts."

"I'm here for the long haul. I hope you're prepared to meet me halfway."

"We'll see about that," I responded, looking down at her. "Let's get to work."

Nine

KARI

I sucked down some kind of orange concoction at a table in the corner of Tikis & Cream. It was late afternoon, and after a few long days in the office, Davis cut out to take a ride, and I texted Dionne to see if she wanted to meet somewhere for dinner. I was already tired of eating at Breakers.

Dionne said to meet her at the shop, where she made me a drink to enjoy while she went through her closing routine. While she was normally meticulous, tonight she was going the extra mile, scrubbing and moving bins around and setting everything just right.

"Girl, what are you doing? This slushie thing is good, but I need food."

"Ameenah is working tomorrow, and I want her to see that I took good care of her shop. This place is her baby."

"You scrubbed the tables and the counters, organized the freezer, took out the garbage, mopped the floor, wiped down all the appliances, and used disinfectant spray on the phone and the point-of-sale machine. It's clean. It looks great. I'm hungry. Let's. *Go.*"

"Fine, I'm done." Dionne put away her cleaning supplies in a cabinet below the sink, then crossed the room to pull the metal shade down over the counter that overlooked the bay. She slung a satchel across her chest and pulled out a set of keys. "I forgot how cranky you get when you don't eat."

I followed her out of the shop, then watched her pull the door shut tight and key both of the locks. Then she flipped the OPEN sign to CLOSED and tucked the keys away. "So, tell me about your first week at work. And don't leave out any hot goss about Davis Scott."

I laughed. "The only hot goss I have about Davis is that he collects miniature Harley models. And he doesn't let people touch them."

"That's not surprising. Or hot."

Dionne and I strolled the boardwalk, a pedestrian-only walkway that ran from one end of the public beach to the other. I was quickly becoming acclimated to island life and liked spending my breaks shopping the high-end stores and eating at fine restaurants at the southern end. I wanted to form a habit, though, of getting out of the hotel and frequenting the northern end, where casual shops and restaurants beckoned tourists and residents alike.

We turned into Seafood Alley and grabbed a booth at the back of the restaurant. Our server took drink orders and left us to browse menus.

"I'm going to eat fresh caught seafood until I'm sick of it," I told Dionne, my eyes already scanning the menu. "I don't even want to know where Austin gets its seafood from."

"Houston," she answered. "Tell me about work. And Davis."

"Tell you *what* about Davis?" I peered at her over the center fold of the menu. "You've known him longer than I have."

"But you're close to him. You see him all day, every day. And don't tell Jason, but that man is *fine*."

"As you've mentioned."

"You don't think he's good-looking?"

I'd been trying not to think about it, actually.

Davis lived on the twelfth floor, on the same side of the tower as my unit. It wasn't lost on me how much emphasis Justin put on Davis' efforts to make me comfortable. He'd given me a coveted corner unit, made sure the view was nice, and the suite had been impeccably cleaned. And he seemed concerned that I wasn't happy when I arrived.

I wanted very badly to chalk up my warm feelings about his effort to being grateful at the attention, but a part of me recognized that the loneliness of the past few years made it easy to take niceties and pleasantries to heart. Davis was just doing his best to be a good manager to someone he desperately needed on staff.

"It's not that I don't think he's good-looking," I explained. "Him in his riding gear?" I tilted my head and hiked my brows. "He acts like he knows it. I'm not trying to jumpstart my love life with my boss. Maybe I *should* let you hook me up with some island dick. What's the dating situation around here?"

"How would I know?" Dionne smirked. "I moved here with a man. But you need to be careful. This ain't Jamaica. You'll end up with some relocated Wisconsin dick." She sucked down a mouthful of water and rolled her eyes with a pop of her lips. "It's...not nearly as exciting of a prospect."

"Good reminder," I said, nodding.

"And a lot of the men you come into contact with won't be staying on the island."

"Maybe I'm looking for a good time, not a long time."

"I'm just saying, don't get caught up with these men looking for exotic island hookups. Maybe you should play it safe with someone you know first."

"Dionne."

"What?" she asked, innocent countenance on her face.

"You aren't slick at all. There is zero chance of anything happening with my *boss*."

My stomach growled a loud protest that I hadn't eaten since an early lunch at Breakers. I returned my attention to the menu.

"I work with my husband. Besides, I'm not saying you have to date him. Just…let him knock some dust off."

A mental image of stiff, quiet Davis Scott knocking dust off of anyone made me burst into laughter. "He'd probably call me *Ms. Savoy* the whole time."

"'kay…that could be hot."

"I can't be thinking about that man knocking anything off of me. I'm still getting used to Davis. He's very…regimented. Anyway, we had a great week. As long as he lets me do my job, Davis and I will be fine. I don't need anything fucking that up."

My first week had been a success, with three events booked and several interested parties reaching out to me for future bookings. My tactic of 'hunting for business' had proven successful at the Fairmont, and I was determined to continue using it in my new position.

The first of my long-range tasks was to update the resort website to showcase all the amenities available. Davis and Vance had commissioned high-quality photos of every tower and event space but never had them uploaded with updated information. We couldn't book features we weren't boasting about. The Black Diamond Bullhorn, a local newspaper, ran short ads for free, as did the online register. I utilized these resources to spread awareness of The Pearl Resort and its offerings.

My stomach growled so loud, it drowned out my thoughts. I quickly glanced down at my menu, a desperate attempt to mask my embarrassment. Dionne, however, just laughed louder and waved over our server.

"I don't know why I get a menu. I order the grilled chicken and shrimp pasta with a Caesar salad every time I come here."

I ordered the lobster bisque and pan-seared scallops with spinach.

"You were always good with events," Dionne commented after the server had left with our orders. "That's why I made you plan everything. You remember how we used to throw ideas around? I bet we still have the same magic. You saved my ass all four years, so let me help save yours."

"I'm mostly focused on an idea to fill the hotel this summer. That will give us a little length on the rope Calhoun has around Davis' neck. I was thinking…what if we had some kind of summer series? Something recurring to bring residents back time and again, but also a reason to bring people to the island?"

"Hmmm. Like a theme that could carry all summer."

"Yeah. Fun, family-friendly programming during the day, something area businesses could sponsor. Food, drinks, concerts at night. If it's someone big, someone popular, it would definitely bring people here."

"Who, though? I know *we* think Black Diamond is the shit, but like I said, this ain't Jamaica."

"But that's just it—we're *not* the Caribbean. The prices are moderate in comparison. No passport required. You could actually drive here. We could advertise it as a budget escape."

"So, all you have to do is reach out to all the famous entertainers you know and ask them to set up on a man-made island off the coast of Texas for the summer."

"Right. If only I knew—"

I froze in place. Goosebumps broke out, racing down my arms. I blinked, staring at Dionne. "But you do. *You* know someone who knows hip-hop's number one artist. The world hasn't heard from Gage Coleman in years. He could do a pop-up concert and his fans would swarm this island."

Dionne twisted her lips to the side. "Wade spends his summers here. Gage...not so much."

"He has a house here, though, right? Maybe they haven't started planning their summer yet? If they could kick off the season for us, I could capitalize off of that and get other acts to follow suit. Maybe they have friends that would like to book a weekend. Maybe they'd even be willing to close the summer out too."

"So I'm supposed to ask my boss if I can talk to her music industry boyfriend about doing a favor for my best friend and her failing hotel?"

"Yes. Yes, you are. What's the worst he can say?"

"He can say no! And then what?"

"Nothing ventured, nothing gained. I'm in the same place. But if he says yes? I'm on my way to being a hero."

Dionne looked at me, lips pulling into a small, begrudging smile. "How do you always know how to make an argument seem completely reasonable when it's absolutely unhinged?"

I flashed her a quick grin, relieved that my recognized cannon of logic had once again made its mark. "It's a talent. And it's not all that unhinged. They have homes here—it's understood that they spend a lot of time here. It won't hurt to ask...or beg."

As the server arrived with our meals, we fell into silence. I ate like I hadn't eaten in days, savoring the rich bisque and flavorful scallops as my mind looped back to our conversation filling with the possibilities if we could get Gage Coleman and Wade Marshall to perform. Opening or closing the summer would put the resort on the map like nothing else could. Dionne's connection to him wasn't ideal, but it was our only shot. If she asked her boss, who asked her boyfriend, who requested a favor from his best friend, and they all said yes… We'd be in business.

"Okay, I'll give it a shot," Dionne conceded after inhaling half of her Caesar salad. "I'll at least talk to Ameenah. This could be big, not just for the resort but for the island. But remember, no guarantees."

"I'll owe you in a major way if this works out."

"Mmmhmm. Keep that same energy when I need you to repay the favor."

"How did I know this would end up in me subscribing to your summer yoga program?"

"Oh, *honey*. As soon as registration opens," she replied with a wide grin.

————

As the arm to the parking garage lifted, I felt the pavement rumble beneath me, then caught a black blur zipping past while I maneuvered between stone columns to my parking space. I grabbed my bag from the passenger seat and exited the car in time to see Davis across the aisle dismounting from his Harley.

He removed his helmet and nodded in my direction, then lifted the seat to retrieve his wallet and a pair of shades from the compartment underneath.

"Good evening, Ms. Savoy," he called, approaching me. "You're out late."

I rolled my eyes at his insistence on being so formal. It was a quirk that I was going to have to get used to. "Good evening, Mr. Scott. You wouldn't know I was out late if you were not *also* out late."

He actually smiled and replied, "It was too nice of a night to not get out and ride. I like to leave the property every once in a while."

"As do I. I had dinner with Dionne. Were you with Jason?"

"Yes."

We walked slowly, ambling toward the elevators. Davis tucked his helmet into his waist, under his arm. He wore similar gear to the outfit I saw him in a few days before, except it was bright green. Form-fitting, outlining every muscle in his arm and torso. I tried not to stare, but Dionne's teasing over dinner was getting to me. I had to work at a fever pitch to put Davis squarely in the 'no way in hell' dating column.

He. Is. My. Boss!

"We've formed something of a riding group with Vance and Justin. Though Justin's bike is more for entertainment, he does his best to keep up."

"It's great to have friends with a common interest."

"It is. I enjoy it. What, uh...interests do you have, Ms. Savoy? And do you plan to...make friends that correspond with them?"

We had reached the elevator. Davis pressed the call button, and the doors slid open. He waited for me to step inside to follow, then pressed the lobby button. "I've been preoccupied with work and family for a long while. I haven't had much time for friends and interests. One reason I moved out here was to... I don't know, figure out what I like to do and do it."

"Hmm," he mused, nodding. "I understand. I also moved to Black Diamond with a goal to change some things about my life."

"Oh?" Was the mysteriously quiet and walled-off Davis Scott about to reveal something about himself? "What things?"

The elevator chimed its arrival at the ground floor of the Paradise tower. As the door slid open, the area seemed unusually busy. People milled around with half-full glasses and appetizer plates. I remembered then that the monthly owners' mixer was in full swing. The group had spilled over from The Bistro to the lobby.

Davis and I glanced at each other before stepping into the fray. A hasty wave from an overeager owner caught my attention. Before I could even nod back, Davis put a hand on my arm. "Would you like me to handle that?" he asked, his voice barely audible over the din of chatter. "I know exactly what they're going to ask about."

I nodded, grateful for his intervention. "I would appreciate that, Mr. Scott. I'm going to head upstairs. I've got to get out of these shoes."

He saluted me with two fingers. "It was nice seeing you, Ms. Savoy. I hope you find what you're looking for."

Davis turned the corner, heading straight for the owner with the face full of questions. I crossed over to the bank of elevators servicing the residence tower and pressed the call button. When the elevator arrived, I flashed the fob across the reader and, as the doors closed, trained my eye on Davis standing in the middle of the lobby, mid-animated conversation, his helmet anchored against his hip and his riding pants creating the perfect canvas for well-formed cheeks.

"Even if I wanted a taste, he ain't got no samples to hand out," I muttered to myself.

My phone chimed as I reached my condo. A text from Dionne read:

> Dionne Woods: Come to Tikis & Cream tomorrow after work. Talk to Ameenah so she can help us sell it to Wade.

The thought of presenting my half-baked idea to someone very close to a music mogul sent my heart skittering around my chest. I headed straight for my computer, booted it up, and carted it with me to the bedroom, where I sat up against the headboard and piled pillows behind me. Not only did I have to sell my idea to people who could literally save the hotel, but I had to convince Davis that it was a great idea to spend money on.

I pulled up my project plan to review and add to it, but first, I fired off a response text to Dionne.

Kari Savoy: I'll be there.

Ten

DAVIS

"You haven't spoken to any of these people about this idea yet?"

"I don't even want to get deep into planning until I hear a *yes*. And then, if they agree, I figure they'll want to plan their own show. And we would plan the events and other entertainment around them."

"And this is all contingent upon Wade and Gage agreeing to your proposal."

"Correct. But we have a very good chance of them saying yes."

I nodded, lips pursed, hands in prayer position with my index fingers against my chin. It was my thinking pose. "Even so, it sounds costly," I mused, after some thought.

"The cost of the event will heavily depend on the opening and closing shows, so we should distribute more funds toward those. Local businesses who want to take part will provide their own materials in exchange for using our space. I'd like to solicit donations of time and materials for anything the resort is sponsoring and ask Wade and Gage to cut their fees if they're willing. We are asking for a large favor, but it will put money in their pockets."

I had seen both men on the covers of music magazines over the years. Though they had been quiet recently, their names still carried clout. The more I thought about it, the more it seemed Kari was onto something. With Wade and Gage headlining, we could draw a considerable crowd, not just from the locals in the area but also from neighboring towns and cities. And if we played our cards right, we might get media coverage.

"I doubt an act like Wade and Gage will cut their fees for us. I don't want you to get your hopes up and start planning, spending money."

"I won't. And I thought that since we'll have people on the island and on property, I'd like to open a few condos for tours. Maybe hold a raffle for a weekend stay each day if people take a tour—"

"The same strategy you used at Fairmont. Kari, we discussed this. That's a smaller resort—"

"And as I told you, *Davis*, it doesn't matter what size property we're talking about. I use these strategies because they have a proven track record. If Ameenah doesn't think Wade and Gage will go for it, we can scale it down and focus on the businesses we have here on the island. We could get Rod from the gym to come teach a summer-themed fitness class. For that matter, Dionne could teach a beach yoga class. The library has a cute little bus—they could do a story time in one of the ballrooms. We have options, but…"

Kari shrugged. "The best bet is to focus on family events during the day and adult events at night with a name to draw crowds. Even if we don't book big stars, that's going to be our ticket to a full and busy summer, all of which we can handle."

I leaned back in my chair and stared at the ceiling, deep in thought. This plan terrified me. But it also created a spark that hadn't been there before. I'd spent so much time dreading the summer. Kari already showed a knack for turning dread into excitement.

If it didn't work, we were sunk, and I would have to find somewhere else to work. But a part of me was excited about the prospect of having a hotel full of people enjoying every end of the property. And watching Kari work was inspiring.

"Fine. Keep me informed of the outcome of your meeting," I said, sitting up again. "I need detailed spending— everything we might need to pay for. I would rather cut events than add to an already tight budget. We're behind if we're kicking off the summer over Memorial Day weekend."

"I'm meeting Dionne and Ameenah this afternoon with a rough draft of the project plan. Even if they don't say yes… the themed summer festival is a go?"

I had no choice but to agree to this plan. It was our best bet. And it wasn't a bad plan, so long as Kari was around to pull it off. I gave a terse nod.

"Yessss!" Kari hissed, then pumped her fist, which was so cute and unexpected that it made me laugh. "Okay, I'm heading out in a few, but…uhmmm…" She stood and leaned against the desk, tilting her head slightly with a fist planted on her hip. "Mr. Scott…"

"Ms. Savoy," I answered quietly, knowing what was coming.

"Oh, no you don't." She smiled. "You called me *Kari*. You can't go backward now."

It wasn't until she used my first name in sarcastic response that I realized I had used hers. By then, it was too late to take it back. I'd planned on not calling attention to it. I stalled, taking a moment to clear my throat before locking eyes with her, noting the amusement and half-smile on her lips.

"Will that be a problem?"

"I've been asking you to call me Kari for weeks. Of course,

that won't be a problem. So I'll be calling you Davis from now on. I think that's fair"

"I suppose so."

"Good," she chirped, then turned to leave. "I'll keep you posted."

Her skirt made a satisfying *swish* sound as she left my office. As soon as she cleared the threshold, I picked up the phone and punched the internal line to Justin's desk.

"This is Justin."

"I called her Kari," I blurted. "I just… It just slipped out."

"It took you long enough. What did she say? Did she notice?"

"Yes, she noticed. She said she felt it was fair that she call me Davis."

"Okay. This is a good thing. The first step to familiarity is when the formalities slip away. It means you're getting comfortable with her. And she's comfortable with you. You're still the boss, right?"

"It's not about comfort or authority. It's about not making the same mistake twice."

"Kari ain't ol' girl, Davis. You got to let that go, and you don't have time to let this trip you up. We have a meeting with Aqua Care to review their bid for pool maintenance. Are you coming?"

My watch buzzed to remind me, and I rolled my wrist to silence the alarm. "Yes. I'll meet you in the conference room."

I stood, adjusted the collar on my jacket and straightened the enamel pin that read *The Pearl* on the lapel, then picked up my notepad and favorite pen. I entered the executive board-room for my lunch meeting with potential vendors with a wide smile and friendly greeting.

My mind reeled from my slip-up, though. I'd let my guard down, and while I didn't feel like I could afford to do that, I also felt lighter, with less to worry about.

I hoped I wouldn't regret it.

Eleven

KARI

I timed my arrival at Tikis & Cream for the end of the afternoon rush. Ameenah and Dionne wiped down appliances and tables while dancing to the heavy drum beat thumping from a Bluetooth speaker on the counter, in cadence to a throaty, rhythmic rap verse.

"Kari!" Dionne shimmied her way over to me as I stepped into the shop. "You made it!"

"You told me to come," I reminded her.

"Never know what might happen during the day to keep you on the high-priced end of town. I'll turn this music down. Wade actually let us listen to something new."

Ameenah was more beautiful in person than in the photos I'd seen. I'd been lightweight stalking her and Wade in the tabloids since they'd begun dating, following their day-to-day life in Brooklyn and when she traveled with Wade for the occasional gig. The Bullhorn was good for posting jobs and summer rentals but unreliable for celebrity gossip, so when they were on Black Diamond, photos popped up less frequently since there wasn't much of a press on the island, just the occasional snap appearing here and there.

Ameenah approached me with open arms. Her bright yellow sundress was paired with comfortable white sneakers and simple gold jewelry. The lone standout piece was a black pendant resting at her neck. Her sweet vanilla scent surrounded me as we hugged. It was already as if I had known her forever. I understood why Dionne spoke so highly of her and wanted to make a good impression.

"It's such a pleasure to finally meet you," I gushed. "Dionne has told me so much about you."

"Sit, sit," Ameenah urged, sliding a chair from another table. Dionne returned with another Frozen Sunshine since I seemed to like it so much. Ameenah beamed. "That's Wade's favorite. He has one every day when he's here."

"But only if Ameenah makes them. He'll drink it if I make it, but he *prefers* if she does it." Dionne rolled her eyes, then replaced playful annoyance with a smile. "Speaking of Wade... Kari has an idea, and she's hoping you can ask about his willingness to participate."

"Dionne mentioned a few details last night over text. She said it had something to do with plans for the summer?" Ameenah faced me, crossing her arms and leaning closer to the table.

"Well...putting it plainly, The Pearl needs a big damn deal to kick the season. I need a lot of people on property, all summer long. I hoped we could capitalize on having celebrity residents. A small contribution could be a one-time donation, or a few items of value that we could auction or raffle off. But I was aiming for something bigger."

"Bigger as in..."

"A personal appearance. A concert performance, a meet and greet, or even just being seen on site for a while."

There was a pause as Ameenah absorbed what I was suggesting. Then she burst into laughter. "Girl, I thought you were about to ask for something wild. Gage has been ducking calls about using the house for a televised concert. You want my man and his best friend for an appearance? A one-off?"

"The vision is a festival, anchored around a concert series. If I had one good, big act to kick it off, I could book others to follow—"

"Because they could ride the wave."

Ameenah seemed to ponder the idea, and from the twist in her lips, I had a good feeling. "Gage loves to be the first out of the gate. It's not a lot of time to prepare, though. Their next album will be out this summer, and they've been priming the artists they've signed to the label they created. In fact, that's why we're in town. We hadn't planned to be back here before June, but Wade works better when he's on Black Diamond."

I popped straight up in my seat as Dionne and I locked gazes. "Wade is on the island right now?"

Ameenah nodded. "Gage, too. They have a mini studio in the house."

"Okay, so…what are the chances we meet with them and ask them to consider it—if not at the beginning of summer, then at the end?"

"Gage will be the hard sell," said Ameenah. "He's a perfectionist and won't want to do it unless he's ready. Wade is a showboat. It's not hard to get him on a stage, and I have a little pull with him. So, I'm thinking…"

She paused, bit her bottom lip, and leaned in. "I have a secret that I need to tell you both, but you can't breathe a word. It's not public knowledge."

Dionne leaned closer, a gleeful smile playing on her lips. "Is this what I think it is?"

"Um…yes. And no." She stopped to laugh, then sucked in a breath and pushed out, "Wade and I are getting married. Soon, because this album is coming, which means they'll be touring right after the release, and we want to be married before that. Because I'm pregnant."

"Holy shit!" Dionne pushed back from the table and hopped up, her chair scraping against the cement floor. "Ameenah! You've been on your feet all day and didn't say shit! I wish I'd known!"

"It's okay, Dionne!" Ameenah laughed and waved for her to resume her seat. "I'm very healthy. My fiancé makes sure I'm well taken care of. But... Kari's proposal is giving me all kinds of ideas about how we can make our summer really special."

"Anything I can do to help you celebrate, I'm all in," I said.

"So, I'm just spitballing here. I think they should take you up on opening the summer at The Pearl. The album will be done, so they could do a show to preview the new music, maybe an exclusive listening party at the hotel, something people have to buy tickets for. That kicks off pre-promotion and gives you plenty to work with."

I slapped my palms together, resisting the urge to get on my knees and bow to Ameenah. "Oh, I like that idea!"

"I already don't have the energy for a summer full of parties— bridal and baby and bachelorette. I'm considering bringing all our people to the island. I want to have one shower and one fancy event, followed by our wedding to close out the summer. It would be perfect if we could just buy out the hotel."

"Can you *imagine*, Kari?" Dionne squealed. "Grammy award-winning producer Wade Marshall and Grammy award-winning artist Gage Coleman partying, hanging out, getting married at your hotel?!"

"It solves all of my problems," said Ameenah. "Everyone near and dear to me will be on the island, comfortable, living in luxury. And out of my hair."

"The penthouse!" I added with a gasp, catching Dionne's excitement. "That would be perfect for your bridal and baby shower."

"I love it. Then I was thinking the wedding would be the next weekend. Between both our families, our friends, Wade's family, all the PR and record label people who want to see and be seen, plus the Tuneage label acts and their families and teams, we are going to deck that place out. Black Diamond is so easy to get to, I can't imagine the place not filling up."

"And once other artists see what Wade and Gage are doing down here," I added, "they'll want a piece of the action."

"What *are* Wade and Gage doing?"

A deep bass voice filled the shack, booming so loud I nearly screamed. I turned in my seat to see the wide-shouldered, bearded handsomeness of Wade Marshall, just casually standing in the door at Tikis & Cream, so tall he blocked the sunlight.

"Wade!" Dionne shouted, then hopped up from her seat. She ran to him and jumped into his arms. He lifted her off her feet and squeezed tight. She laughed as he set her down, adjusting her t-shirt. "I haven't seen you in forever!"

She gripped his bicep and he flexed, just to show off. "Damn, boy. You found a gym in New York, huh?"

Wade laughed hard. "You tryna say I was puny, D?"

"You trying to take on Method Man? Looking real beefy right now."

He sucked his teeth, smirking. "I ain't got nothin' on Meth."

"That's too many ribeye and whipped mashed potato dinners at Porter's Steakhouse," said Ameenah. "That's what that is."

"There she goes," said Wade. "Like her parents don't invite us to dinner every week." He wandered into the shop and bent over Ameenah, dropping a long kiss on her lips. "Hey, pretty."

"Hey, handsome. You're right on time."

Wade extended a hand in my direction. Mine drowned in his as we shook. "You must be D's friend that just moved down here. How are you liking the island?"

I nodded. "Uhm, yeah...th-the island. I'm..." I drew a blank suddenly. *Fuck.*

"This is my best friend since college, Kari Savoy," Dionne said, jumping back in with an arm around my shoulders. "She runs events and marketing at The Pearl, on the south end of the island. Give her a few minutes and she'll be smart again."

"Are you two done for the night already?" Ameenah asked Wade.

He grabbed a chair and sat around the table with us. "Sheree just showed up with the kids for the weekend, so Gage took everybody out. Besides, I felt you talking about me all the way back at the house, so I decided to come down here and see what was up."

"We were discussing summer plans," Ameenah said. "*Our* potential summer plans." She glanced at him and winked.

He reached for her hand, winding his fingers between hers. "You heard our good news. What does that have to do with Gage?"

"I was priming Ameenah to ask you for a favor," I said, butting in, finding my voice and remembering why I was in this shop. "I'd like for you and Gage to perform at the resort this summer. I'm hoping you'll hear my proposal and agree that it's a great idea, because I could really use a yes."

Wade glanced at Ameenah, who beamed a smile at him. Then he returned his warm brown eyes to me. "Feels like I'm getting ganged up on, but...lay it on me. Can I get one of those Frozen Sunshine things first?"

———

Wade sucked down the last of his frozen drink and dropped the empty cup to the table.

"The timeline is aggressive," he said, rubbing a finger under his bottom lip. "We've been heads down on this album and sketching out some promo plans. Setting this up will take time away from perfecting the rollout. Gage doesn't like distractions."

My heart sank; I saw at least half of my visions of a packed-out hotel swirling down the drain.

But then Wade waved a hand in the air. "You know what? Fuck it, I like it. I've done more with less time. Let me run it by Gage. I need to couch it right, talk about the benefits, hype it up. He'll go for being the first celebrity act at the hotel, plus making a big deal about the album. And," he added, "we have new acts that we just signed to the label. Give us the first run at the schedule and I can damn near guarantee Gage will be in."

"I told you," Ameenah said. "Gage wants to be the first to do everything."

"Wait…" My heart threatened to gallop out of my chest. "Can you clarify that? You might have more than one act? So we could do a show a month? Or more?"

"Correct," Wade replied. "Matter of fact, give us free rein to hook up the concerts. It'll be a Tuneage Records summer, baby. Between us and our management, evening entertainment won't be a problem."

"I came up with this idea two days ago. I have the local library minibus scheduled, and I was going to beg Dionne to offer a summer yoga session. I have nothing else booked. If you want to take control of the concert schedule, I'd love that. I can work on the daytime activities."

"Bet. Now…" Wade rolled his head dramatically in Ameenah's direction and tried to scowl. "You're already running me about this wedding, Meenah. You don't have to do this shit all by yourself. Let me make some decisions."

Ameenah's brows shot up. "You can pick your tux. That's what you get to decide."

"For real, though? I like the idea of doing everything down here, all at once. Brooklyn would be a circus, even if we let somebody else take care of the details."

He laid eyes on me, his tone and his gaze dipping to a serious level. "If you ask me, Ameenah shouldn't be doing shit but laying on the beach, working on her tan and growing a person, but I can't tell her nothin'. I'd rather have a healthy baby than a big ass wedding and whatever else she's trying to set up."

"But if we can have both—"

"I hear you, Meenah," he soothed. "I want you to have the wedding of your dreams, but there's no rule that says we have to be married before the baby gets here. You and this child are my priority. Hire somebody to run the show and work with Kari, and I'm good. But the minute you seem stressed, I'm pulling the plug. We're grabbing our parents and heading to the courthouse, and I'm not playing."

"Deal." Ameenah shot a tired but satisfied smile in my direction. "We'll talk with Gage and get him nailed down on the concert series. I know I don't need to say this, but I'm going to, anyway. Absolutely no one can know about our plans until we announce them. We're counting on you both."

"Oh, of course. Absolutely." They both stood, so I stood as well. "I *so* appreciate this, Wade. And Ameenah. You have no idea."

"Don't be appreciative yet," said Wade. "I still have to talk Gage into it. And if he says yes, I'll hook you up with our manager, Fontaine. He's not easy at all. You'll work for this."

I held my breath, watching them walk out of the shop hand in hand. Once they were out of earshot, I twirled around to grin at Dionne and finally exhaled, then dramatically fell back into my chair.

"A wedding, two events, and a summer concert series.

What just happened? Did that just happen? Did you know he was here?"

"No! She didn't say shit! I'm so excited!"

I pulled out my phone to scroll through notifications. "Oh! I need to go," I said, tugging the strap of my bag over my shoulder. "I need to update Davis. Mo left a message. And I should probably check on my sister. Thanks for today, Dionne."

"I like being the connect. Make sure I get VIP all the way. And tell Davis you already need a raise. This is huge!"

Twelve

KARI

Back at the hotel, I went through the ritual that had now become routine: park in the garage, take the elevator to the lobby, then cross the hall to the residence tower to my condo, where I'd spend the evening on the phone with Dionne or chatting with Moses.

Less often, I spoke with Reyna, who made it clear she only talked to me because I controlled the trust that held her money.

"Reyna talks to me because she *has* to," I whined to Moses, phone tucked between my ear and shoulder. I reached my condo, locked the doors, and kicked off my shoes, sighing in relief.

"Take what you can get, Kar," Moses was saying. "At least you're hearing from her."

"It doesn't do anything for our relationship if I can't get her on the phone unless she wants money."

"Reyna Savoy is gonna Reyna Savoy," said Moses. "She

ain't ever been easy, and you're not going to change her or make her do what you want. Deal with what she gives you. If you have to withhold her allowance until y'all speak, that's what you have to do."

"See, Reyna will decide that's too much effort and try to make money some other way. Some illegal way, you know what I'm saying? This new guy she's hanging out with is all bad, Mo. All. Bad."

The dispatch from my spies around campus was that Reyna's new boyfriend was the oldest sophomore ever. Apparently, he had problems staying enrolled at SMU. Over the summer, he'd been arrested and released, but since it was between sessions, the university opted to do nothing. He was skating on thin ice and taking my sister with him.

I hated being helpless. Even more, I hated watching my sister throw so much away for a dusty man that couldn't put down his bud long enough to drag his ass to class.

"I know, Kar," Moses said. "But what can you do? Fly up there and sit on her? She'll call you when she needs you, and knowing this dude, she will eventually need you."

"I know you're right, Moses. I don't have to like it."

"Yeah. That's how it goes, usually. So…how's five-star hotel living?" he asked, changing the subject. "The new job still good? And when are you gonna host your little brother and ten of his friends down there?"

I laughed. "I don't have that kind of pull yet. But the new job is great. You will not believe who I might be working with."

I changed into a pair of shorts and a tank top while talking to Moses on speakerphone, sharing everything that wasn't confidential about what could be an exciting summer at The Pearl. He seemed as hype as I was about it. Moses and I were so much alike. He really got me.

"That's dope! Make sure I get a ticket to that exclusive

listening party. I got friends in high places and I'm calling in all the favors."

"If you and your friends come down here, I'll make sure you get a nice suite. I can't comp a room for you, but I can probably get you into everything. I have to clear it with my boss, but—"

"Aw, it's gotta go through ol' puckered?"

I laughed hard, then felt bad that I'd called Davis puckered, then laughed again.

"He's loosening up, actually. I—"

The words I was about to say flew from my mind as soon as I stepped onto the patio outside my bedroom and took my usual customary glance at the outdoor pool. Davis, who was rarely out after hours, was lounging by the pool, barefoot and shirtless, wearing knee-length deck shorts in a blue and white floral print.

"Kar? Kari, you there?"

"Yeah, I'm here. Listen, speaking of ol' puckered—you cannot call him that when you meet him. He's sitting out by the pool, and he's never sitting out by the pool, so I'm going out there."

"Go disturb his peace, girl," Mo teased.

"I need to update him about my meetings today. I hope I hear from Wade or Ameenah soon."

"Me too. I want to party like a rock star. Love you. Be easy."

"Love you too, Moses."

Moses ended the call. I tucked the phone into a pocket, grabbed my keyring with my fob, and left the suite, padding down to the pool in a pair of slides. The weather was mild, just warm enough for shorts and a tank top.

"Davis!" I called as I approached.

He practically leaped into the air, almost tossing the magazine into the pool. "Miss—" He sighed, then closed his eyes.

A moment later, they reopened, and he tried again. "Kari. Hello."

"Good job." I picked up the magazine and handed it back to him. "Didn't mean to scare the shit out of you. Mind if I join you?"

He gestured to the lounge chair next to him. I dragged it closer and sat. "I rarely see you out here. A change in routine?"

"I'm…trying something new."

"Mmmm." I noted he was working hard to look casual but was, in fact, not casual. "And how is that going?"

He frowned at the rowdy guests in the pool, the lounge chairs scattered around the patio, and the line at the bar, then returned his gaze to me.

"Not well. It's hard to relax when I see work that needs to be done and the responsible parties not doing it. I'm stressed and I'm considering returning to my condo."

"Yeah, that about describes how you look. Can I distract you? I have an update on my meetings today. Sort of."

"Do you want to share if it's not definite?"

"There are some developments, and I'd rather keep the lines of communication open."

"I'm listening," said Davis. He set the magazine aside, then pivoted his long legs so that he sat sideways on the lounger, facing me.

"So, I was all set to pitch Ameenah so she could help us convince Wade and Gage to throw a show for us. Then Wade shows up out of the blue and hears us talking. He sits right down with us, and I decide to shoot my shot. He said the timeline is tight, but they might make it happen."

"That sounds promising."

"It does, right? He said he's going to talk to Gage, and if he's a go, he'll get me in touch with their manager. And get this—Wade and Gage launched a label last year, and they're interested in featuring their artists over the summer. It'll be like…a residency. Before you know it, this whole thing will domino and we'll be full to the brim."

Davis' head bobbed up and down, but his eyes were far, far away. Suddenly, he poked up a finger and stood.

"Follow me," he said, slipping his feet into a pair of slides, and began racing toward the main building.

I grabbed the magazine he'd left and followed. "Where are we going?"

He didn't answer but held the door open as he entered the management suite, then stalked down the hall to his office. The room was in its usual state—clean and bland except for his Harley models on display.

He went right to a filing cabinet, pulled open a drawer, and plucked a folder without flipping through the tabs. He tossed a folded wad of pages to the table, then unfolded until a large drawing representing the footprint of the entire resort was laid across the table.

"Pavilion," he said, stabbing a finger at one end of the drawing. "Crowd would probably gather around here, spill out to the beach. If they want to do a VIP section, it would be here…"

He pointed to an area to the right, nestled between the stage and the hotel.

"That would mean hiring someone to manage that section."

"I could talk to Calhoun."

"Or…just go for it. He'll have Grammy award-winning artists at his hotel. Is he going to say no?"

He leaned onto the table, surveying the plans, eyes bouncing back and forth, his tongue running over his teeth beneath closed lips.

"I can't read your mind. What does this face mean?"

"I'm calculating. When Calhoun says pack it out…" He

glanced up at me. "Exactly how packed is that? How many people can we fit in this place?"

"Doesn't the fire department determine that?"

"Max capacity is five thousand in the pavilion, but that doesn't include the beach overflow and what we've decided will be our VIP, so that's another few thousand, easy. Not to mention people will be on the rooftops here," he said, pointing at one penthouse, "and here," he finished, pointing at the other.

"Doesn't someone own one of the penthouses?"

"They don't own the roof."

"So… fifteen thousand people? At the very most? You think we'll sell that many tickets?"

"That's the most we can sell without the fire marshal shutting us down. But if we sold out…" He paused, then rolled his eyes up to mine again.

I grinned. "That would be a *nice* crowd."

"I'd like to send that photo to Calhoun, just because he thinks I can't do it. *We* can't do it."

"One other thing. Ameenah and Wade want to buy the hotel out over two weekends at the end of the summer. Possibly renting the penthouse for a special event and using the entertainment complex or the ballroom for a large party. They would have an extensive room block for friends, family…friends of the family. The following weekend would be…uh…a large, *momentous* event."

Davis seemed confused. Eyes narrowed, he tilted his head. "Are you speaking in code?"

I sighed. "It's a secret. It's big. And…*personal.* For Wade and Ameenah." I stared at him with huge eyes. He stared back, his expression blank. I gave up, tossing up my hands. "It's a good thing you're pretty. I'll get permission to tell you because you suck at picking up hints."

Davis' brow furrowed at my playful jab. "Wait, are

they…?" The realization suddenly dawned on him, and he laughed. "Why didn't you just say it's a wedding?"

"Because it's a secret! And that's not the only secret."

"Is she pregnant or something?"

I squealed, then slapped a hand over my mouth but pointed with the other.

"Why is that a secret? Won't people figure it out when she starts to show?"

"Yes, but not from us. So we can't label anything *wedding* or *baby*. Calhoun wanted a full hotel. This place is going to be overflowing. All summer long."

"Nice," said Davis. "Very nice."

"Thanks," I replied, beaming with pride.

"I mean that, Kari. I was skeptical, but if you pull this off, you'll have bailed me, MGMT, and Calhoun out. And hopefully, you didn't have to work with an asshole to do it."

I blanched, then blushed at his recall of my flippant comment on my first day at the resort. "Davis… I was really cocky that day, and I shouldn't have said that."

"No, you were right," he conceded, leaning against the table. "I was sure Calhoun was trying to undermine me and I was upset that you were hired behind my back. You've only been here a few weeks, and now I'm wondering if we'll have any space left to book this summer. Which is a very good problem to have."

Surprised, I stepped back and crossed my arms, shifting my weight from foot to foot out of…nervousness? "I can honestly say I did not expect to hear kind words from you, Davis. I think I'll head home before you bluntly say something to ruin the moment."

Davis chuckled, then began meticulously folding the plans back into a neat square. He pushed himself off the table, muscles rippling ever so slightly. The heat that flushed through my body shouldn't have been a surprise, but it almost knocked me off of my feet. I tried not to watch as he stretched to return the folder to its rightful place, the muscles in his back flexing under sun-bronzed skin.

I looked awkwardly away, fumbling with the key fob in my pocket. He'd suddenly gone from Davis to *Davis*. I had to regain control of my emotions before things got complicated.

He's my boss. He's my *boss*. He's my puckered, stern, didn't-think-I-could-do-it-so-I-had-to-prove-I could boss.

Falling for him, in all his quirky glory, was not an option.

Thirteen

DAVIS

"Sorry, everyone," I called out, walking into my meeting a few minutes late.

The low murmur of chatter died down as I took my seat at the head of the table. The spacious conference room was set, as usual, with light bites, since the weekly management standup was scheduled during the lunch hour. The aroma of ham and cheese or beef sliders, curly fries, freshly baked pastries, coffee, and a fruit salad filled the air.

My stomach rumbled so loudly that Justin laughed and pushed his chair away from the table. "I'll load up a plate for you. We're ready to go when you are."

On the table in front of me was the Operations log, a manual of sorts that told the story of every happening at the resort, by department and overall. I flipped through it absent-mindedly, noting that the next few weeks were packed. Kari's vision was coming together, the staff was energized and inspired, and the resort was thriving. I couldn't take all the credit, but I felt pride when I looked at the faces around the table.

"I've been informed about how hectic last week was and how well the teams performed together. This week will be just as busy. I'd like to spend a few minutes hearing what's happening in each department. Who would like to volunteer to begin the report out?"

My eyes scanned the faces around the table, but everyone avoided my gaze. Kari's usual seat was empty. I noted a pang of disappointment at seeing the open spot around the table. She hadn't mentioned anything about not being able to make it to today's meeting. In the few weeks since she came on staff, she had revamped her organization, rallied her team, and brought life to the resort, taking my skepticism and using it for fuel. She was often booked and busy, so the weekly management standup had become my favorite part of the week.

"Since when are you all shy?" I asked, after a few moments of silence.

As I spoke, Kari slipped into the room and took her seat, placing the large binder that she could regularly be seen toting around the property on the table. She shot a sheepish smile in apology for being late and disrupting the meeting.

Heather, head of catering, spoke up first. Her thick Southern accent flowed slow and sweet like syrup. "This is nothin' on Kari because we need the business, but we're about to break, we're stretched so thin. If more than one person calls out, it's a nightmare. I know we've said we can't add headcount—"

"That's the current situation," I interjected. "However, I want to discuss this with management and propose provisional funding for additional staff. Kari has planned a busy summer for us, and if we need temporary help to get through it, I need to know how that will affect our budget. Are all of you in the same situation?"

"The front desk is slammed most days, and my back office has never been busier," said Christopher, head of guest experiences.

"Accounting is struggling to keep up," Frances, director of finance, added. "It's a good problem to have, but it's about to teeter into the danger zone."

"The weather has been nice lately, but we're still mid-rainy season," mentioned Tim, general manager at Breakers. "That puts pressure on all the services here, but also affects deliveries, especially to the restaurants. I've learned my lesson—if you're low on anything, get it ordered now. The trucks are the first thing they hold at the bridge."

I took a moment to review the latest labor report. "I need everyone to provide a projected headcount and note any potential shortages by the end of the week." I turned to Robin Paul, Director of Human Resources. "Let's schedule some time for you and Frances to discuss personnel ahead of our quarterly meeting with MGMT."

Robin nodded, her pen scratching the task across the bottom of her notepad. At the sight of heads nodding again, I smiled. Justin slid a full plate over to me and resumed his seat.

"Continue the report out."

I scarfed down lunch while my team detailed the past week of business in their departments. When it was time for Kari to share, I paid close attention.

"First, sorry, not sorry you all are so busy," she joked. Thankfully, everyone laughed. "But just like every other department, events is slammed. We are prepping for a wedding this weekend, Vance has a group coming for a birthday celebration, and I've booked a corporate event that begins tomorrow. It overlaps with the business summit that ends today, but tomorrow's group will begin with nine holes of golf. That will give us time to turn over the meeting room—"

"And guest rooms," Mason, head of housekeeping, added.

"Vance also caught me in the hallway to tell me he has a large party booking in a few weeks, so heads up. It's been nonstop lately, but that's why I was hired, right?"

"Indeed," I replied, acknowledging Kari's efforts to get the staff on board. "Focus on selling the resort. I'll handle the details."

"The summer festival is coming up," said Kari. "I've given everyone a bare-bones description of what will happen but assume you will need full-day and evening coverage in each of your departments. I'll set up an information session as soon as the schedule is completed, so you'll see how it impacts you and your teams. Davis and I will need everyone in this room to pull it off. I know we've got it, and we're about to have a lot of fun doing it."

"I heard there might be celebrities coming," Robin mentioned.

"If everything goes according to plan," said Kari, "this place will be *swarming* with celebrities."

As the room cleared, I pushed my plate to the side and did one last flip through the log. I recognized the feeling of being pleased, of enjoying my job and looking forward to going to work each day. It was the first time I'd felt that since my first week at The Pearl.

"Davis."

I came to, realizing I wasn't alone in the room. Kari had added a few sliders and a pile of curly fries to a plate and taken the seat Justin vacated. Her white blouse, cropped black slacks, and low-heeled sandals were classic, understated cuts but also...so *sexy* on her. She licked her lips, which led my thoughts to what else she could do with her tongue.

Shit. *Keep it together, man.*

I cleared my throat. "Kari," I replied, using the same tone she'd used to alert me she was in the room.

"Do you have to leave right away, or can we talk?"

I looked at my watch as if I had to think about whether I had time. In truth, I had all the time in the world for Kari Savoy.

"We can talk."

She scooted the chair up to the table. The way she looked at those mini sandwiches, golden and cheesy, she must have been starving. "I just wanted to remind you that Gage, Wade, and their manager will be by this afternoon to tour the resort. They want to see it in person so they can put their shows together."

I bobbed my head in a nod. "I saw it on my calendar. I have a few copies of the resort blueprint if needed."

A sheepish expression crossed her face. "I appreciate that, but I had tour booklets designed, which includes a miniature version of the blueprint we looked at a few weeks ago. If they prove useful, I'll make them standard for on-site proposals."

"Ah." A light chuckle escaped my lips. "So I should mind my business?"

Kari laughed, biting the end off of a curly fry. "I didn't say all that."

"But you're not arguing." After a moment, I tapped her hand. "I'm realizing daily that my Cornell degree doesn't mean much when I am up against a younger, smarter, more innovative version of me."

Kari reared back at the last part of my statement. "Version of *you*? Beg pardon? You think *I* am like *you*?"

"You don't? Resourceful, intelligent, approachable—"

Kari laughed, pounding the table with the heel of one fist. "Now I *know* you're joking. Davis!"

"I'm not approachable?"

"Ummm, do I have to answer that?"

Judging from Kari's expression, she assumed I would be upset to hear the truth. It didn't bother me as much as she surmised. The past eighteen months at the resort had been challenging, and the years leading up to my arrival at The

Pearl were unnecessarily stressful. In just a few weeks, Kari had already made such a positive impact on the atmosphere of the resort that I hoped to end my tenure as a terse and demanding property manager.

"I'm not unaware of the staff's perception of me, and it's not a problem as long as they don't let that perception destroy their faith that I can run this resort efficiently."

"I've never heard a complaint," said Kari. "Your staff has a great deal of respect for you, actually. And maybe it's because I'm the new kid on the block, but they don't discuss you as much as you think they do."

"I suppose that's good news."

"Tell me about me being like you, though. I'm not fishing for compliments, I promise. I am intrigued that you feel I mirror you."

"I was attempting to compliment you while also patting myself on the back. Everything you've implemented has been a great idea, long overdue, and much needed. They're also ideas that I've had, even if they were fleeting, but didn't have the time or energy to carry out. I see you as an extension of me, so to speak."

"Thank you for the compliment," she said, "but...an *extension* of you, Davis? Don't you mean a fully autonomous being with education, experience, and a vibrant mind, with the added benefit of beauty and style to go along with it?"

"Added benefit of beauty and style? You're not trying to come for my looks, are you? I'm not a humble man, and if pressed, I'll brag."

"I am not coming for your looks. And if you were pressed to brag, I would not argue."

Something...shifted. The easy banter and professional distance between us was quickly disappearing, replaced by deceptively easy banter and a charged energy humming just under the surface. Kari's words hung in the air, thick with unspoken implications. I watched her bite her lip and lower her gaze. I couldn't resist the urge to lean in closer, my eyes locked on hers.

"I am quite sure you could hold your own in a bragging contest. I would also not argue."

My heart thumped a loud, steady rhythm as we stared each other down, both daring the other to cross an imaginary line. After a few moments, I came to my senses, wrestling myself for some sense of control.

Kari cleared her throat. "I—I've been reading back on the quarterly reports you've sent to MGMT over the last year. There is a marked changed—occupancy has increased steadily, and employee turnover has noticeably decreased. No matter what Calhoun calls you to bitch about, you do a great job here, Davis."

Suddenly shy, I traced the wood grain pattern on the table to avoid her piercing brown eyes. "Every day we aren't going under is a good day to management. I don't know if they consider my numbers an improvement. Acknowledgment from MGMT or Calhoun is infrequent at best."

"Well, consider them acknowledged. But you know this information. You are too smart to not know you kick ass. You don't celebrate your victories?"

"I do. But I don't want to seem like I'm thirsty for compliments either."

"Accolades aren't *compliments*, Davis," said Kari. She brushed her hands together to rid them of crumbs and pushed her chair back. "I'm not just being polite. Don't downplay your hard work. Don't transfer it to me or to Vance or to Justin or the staff. You're good at this. And you know you are, so before you go all humble on me, just say thank you."

As she gathered her things, I leaned forward and covered her hand with mine. "Thank you, Kari. I appreciate your words."

Time stood still for a few seconds, but it may as well have been hours. The electricity that flowed between us made the air crackle. I wanted nothing more than to pull her up from her chair and kiss her until neither of us could breathe. I wondered what it would feel like to touch more of her, to explore the softness of her skin, to memorize her curves. In my imagination, I led her away from the building to a secluded spot where the only sounds were those of our ragged breathing as we consumed each other.

Silence hung heavy between us, punctured only by the distant hum of a hedge trimmer and the scent of freshly cut grass wafting through the vents. I shook my head, scattering the visions that tumbled around inside my mind.

I released her with a friendly, gentle pat and stood, grabbing her plate before she could, stacking it on top of mine. "Thanks for the chat. I'm—I have a meeting."

"I'll see you later, Davis," Kari said, her voice soft and slightly husky.

Did I imagine the spark? The way she looked at me? The tease and lower tone in her voice?

I swallowed hard and forced myself to walk away, my heart pounding, drowning out the lecture that was already building. I made it to my office and closed the door behind me, leaning against it and inhaling a deep, steadying breath.

I could not fall for someone I worked with. I could not repeat past mistakes. I could not destroy the mutual respect that Kari and I had developed for each other. I could not afford to lose focus.

And yet, as I sat behind my desk, the image of Kari with her bottom lip between her teeth permanently imprinted itself in my mind. There was something about her that made me feel alive in a way I hadn't in years.

I recognized that feeling. I also recognized that for me, that feeling was dangerous territory.

Fourteen

KARI

Davis and I waited at the entrance to The Pearl as we watched a shiny Escalade make its way down the drive from the major thoroughfare through Black Diamond. As the vehicle glided to a stop, he stepped forward to open the passenger door.

A stocky man in a caramel-colored shorts and shirt combo emerged. His chiseled features were accentuated by a well-groomed goatee and beard.

"Afternoon," he said, offering a fist bump to Davis. "I'm Fontaine. I hold the checkbook, so whatever gets thrown around today, make sure it's good with me. We cool?"

"Understood. Looking forward to working with you."

"Good deal. Now that we got that clear…" He leaned back into the vehicle and shouted, "Y'all napping? Get out of the car. We got shit to do."

Two of the most deliciously brown-skinned, muscled, bearded men I had ever laid eyes on strolled around the vehicle, oozing sexiness in fitted t-shirts and distressed jeans paired with pristine white sneakers.

"We comin', we comin'," grumbled one.

"Chill out, tryna boss me around, man," said the other.

Gage and Wade introduced themselves to me, then Davis, before each slipping a pair of shades over their eyes. Ameenah followed, giving off cool and comfortable vibes in flowy floral pants and a white tank top with a short-sleeved shirt layered over it.

"Who's in charge here?" asked Fontaine, his eyes moving from me to Davis. "I need to know who to yell at when shit ain't right."

"This event is Kari's brainchild," said Davis.

"You have my full attention, Kari," Fontaine said.

Davis led us through the sliding doors with *The Pearl at Black Diamond* etched across them. I fell into step with Fontaine as we walked through the main building to the outdoor stage near the entertainment complex. I handed each of them a tour booklet to refer to during our discussion, noting where Gage, Wade, and the Tuneage label artists would be featured and could shine.

"This is slick," said Gage, slowly bobbing his head. "I was wondering what it looked like in here."

"This is where all the concerts happen, right?" Wade asked. "No side stages?"

"Weather permitting," I confirmed. "We have an indoor stage as a weather backup, but we plan to hold all the shows on this stage. The back of the house has standard lighting and sound equipment, but we can meet any added requirements to round out your show. If you need fireworks and special lights, you'll provide those, of course. We have an in-house engineer, but you should consider him as oversight and basic production. You'll want to provide your own crew for special circumstances."

"We run our own show," said Fontaine. "What's the capacity of this spot?"

Davis took the group through the numbers, pointing out

areas we thought would be best for VIP ticket holders and sponsors. I walked with Fontaine, providing him with the basic details of accommodations, food, beverage, and hospitality services.

"We'll have green rooms in the pavilion with a secure path to the stage. We'll also ensure your crew have rooms reserved."

"The fire department and Black Diamond EMS will be on site," said Davis, "and I'm working on a contract with a private nurse to be on hand if needed."

"Take a test drive, fellas," said Fontaine, waving Wade and Gage to the center of the stage. "Get a feel for it. Start thinking about the approach—you have room for a live band."

Gage pulled his phone from his pocket, queued up a song, and held it aloft so we could all hear as he and Wade began an impromptu performance of one of their biggest hits, "Flow Fusion." The up-tempo song featured a relentless beat that carried clever wordplay delivered with rapid-fire speed and precision.

They moved fluidly across the stage, pretend mics in hand as if performing was second nature to them. Fontaine walked behind them, measuring the area and noting where instruments and people would be placed.

Davis stood back, observing the scene. Despite the mid-afternoon heat, he was dressed in a jacket, collared shirt, and tie. His head nodded along to the rhythm, even as sweat dripped down his forehead.

Ameenah moved to stand next to me. "How do you think it's going?" I asked her quietly. "I don't want to assume."

"Oh, they're in the zone. This was a great idea, Kari. It completely upended their original rollout plans, but they like this better. Plus, it gives them a platform to showcase artists on the label."

"I'm honestly surprised. I expected a hard and fast no."

"Oh, please. A chance to design a show from scratch where they headline and aren't controlled by promoters?" Ameenah snorted, watching Gage and Wade play off of each other. "They're like children who found a new playground."

"Well, we don't mind sharing our toys."

"Wade and I used to drive down here to watch the crews build this place, wondering how it would turn out," Ameenah said, taking a moment to admire the view from the stage. "It was neat watching it come together. I've been coming to Black Diamond since I was a kid visiting my grandmother. It's so different now."

"Is different a good thing?"

"Well…yes and no. I miss the days when it was a hidden gem, slow and quiet. This festival is about to put Black Diamond on the map. I hope my favorite place isn't going to become overrun with tourists. I've seen spots like Miami Beach discourage Spring Break crowds."

"Our goal is to maintain the island's charm while also offering a luxurious vacation experience," Davis explained. "Creating a fun and exciting but laid-back vacation atmosphere is important to us. We hope this show—and the festival overall—will contribute to that."

"What do you think about having the wedding at the Pavilion?" Ameenah asked.

I glanced at Davis. That would mean an even larger-than-predicted crowd.

"It would work, especially if you're concerned about the event being too large for a ballroom. It would also mean your wedding would be more like a show and not an intimate event."

"Have you seen who I'm marrying? The business I'm marrying into? I'm only doing this thing once, so we may as well do it up. Man, it's so hot out here." Ameenah fanned herself, and I jumped into action.

"Let's go look at the penthouse we plan to use for your

bridal and baby shower." I took her elbow, leading her back to the air-conditioned main building.

"Great idea. Wade and I are already working with a planner, and I want to give her a better idea of the space."

———

"My blisters have blisters," I moaned, falling onto Dionne's couch hours later. A plate of soft tacos, rice, and black beans appeared in front of me. "I don't think I expected to be *quite* this busy. I have worked every day for the past two weeks. I haven't even used the new patio chairs I bought."

"Aren't you the person who books the events?" Dionne dropped to the couch next to me with a plate. She tucked one leg under the other and moved around to face me.

"I'm complaining, but I wasn't missing today for the world."

"So, tell me everything. Ameenah said she was hoping to see the penthouse space you said she could use."

I picked up my plate and got comfortable. I hadn't had a bite since those sliders and fries during the meeting, and Dionne's tacos were always good.

What was set to be a standard walkthrough of the resort turned into a full tour plus hours of contract stipulations with Fontaine. They only called it a day when Ameenah declared she was sleepy, but we made plans to work on the end-of-summer events—the bridal and baby shower, the weeklong family celebrations, and the wedding. Ameenah's planner had already called to set up her site visit.

"It was honestly the most exciting day I've ever had on property. Fontaine is…well, he's a manager. Bossy with high expectations, but reasonable. Wade? Gage?"

I fluttered my eyes and pretended to faint. "It should be illegal to be that fine. Not…*celebrity*-like at all. As close as I'm going to have to work with them this summer, I'm glad they aren't full of themselves."

"So, you're happy you made the move, then?"

"Overwhelmingly. Davis has given me leeway to run my department the way it needs to be run. He doesn't have time for much micromanagement anyway."

I took a monster-sized bite of taco and shoved a forkful of beans into my mouth behind it. After I grunted a few appreciative sounds at Dionne, I washed it down with a frozen margarita.

"How is Davis, by the way? Jason mentioned he hadn't seen much of him since you started. Tonight is the first night they've hung out in weeks. You're keeping him to yourself?"

"Davis is in his office when I get in, and he's still there when I leave. He attends almost every event and he's always...*around*. You know what I mean? I just see him wherever I am on property."

"Oh. Does it, like...creep you out?"

"No. I just think..." I shook my head, conveniently filling my mouth with the last bite of taco instead of finishing my sentence. "I don't know."

Dionne refused to let me off so easily. "You just think that man is *fine*, and you don't mind him being around. That's what you're trying not to say."

I hummed, chewing. "When I first came to the resort, he did not like me, didn't want to get to know me, wanted nothing to do with me. He showed me to my office and stayed away. But like, ever since we've been working on this festival, he's...*interested*. He asks questions and gives compliments, and he seems way more relaxed."

"Did I or did I not tell you that the real Davis Scott was not the man you met when you arrived at The Pearl?"

I hung my head, dreading the realization that Dionne had been right. "Okay, so...a few weeks ago, he was out by the pool. He was trying to be casual, but it wasn't really working.

He seemed uncomfortable. Anyway, that was the day that I started...*noticing* him."

"Noticing him. Like hanging around?"

"No. Noticing...*him*. The way he tries so hard not to laugh that his lips twitch. The way he's so particular about certain things. The way he walks. The way I can tell if he's in a good mood by the tone of his voice. His hair, his physique, the softness of his hands—his hands are so soft."

Dionne set her plate down on the coffee table and scooted closer. "How do you know how soft his hands are, Kari? I need all the juicy details."

"Earlier today, he grabbed my hands, and I swear, if we were not in the office and he was not my boss—"

"Y'all would have been fucking up some sheets in the penthouse suite?"

I laughed, then groaned, tossing myself back onto the couch cushions. Dionne laughed, loudly clapping. "This shit is not funny. I cannot have a crush on my boss, Dionne!"

"Sure you can, so long as he doesn't find out."

"I think he might already know," I confessed, sitting back up. "Today, I meant to just...agree with a comment he'd made. I might have insinuated that he was good-looking. To his face."

"And he is. So?"

"It was the *way* I said it. And the *way* he responded. It was...it was the mood and the energy between us. It was so... he got nervous and walked out like he was afraid of what might happen if he didn't leave the room."

"If he made an attempt, would you refuse him?"

"On the right day, at the right time, in the right place? When I'm ovulating?" After a few long, thoughtful moments, I shook my head. "No. And that scares me. I think it scares him too. He lost a job behind messing with someone at work."

"Okay, there's a difference between leaving a job because

of a work situation and losing a job because of a work situation. Davis *left* that job."

"But we—"

"Work together. So? You're together all day, every day, and that wouldn't change whether or not you're dating him. You're both good-looking people in the prime of your lives and *obviously* attracted to each other. I'm not saying you should run back to the resort and ride that pony, but if the opportunity—and anything *else* arises…"

"Dionne…."

"Why not?"

"Because if it doesn't work out, then I have to work with him *all day, every day*."

"And if it works out, you don't have to go far to see your man. You are letting what-ifs and shit you made color your judgment."

"Your judgment is colored from jump."

"Okay, girl. Be miserable. Work with that handsome, well-built, intelligent, dedicated man all day every day and don't do shit about it. Let them loins burn."

"You are so dramatic."

"Look, I'm not pushing you toward him, but…" Dionne shrugged. "Seems like you have a golden opportunity to at least knock some cobwebs off. Let him get a sniff. Hit it real good one time."

"And here is where I go raid your refrigerator for something sweet because you've started talking nonsense." I hopped up, exasperated, but then came back to add, "And if I remember right, you worked for Jason at Houston Parks and Rec. You were supposed to have sex with him *just the one time* to get it out of your system."

Dionne laughed. "I know what I'm talking about, Kari."

By the time I dragged myself home and onto the elevator at the Paradise tower, I was running on fumes. I was so looking forward to having a day off. I leaned against the wall of the cube as the elevator slowly closed…then reopened when a foot stopped the doors from closing.

I suppressed a groan. I did not want to share my elevator. When I noticed it was Davis in his riding gear, I was reminded of how the fabric clung to his arms and torso, and how I could make out the definition in his thigh muscles as he stepped into the elevator.

This was not what I needed to see before I crawled into bed. Alone. With nothing but a vibrator that I forgot to charge.

"Ms. Savoy," he said, greeting me the way he used to. He flashed his key fob and punched in the round button marked 12. The doors slid closed, and the cube began to climb.

Davis leaned casually against the wall opposite me, his eyes finding mine.

"Mr. Scott," I replied. "I thought we did away with Ms. Savoy."

"Have to keep you on your toes."

"I'm being hazed, aren't I?"

"How was your evening?" His tone was smooth and low, making my skin prickle with a familiar heat.

"Good. Dionne and I watched a reality show about people who marry strangers. And yours?"

"Bikes and beers, as Justin and Jason call it. It's always just what I need, especially at night."

"Sounds like a great time."

"Did your brother ever take you for a ride on his little sport bike?"

A delirious giggle spilled from me. I hated myself for how flirty it sounded. "So much shade in *little sport bike*, Harley rider."

Davis lifted and lowered his broad shoulders in a shrug. "I call them like I see them. They look like Fisher-Price *My First Motorcycle* to me."

"Note to self—don't let Moses bring his little sport bike down here. Uh, no. He's never taken me out on one."

"It's a nice way to take in the sights. Have you seen much of the island since you arrived?"

The elevator stopped at my floor and the doors glided open. As much as I wanted to get out of that box, go into my condo, and pass out, I also loved that I could have a casual conversation with Davis.

A casual, flirty, *personal* conversation with Davis.

He held the door open, then stepped out behind me. "I'll walk you."

"Thanks. Uhm…" I walked slowly, dragging out the conversation. "I actually haven't seen much except the board-walk and Dionne's house. There just…hasn't been time."

"You have tomorrow off, correct?" Davis asked. I nodded, hoping he wasn't going to ask me to work. I was exhausted, and I was hoping to actually use the new patio chairs I'd ordered.

"How…" He paused, shyly bobbing his head side to side. "How would Moses feel about his sister touring an island on the back of a *Harley*?"

"He would be jealous as hell, and I would love to brag about it."

We ambled slowly to my door and stopped there. I was not inviting my boss inside my condo. Right?

"We could go for a ride tomorrow. I have an extra helmet. We'll head out a bit before lunch, eat at a little out-of-the-way spot I like, ride up the coast and back. If…if you would like, that is."

Was this a date? Hanging out? Team building?

Did it matter? As if I planned to say no.

I smiled, then waved the fob over the sensor at my door. "I would really like that, Davis."

Fifteen

DAVIS

I had hoped that the sights and sounds of a morning at my favorite table on the patio at Breakers would quell the voices in my head telling me that today's plans weren't a good idea and I still had time to preserve my dignity and cancel my ride with Kari.

No such luck.

In fact, I willed time to move faster so I could see her again, this time on an even playing field. Not as the event planner who strutted into my office with her confidence on high, but as the woman I had been getting to know over the past few weeks, whose contagious laughter could be heard throughout the management suite, and whose captivating brown eyes had the power to distract me.

"Davis!"

Justin strolled toward my table in a resort polo and shorts, his legs glistening as if he had applied too much body oil after his shower. As always, he wore black loafers without socks.

He pulled out a chair and sat, leaning forward with his elbows resting on the table.

"Do you ever eat anywhere else?"

"No." I loaded the last bite of pancake onto my fork, ready to finish my plate. "Meals are part of my compensation and I enjoy the food. I save my money for other things."

"I guess if I lived on property, I wouldn't bother leaving for breakfast either."

"Mmmm," I grunted, chewing. "Is there a reason you're here interrupting my breakfast? It's Sunday. You should be out doing…whatever it is you do on Sunday mornings."

"I work on Sunday mornings so I can take off early on Friday. Remember?" I recalled, then, that we had arranged his schedule so he'd have Friday evenings open to watch his little brother play basketball. "I saw you sitting here on my rounds, so I dropped by to say hey."

A member of the waitstaff stopped to offer Justin a cup of coffee. He declined, instead asking for a soft drink. I gestured to my cup to indicate that I'd like a refill.

"The question," Justin continued, once the server filled my cup and left, "is what are *you* doing with *your* Sunday?"

Sometimes it was like Justin had radar, as if he knew I was trying to keep my plans on the low. I watched curiosity pique in his eyes as he leaned back, sipping his beverage.

"Nothing much," I lied, avoiding his gaze. "Typical Sunday."

An eyebrow slowly rose, clearly not buying it. "Just… hanging out? On property? All day? By yourself?"

Impatiently, I dropped my silverware onto my plate. "What, Justin?"

He shrugged, but his lips curved into a smug grin. "I'm just ask—"

"*Justin.*"

"A'ight, a'ight," he said, holding up his hands in surrender. "I ran into Kari and Dionne. She said she had to borrow an outfit and asked me if it was cool to ride in."

I stared at Justin. He stared back, an expectant expression on his face. "What?"

"What do you think? Are you taking Kari out on your bike today?"

I tempered my breathing, keeping any emotion—excitement, nervousness, anticipation...exhilaration—at bay. "Kari has never seen most of the island. Yes, we're going for a ride."

"Ah." He grinned wide. "A romantic ride up the coast—"

I rolled my eyes, not wanting to encourage any assumptions. "A tour of the island. Don't get any ideas."

"Then why couldn't you just say you were taking her out on a ride? Why's it a secret?"

"Because..." I glared at him over the rim of my cup as I sipped. "You are *this way* about it."

"All I'm saying is that you two have been getting along really well the last few weeks. The way you work, you fit together like two pieces of a puzzle. Don't think I haven't noticed you hanging around her events."

"She is still new," I reminded him. "I've ensured she's on solid footing."

"Still new, but she's spearheading the summer festival—"

"With my full support."

"Right, right." Justin bobbed his head deeply forward and back, then gave me a slow, sly wink. "I believe you."

"You don't, but it doesn't matter. We'll be heading out before lunch. It's my first day off in weeks, so don't need me. Or Kari."

"Consider the resort handled," Justin said, finishing his soda and crunching the residual ice in his cup before standing. "Can I work out of your office?"

"Don't push it."

"Fine," he whined, sucking his teeth.

Justin's dramatics could be frustrating, but he was mostly amusing. He knew me too well for his own good. His well-timed suggestions and hints had worked their way into my subconscious, giving me dreams and ideas about what could be possible if I had no scruples.

Kari and I *had* been getting along really well lately, and while we were colleagues—technically boss and employee—there was a chemistry between us. I wasn't sure how long I'd be able to deny it.

I finished my coffee and pushed my plate away, then pulled out my phone to scroll through emails, being careful to avoid the mobile app that tracked open work orders and issues across the resort. Today, they were Justin's problem.

Most of the forums and group chats I visited were slow, as it was the weekend, but Throttle Therapy, a group of Harley and motorcycle enthusiasts, had a few threads of bike-related banter in progress. Satisfied that I'd reached the end of the internet, I stood, leaving a healthy tip for the server, and headed back to my condo. Being an early riser with plans later in the morning was both a blessing and a curse. I had several hours before my scheduled meet-up with Kari.

Back at my condo, I dropped the key fob into a bowl that sat on my entryway table and headed to the living room, where I grabbed the remote and pointed it at the TV. I turned down the volume and dropped it on the table, then pulled a bottle of water from the refrigerator and settled into the stiff, hotel-style couch. I scowled, realizing the TV was tuned to the news.

The tone and timbre of the anchor's voice reminded me of my father.

My mother had kept some of his things, including a few VHS tapes, the miniature bike models, and the Harley, which she'd passed on to me. My stepfather was a great man, but he could never take the place of the man who had a part in making me. I couldn't explain how much I missed a person I'd never known, how I longed for a relationship with a man I hadn't seen since I was a toddler.

I changed the channel, landing on an episode of a documentary about how everyday objects were made.

But I wasn't watching. I was daydreaming, playing the what-if game.

Thoughts of Kari consumed me, though I tried to push them away. A reel of running my hands up her smooth, caramel brown thighs resurfaced time and again, like a record on repeat. I'd been avoiding thinking about what it would feel like to pull her warm body up against mine, to cup her face in my hands and look into her eyes.

What if it felt like heaven? What if it was everything I'd ever wanted? What if, despite wanting to believe that today would be just another day, that I would simply be showing Kari around the island, I decided to stop ignoring the flicker of hope that maybe it could be more than that?

My fingertips tapped nervously on the armrest of the couch while I berated myself about professional boundaries and responsibilities.

What if I threw caution to the same wind that carried the scent of salt and sand? If the feeling was mutual—and I suspected Kari wrestled with the same thoughts—and we resisted the attraction between us, we'd be dancing around each other just as awkwardly as if we gave in.

What if we had something exciting and beautiful and untamed and sensual, something that would be unconventional at best, messy at worst, but could also be so... *right*?

———

Kari and I had agreed to meet in the parking deck, but I wanted to make sure the extra helmet I had would work for her. I left my condo a few minutes early and rode down to the ninth floor. Just as I rounded the corner to her condo, her door flew open.

"Alright, girl. Do everything I would do and then some. Sex on a bike is *hot*."

I recognized Dionne's voice. In a panic, I ducked back around the corner and waited for her to pass.

"Dionne, get from around my door."

"I saw this video where this author was doing research on engaging in hoe-tivities on a motorcycle. He was doing all kinds of rocking and moving around, and that thing stayed put! I can attest to them being very sturdy—they can hold up to a lot of movement—"

"Girl, *shut up!*" Kari hissed.

"Fine, act shy. You're welcome for the leather pants. They're safer to ride in. And they'll slide down your thighs—"

Kari giggled. "Go! Away!"

Dionne snorted, then walked down the hall. I heard the elevator arrive before the doors slid open with a melodious tone. I waited to be sure she was gone, then resumed my trek to Kari's apartment. I knocked twice, holding my helmet in one hand and tucking the one I'd planned for Kari to use against my hip.

"What did you forg— Oh."

Kari stood in the open doorway in a long-sleeved shirt and black leather pants, her mouth frozen open in surprise. I was sure she hadn't been expecting me, especially after whatever she and Dionne had been discussing.

"Davis. Hi."

"Did I catch you at a bad time?"

"No," she said, finally snapping to reality. "It's just... Dionne just left and—" She waved a hand as if to say never mind, then stepped back to let me inside her condo.

She'd done a great job turning the place into a perfect blend of her unique style and the hotel's laid-back beach decor. Along the walls were framed photos of her with friends and family, some of the beach, and even a stunning black-and-white rendering of a lioness, a nod to her zodiac sign. She had added a few accent tables and various knick-knacks so the condo no longer looked like a spruced-up hotel suite but a cozy beachfront home.

"I'm early, but I wanted you to try this helmet on." I showed it to her. Her eyes dipped to it, then back up to me. "I thought it would be better to know before we get on the bike. If it doesn't work, we can drop by a shop nearby."

"I was overthinking about wearing a helmet, actually, so I had Dionne braid my hair." Her hair had been twisted into neat rows that hung past her shoulders. "She also brought me these pants. Will they be okay?"

I surveyed her look, nodding my approval. The pants fit well and molded to her body. "Your brother must have taught you about appropriate riding gear."

"Moses? No. Worrying about Moses never wearing proper riding gear taught me that. I just want to be sure I'm safe in case something happens."

"I always ride responsibly."

I handed her a full-face helmet and watched as she lowered it onto her head. It was slightly too big, but not enough to go to the trouble of renting another helmet. "Fasten your chin strap." I watched her fingers feel for the clasp, then pull the strap through the opening and snap both sides together.

"Looks good. How does it feel?"

"Like I have a gigantic head," she said, muffled behind the fiberglass shield.

"Good. That'll keep you safe. Here's the fun part. Take that off and look inside."

She pulled hers off and peered inside the dark cavity. I pointed at a few wires and devices.

"See these? Speakers. And that?" I pointed to a microphone mounted near the mouth of the helmet. "That's a mic. When the Bluetooth is on, we can talk to each other. That's how you'll hear me over the sound of the bike. We'll test it once we're outside."

She squealed with unbridled excitement and clapped. "I can't wait! I need to put on my shoes."

"I'll, uh…" I pointed toward the door with my thumb. "I'll meet you by the bike."

A few minutes after I made it to the parking deck, the elevator sounded its arrival. When the doors slid open, Kari appeared. She had slung a small pouch across her body and carried the helmet.

"Wow," she breathed out, taking in the machine in front of her. "It's…bigger once you're up close. What a beauty."

"Thank you. I take good care of her."

"Her?"

"*Her*. Powerful, loud when she has to be to get the job done. Can be temperamental, but if I treat her well, she's good to me. She's definitely a woman."

I sensed her trying not to laugh, and I didn't blame her.

"Can we hook up the Bluetooth? And can we play music?"

"I'll even let you pick the tunes."

I connected my helmet and put it on, then turned on both units. While Kari put hers on, I unlocked the ignition switch, then turned the gear and pressed the start button. Immediately, the engine kicked to life, the rumble echoing through the concrete structure. I gave a pat to the seat and watched Kari struggle to kick her leg up high enough to straddle the bike. After a few moments, I stepped in close, gripped her hips, and lifted her, giving her enough clearance to settle on the seat.

"Thanks," she said.

"No problem," I replied. "Your mic is working fine. Speakers okay?"

She gave me a thumbs up. I climbed on the bike, settling onto my seat. "Scoot up close and wrap your arms around me. There's no such thing as personal space on a bike. Get as close as possible."

It had been years since I had a woman on a bike with me, since I'd had a woman this close to me. Between the vibration of the motor under me, the scent of her perfume wafting over my shoulder, her breasts pressed into my back, and the warmest part of her plastered up against my ass, I was powerless to stop my body's reaction to her.

Man… What the fuck are you doing?

"Hold tight and move with me," I instructed. "If I lean, you lean. If I don't, you don't. Follow me, okay? Otherwise, the balance is off. You'll always be safe with me. Got it?"

"Got it."

I twisted the throttle gently, and the bike surged forward. We began our ride down a winding dirt path, bringing us closer to the coast. The wind picked up, whipping through our clothing. Kari leaned in, her body tensing for the occasional changes in the terrain.

"You doing okay?" I asked through the mic.

"Yep!" she replied. "Are you okay? Am I holding too tight or anything?"

"No," I answered, laughing. Even if she didn't hear it, she felt it. I heard her singing along to the music blaring through the helmet speakers. The display on my handlebars showed the bike eating up the miles, my racing heart pounding in sync with the roar of the engine.

After a winding twenty-minute ride, I swerved into an uneven, divot-pocked parking lot. I'd been eating at a little hole-in-the-wall spot called The Shack since I'd arrived at The Pearl. Patrons often lined up behind one another for a juicy burger on a buttery toasted bun or a crisp green salad from this tiny, unassuming restaurant.

I parked the bike and we both dismounted. I guided Kari to one of the wooden picnic tables by the water's edge.

"Hope you're hungry," I told her, handing her a plastic-covered menu. "The portions are huge."

"I am starving, actually." Her eyes lit up as she scanned the menu. I was reminded of my first time eating at The Shack. I couldn't decide what to have, so I ordered three meals. I did not regret it. "Your choice of dining establishments is…interesting, Davis."

"How so?"

Kari looked around, her eyes taking in the lush greens of the palm fronds swaying overhead and the distant rolling waves of the Gulf of Mexico beyond the shore. "I guess I didn't picture a man whose shirts never wrinkle to hop on his Harley-Davidson and ride twenty minutes up the coast to a restaurant that might collapse if a hurricane-force wind blows in the wrong direction."

I laughed, nodding. She was right.

"Working at a resort that charges hundreds of dollars a night, eating all of my meals at a Michelin-rated restaurant with access to all the fineries of beachfront living spoils a person. Every so often, I like to remind myself that I, too, started from the bottom."

"Did you, now? How low of a bottom?"

"Night clerk at a Ramada Inn."

"Wow," she replied with a laugh. "Do those even exist anymore?"

"They do. Over eight hundred locations. It was a summer job that turned into a college job. I decided I really liked hospitality. I did grad school at Cornell, then I worked a few smaller chains before I landed at the Maison in New Orleans."

"That's where you met..." Kari's voice trailed off, but I knew where she was going.

I acknowledged her guess with a slight nod. "Charlotte. Yes."

"I— We don't have to talk about her. I wasn't asking, just clarifying."

"I'm okay to talk about her if you have questions. Or... would like to further clarify."

"The gossip is that she fucked you over."

I placed both hands on the table and clasped my fingers together. "She showed her true colors when her method of getting the job she wanted meant throwing me under the bus. Then she was going to be magnanimous and give me a promotion and a raise?"

My smile was bitter as I shook my head. "I decided to take my talents elsewhere. I'd rather help build a business, so I took on several properties that needed a guiding hand and structure."

"If you know nothing else," Kari said, her tone dry, "you know structure."

"I refuse to take that as an insult. I left those properties better than I found them."

"So then, how did you end up with Calhoun's ugly boot in your ass?"

"My reputation preceded me, I suppose. I was referred by one of the hotels I had worked with in the past. Calhoun had already fired two GMs. I was between jobs and considering going back to New Orleans, but I felt like I'd be moving backward. The Pearl was in dire need of what I do best. The challenge was tempting. So I bit."

"Know what I think?" Kari hummed, then crossed her arms and leaned forward. "You love that this isn't easy work. We're supposed to think you hate it, but you don't. You love working night and day, six to seven days a week. You're having a *blast.*"

I laughed louder than I had intended. How had she figured me out in just a few weeks?

"You're not wrong," I conceded. "But honestly—and I'm not sucking up here— it wasn't until you came to The Pearl that I started to really enjoy the job. When I felt like I had a partner, someone who could take the load off, who understood the vision and what I'm trying to do with the little money we have to do it, work became a pleasure. I have time to do what I really like doing. Thank you for signing on."

I averted my gaze, unsure if Kari would see my true intentions or feel like I was blowing smoke up her ass. Regardless, the words had to be said.

"You're being honest, so I'll be honest too," Kari said, tapping my hands, then pulling at my fingers until hers wound with mine. "You are the sole reason I didn't pass on this job."

"Kari…" I chuckled, remembering her interview. "You are *not* being honest."

"The hell I'm not! I walked into that office, and you were like, 'Bitch, who is you—'"

"I was *not*."

"I knew I would have to prove myself. I've loved earning your respect and your trust. And, I hope, your friendship."

I wondered briefly if Kari really meant friendship. "Certainly," I finally replied.

"I'm sorry about what happened in New Orleans. It actually makes me sad to think about not being able to trust a person I work so closely with."

"I appreciate that." I wasn't sure if she realized it, but we were still holding hands. I didn't dare move because I didn't want to remind her. "So…is there someone back in Austin waiting for your return?"

She shook her head, drawing her mouth down into a frown. "No one worth thinking about. Moving to Black Diamond was a new start. On all fronts."

All fronts? Even...the personal?

"I noticed you don't appear to date anyone. Are you, uhm...interested in dating?" Kari asked. Her tone was soft, quiet, the most timid I'd ever heard her.

"If a situation presented itself, I would not mind having someone in my life. She would have to understand this life. This schedule." After a pause, I lobbed the ball back in her corner. Feeling this out. Moving this...whatever it was... forward. "And you?"

"Same," she quickly bit out. "The schedule part—I feel you. We work long days and that can be hard for people to understand. Dionne offered to fix me up, but her criteria is anyone on two legs with a pulse and a penis."

I laughed long, loud, and hard. Kari was the best thing that had happened to me in a long time. I was going to enjoy this day with her.

"Y'all know what ya want?" a server asked, hands on generous hips. The Shack's logo stretched across an ample bosom clad in a tight, dingy white t-shirt. I reluctantly let go of Kari's hand to pick up the menu.

Kari chose a fried chicken sandwich with sweet potato fries. I ordered a double-decker cheeseburger with thick-cut steak fries. The server nodded, scribbling our orders before heading back to the kitchen. While we waited for our food, we kept the conversation light, purposely not talking about work. If we started, we wouldn't be able to stop, and I didn't want to spend close, personal time with Kari talking about work.

I felt relaxed, able to withstand her teasing and even throwing a few barbs back at her. I felt like I could truly be myself, knowing that Kari wouldn't judge me for being ambitious. I wasn't afraid to show her my vulnerable side, but I also wanted to get to know her a little better.

"I've been trying to think of a non-invasive way to ask

about your family. You don't have to talk about it if it's too difficult—"

"Davis, you're not nosy enough," she interrupted, laughing. "I assumed you knew all about my family situation. You don't hang out with Dionne at all, huh?"

I shook my head. "I haven't asked, actually, because I don't want an interpretation of what's going on. I want to hear it from you."

Sixteen

KARI

"Was Reyna always like that? Or did it get worse as she got older?"

The day had been perfect so far—a scenic ride up the coast on the back of a Harley-Davidson with my arms around the sexiest man I'd met in a long time, followed by a laid-back outdoor lunch with the ocean waves as a soundtrack. Over lunch, I explained why I was raising my half-siblings. As I recounted the story of losing our parents, Davis listened intently, his eyes never leaving mine.

"Reyna was always headstrong. We thought it was cute until she was a strong-willed pre-teen. After our parents passed away, she retreated into herself."

I swirled the last of my sweet potato fries in ketchup, popping it into my mouth. "After a while, she came around, but then she was in touch with her feelings of anger and abandonment. I got the brunt of it. She'll listen to her brother, though. He's been our saving grace, which isn't fair to him."

"Coming from a person who lost their father at a young age, do you understand why she acted that way?"

"I do, honestly. But she was not the only sad person. She was not the only angry person. I lost parents too. I get she felt herself spinning out, that she needed to exert control wherever she could. It's just…I guess I'm thankful that Moses adjusted pretty well. Reyna takes all of my attention."

"Do you think that's why he chose to go to Louisiana?" Davis asked quietly.

"He's always wanted to go to Xavier. He offered to stay behind, to do community college until Reyna was finished with high school, but I couldn't do that to him."

I shook my head slowly, sadly. "Dad was a physician, and Mose wanted to be just like him. After we lost him, Moses doubled down. Aside from Howard, Xavier graduates the most Black doctors. He's determined to be one of them."

Davis nodded at me, a glimmer of empathy in his eyes. "You've been juggling a heavy load for a long time, taking care of everyone's needs and managing their behavior, their feelings. Who takes care of you?"

"Between work, taking care of the kids, and life, there was no room or energy for that. On my days off, I checked out, became one with the couch, binged Netflix. I was getting old fast. That's one reason Dionne suggested I apply for this job— to be closer to her and to keep me too busy to disassociate."

My laughter had a touch of irony to it now. "I'm sure she'll make me take one of her beach yoga classes as penance."

"I'm glad you were there for your siblings. Who knows where they would have ended up?"

"I pretended to think about it, to deeply consider all the options, but there was no way I was turning them over to family that they didn't want to be with, that didn't know them. Reyna might not like me, but I have her best interest at heart. And I love her."

"You wouldn't put up with all of this if you didn't."

"Right now, she's on the verge of being kicked out of school, but she won't talk to me. I'm so frustrated and I don't know how to get through to her. I don't think letting her flunk out of college is what my dad meant when he asked me to take care of his kids."

My throat closed up, tears pricking at my eyes. Davis set both hands on the table, then turned them palms up. Without thinking, I laid mine in his. I felt my emotions roiling up and taking over. This was not what I wanted this afternoon to turn into.

"Kari, listen. *You* are what your father wanted for them. You're doing everything you can for your siblings, and we both know that. Sometimes, kids have to learn things the hard way. You might have to let her fall a little, but as her big sister, you'll be there to catch her, won't you?"

I nodded as the swell of tears, which had abated, started back up again.

"You don't have to be perfect. You just have to be there when she needs you. There will come a time when she will need you. She will call, and you will answer the call. That's what matters, right?"

"Yes, right."

When the check came, he removed a few bills and carefully placed them in the folder, then stood, holding a hand out to help me up. I held onto him tightly as he gripped both helmets with his free hand and guided us back around to the front of the restaurant.

When we reached the bike, he placed both of his hands around my waist, lifting me onto the seat facing him.

In a blur of movement, Davis stepped between my legs, his masculine scent making my head spin in all the right ways. He reached out to cup my face gently, tilting it until his lips met mine. The kiss was sweet yet demanding, slow yet feverish, filled with passion and raw emotion and a promise of more if I wanted it.

I wanted it.

The sun was high, and the day was hot, but the sensation of soft lips on mine sent shivers down my spine. My mouth opened, and the kiss deepened as we melted into one another. His tongue stroked mine in a slow, languid fashion, as if we had all the time in the world. That we were in public, in view of the road and the restaurant and everyone walking by was not a concern as my hands instinctively climbed his body until my arms rested on his shoulders.

His tongue traced the outline of my lower lip before dipping again into my mouth. Davis moved in closer, sliding his hands around me and pressing his body into mine. I gasped, feeling a solid length that lit a flame and fanned it into a more of a fury. Davis's heart thumped wildly against me, his breathing more ragged the longer we were intertwined.

When we finally broke apart, we were panting and flush with no desire to stop, but also knowing that we could go no further. At least not here, not now.

Davis sucked in a few breaths through his nose before he opened his eyes. My eyes met his, the heat of the moment evident between us.

"I hope I don't have to apologize for that. I will if I need to."

"You'd better not."

He smiled, then leaned in and dropped a kiss on my forehead. "You know, having you sit behind me, pressed up against me is the last thing I need right now."

"A tour of the island on your bike was your idea."

"I recall," he replied, then handed me my helmet. I put it on and gave him the thumbs up sign, swinging my legs around so I was ready to ride. He slid the visor up, so my face was visible, then leaned in and kissed me again before sliding it back down, strapping on his helmet, and hopping on the bike. I scooted close and wrapped my arms around him, just as I had on the way to the restaurant.

But this time, it felt much, much different.

We took our time motoring around, venturing into nooks, crannies, side streets and routes that we'd never be able to go on were we in a car. We had stopped at an isolated beach and leaned against the bike, enjoying the shimmering blue-green hue of the water. While we watched the waves rush in and out, he shared stories about his past and his own family history.

He'd lost his father as well, but he'd died when Davis was young. The Harley belonged to his father, and as a hobby, he built models of them. As a connection, Davis began building them, too.

"So that's why you almost bit my head off when I wanted to touch one of your models."

"I apologize for that."

"No, you were right. I shouldn't be touching people's things."

"I could have been friendlier. Less like a tyrant."

"You're not so much of a tyrant lately, Davis. I dare say you've been...*pleasant*."

"Pleasant?" He scoffed. "Don't let that get around. I have a reputation to maintain."

"Are you all twisted up inside about it? The kiss? The *kisses*."

He shook his head. "I'm not, actually."

"Okay, you're *concerned*. Or whatever the unflappable Davis Scott equivalent of concerned would be."

"Concerned would be a good word. But I'm not concerned about what you think I am concerned about."

"Oh? Then what are you *concerned* about?"

Davis laughed, then moved to stand in front of me. "Do

you know that I have laughed more in the time you've been here than I have in the last year?"

"I'm honored, I think."

"I can be intense, I know." Davis reached for me, sliding his hands around my waist, daring to slip his fingers under the hem of the long-sleeved shirt I wore.

"*Intense* would be a good word."

"There's a side of me I would like for you to know. That is the side that lets me relax enough to give in to how I feel."

"Mmmm. And that would be…"

He paused for a beat, then uttered the words I'd been waiting weeks to hear. "Against my better judgment, I like you. A great deal. If you're amenable, I'd like to spend much more time with you."

"Mmmm." I frowned playfully. "That's such a stiff way to confess that you follow me around the resort and stare at me all the time like a lovesick teenager." When Davis laughed, I continued. "And I only know that because I pay very close attention to everything you do. The feeling is mutual."

"I don't want to take advantage of our situation," he said, his tone low and seductive. "Our proximity, the potential for drama on the property. I also don't want to deny what's happening between us anymore."

I never craved a kiss from someone like I craved one from him, and it had only been a short time since he'd last kissed me. This time, when he leaned in, there was no timidity or gentility. He was aggressive and passionate. Davis had been a closed book, never one to show his feelings, but the ferocity of his emotions came through in this kiss.

I let out a soft moan, my hands wrapping around his neck as I lost myself in the moment. His hands slid beneath my shirt, his fingers trailing up and down my back, then around until he cupped a breast in one palm. His thumb found the hardened nub of my nipple poking through a thin t-shirt bra. I arched into him, mentally begging him to never stop while his other hand slowly crawled lower, egged on by the whimpers I sent to his ear.

His touch held a burning intensity that spoke volumes to how much he wanted me. I felt it in the way he was in no hurry to get where he wanted to go but enjoyed every swipe of skin on skin. He teased the button of my pants loose and lowered the zipper, growing harder against me as his fingers dipped between my thighs, finding my wetness with a groan.

"You're so warm," he rumbled against my ear as his fingers teased.

I gasped, bucking against his hand. He pushed two fingers inside of me, curling them in a way that made my eyes roll back in my head and stars come out in broad daylight. My legs trembled as he alternated strokes of my clit and long, deep plunges of his fingers with a building rhythm. Our bodies moved together in a dance that left me aching for more.

"Tell me you like this, Kari."

"Oh...*shit*. I like it. I like it so much. Stay... right... there..."

I moaned softly against his lips, my hands clutching the nylon riding shirt. Davis pulled back to find my eyes. In his, I saw such a volatile mix of vulnerability and want that it made my chest tighten. His fingers moved faster, his hips matching the rhythm as he hunched into me.

As much as I wanted this—his warm, soft lips, his fingers bringing me more pleasure than I could handle—I wanted to drag it out, to not to fall over the cliff too soon.

I couldn't stop it. With a moan, I unraveled, the sensations he'd coaxed reaching a peak.

"Oh my God, oh my God, oh my God... don't stop," I whimpered, body shaking, hips rolling in time with his fingers. "Unh! I'm coming! I'm coming!"

His breaths came in harsh pants, his hips pumping sensuously against me. "Kari! Shit! Oh, G—*uhhhhhhhh*..."

Our orgasms crashed together, spilled over one another in a chorus of sultry moans. We clung to each other, riding wave after wave. We heaved loud, full breaths of salty air, leaning against the Harley, our bodies pressed together.

"Fuck, Davis," I pushed out, breathless. Then I laughed. "You…you really know how to show a girl around the island."

"So, I have a confession," Davis muttered, his forehead against mine.

I raised an eyebrow in question, curious as to what he could possibly need to confess after what had just happened between us. "And you're telling me now because I'm so light-headed I won't remember it later?"

"I…I heard Dionne earlier. Something about *activities* on a motorcycle. I've been biting my tongue all day but I can confirm that she is correct—once locked in place and anchored by a kickstand, this bike can withstand quite a bit of movement."

"Obviously," I replied dryly, then burst into laughter. "You could have said something, Davis."

Slowly, he shook his head. "No, I couldn't. I needed to be certain that we were on the same page."

"I hope it's clear now that we're in the same paragraph."

"I'm not apologizing for that, either," he mumbled, stepping back to adjust himself in his jeans.

"Once again…you'd better not."

"So…" Davis glanced around as if there was anything we could do if someone had seen us. Any attempts at composure would be futile. "Do you think you've seen enough of the island?"

"You know what part of the island I haven't seen?" At the question, one of his brows hiked in curiosity. "Your place."

After a few moments of hesitation, he asked, "Are you sure that's the move you want to make?"

I imagined his home would reflect his personality—

orderly and precise, immaculately clean—but I wanted to see him in his natural habitat, where he spent his days and nights. I nodded.

Davis held my gaze for a few lingering moments before giving a confirming nod. "Alright then, let's go."

He helped me back onto the bike, then climbed on and snapped his helmet into place. I wrapped my arms around his waist and squeezed myself tight up against him.

We rode back to The Pearl with the local radio station in our ears. Davis eased the bike into his usual spot, then cut the engine. After helping me off of the bike, he gestured for the helmet he'd lent me, but I held it out of reach.

"You're taking it back? What if I want to go for another ride?"

"You'd want to ride again?"

"If it ends up like this one, I'm open to it," I replied, then had a second thought. "Oh. Is this...sentimental? I'm sorry, I thought it was—"

"Keep it," insisted Davis, his voice cutting through my apologetic rambling. "It's just...I planned to get you a custom, properly fitting helmet."

"Oh." I smiled, feeling my heart bloom in my chest. "That's so thoughtful, Davis."

"Well, it'll be safer for you to ride with me if the helmet fits well."

His intense interest in my safety was so endearing and I didn't want to discourage it. "In that case..." I handed him the helmet. "Let's plan on getting me a new one soon. I'm looking forward to more rides with you."

His eyes flashed with a fire that burned me down to my toes. "Why don't you drop your things at your place and meet me upstairs?"

———

I'd had ample time to second-guess my intentions.

While I tore off my clothes, took a shower, redressed and slipped my feet into a pair of shoes, I had so much time to think, back up, asses the situation. When I stepped off of the elevator on Davis' floor and walked the hallways to his condo, I could have turned around, took my horny ass home and reminded myself what I was here on this island, at this hotel, to accomplish.

I could have easily backed out. If I'd wanted to. But I didn't.

I wanted this. *We* wanted this. As stiff as Davis had been with me in prior weeks, he had been unable to fight his attraction. His desire lit something in me that I didn't want to tamp down. If we went through with this, there was no turning back. This was a point of no return.

But if we didn't take this step, the what-ifs would haunt us.

"That was quick," said Davis, swinging the door open, the scent of masculine body wash wafting out.

"I didn't want you to change your mind."

He smiled, stepping back to let me inside and closing the door behind us.

His condo was just as I had imagined it would be. Photos of him and his family on the mantle, a neat stack of books and motorcycle magazines on the coffee table, a small but well-stocked bar in the corner of his living room. His home mirrored him: structured and private.

I also understood the difference between a standard unit and the units owned by Calhoun. My place was modern and updated from the flooring to the appliances. Even the paint was more upscale than the bland layer of beige that graced his walls.

"Do you need anything?" he asked, his hands tucked into the pockets of loose cotton pants. His gaze was intense as he took in my attire. The tips of my nipples made themselves known through the off-the-shoulder cropped top. My leggings were tight, clinging to the apex of my thighs.

"Do you mean sustenance? I'm fine where that's concerned. But you asked me up here for a reason, so maybe you meant sexually…"

"I had meant sustenance, yes." Davis moved in, closing the space between us, his breath fanning against my lips as he spoke. "But since you asked, we could also apply that question to your sexual needs. And technically, you invited yourself up here. I didn't argue with your suggestion."

"You literally told me to meet you here. I was following your lead, Mr. Scott."

Davis cocked an eyebrow, then pulled me to him, mashing our bodies together. I felt him through our layers of clothing, pulsing and rigid. My body flushed with heat as I realize I was very much looking forward to being fucked.

"Before we make any moves," he started, "I'm fine doing… or *not* doing anything you'd like. I know we have already had a few moments and I don't regret them. And if that's all we ever have, I will be happy to have shared those moments with you. But I hoped that—"

"Davis." I laughed as I broke in, drawing my arms around his neck and stretching up to kiss his lips. "I don't need a dissertation. I'm here. I'm ready for this and whatever comes after it."

I was sure I saw relief in the flash of emotion that crossed his face, but it was the fire in his eyes that I couldn't ignore. He took my mouth with a passion I hadn't thought Davis was capable of expressing. Without breaking the kiss, he began shuffling us from the kitchen to the living room, then around the corner to the small but neatly comfortable bedroom. The soft click of the door as he closed it behind us punctuated the turning point in our relationship.

We weren't gentle with each other as we crumpled onto the bed. Our hands were greedy and rough as they roamed, and there was no small talk or artful seduction, only a primal hunger for what had been brewing between us for weeks.

Our breathing was labored as Davis pushed my shirt up over my head, revealing bare, full breasts. My fingers traced the play of muscles through his t-shirt before trailing my nails down his abs.

He sat up to pull the shirt over his head and toss it aside and hovered above me, his eyes burning into my skin. "Is now a good time to confess how much I've been thinking about this moment?" Davis rasped, his voice thick with barely restrained need.

I smiled as I confirmed, "It's always a good time for that," and pulled him down on top of me. His weight pinned me to the bed, the heat of his skin warming mine. His lips found my throat, trailing kisses down to my collarbone, his tongue flicking and whipping my nerve endings into a frenzy. His hands were everywhere at once, stroking my skin, rubbing my nipples, making my back arch.

I ran my fingers through his tight curls, felt the stubble of his beard brush against my skin as he moved from my neck to my breasts. His mouth closed over one nipple, teasing and sucking before moving to the other. He dipped to kiss me again before venturing past my navel.

Slowly, deliberately, he tugged down my leggings. When I was naked underneath him, wet and wanting, I guided his mouth to me. The first brush of his tongue caressing my skin awakened every nerve ending. I tilted my hips, yearning for more. A pleasured, lustful moan rolled from him, his hands gripping my thighs to hold me where he wanted me.

He took his time, lapping at my most sensitive spots, ramping up the heat and anticipation until I grew restless and impatient. I gripped the back of his head and rode his face, grinding against his tongue, emitting quiet, desperate whimpers until my hips jerked in uncontrollable convulsions.

Davis watched my face, his eyes dark and intense. He

replaced his mouth with skilled fingers and kissed his way back up. He was quiet, but his body language screamed that he was more than ready for this moment.

"Don't tease me...*please*... I need you," I moaned as a warm, liquid pleasure coursed through my core, stirring a craving for more. He sat up, reaching to pull open a drawer in the nightstand, retrieving a small foil square. He tore it open with his teeth, his eyes never leaving mine as he yanked his pants down his thighs and kicked out of them, then rolled the condom on.

As he returned to the bed, I wrapped my fingers around his warm length, gently stroking him. His eyes lit up and his nose flared as he entered me slowly, sinking deep, hips rolling against mine. Our bodies moved together in a sinuous dance, each thrust eliciting a sigh from one before being answered with a gasp from the other.

I grinned, allowing my eyes to slide closed so I could just...feel him. Feel this, enjoy him, be present in the moment.

"Are you okay?"

"I...am *great*, Davis," I mumbled. "Are you?"

He groaned, which forced my eyes open to find his eyes closed, his bottom lip tucked between his teeth and a deep line of concentration across his forehead.

"Davis, seriously. Are you okay?"

"Yeah—yes." He huffed a hard breath, then suppressed a shiver. "I don't want this to end too soon, but...it's been a while, and you— You feel so—"

"You don't have to hold out, Davis. I already came. Twice."

I raised my knees, locking my ankles behind his thighs, then grabbed his face and brought his lips to mine. Our mouths collided, tongues dancing together, grunts and moans filling the air.

Davis drove deeper, faster. My hands moved to grip his

ass, to drive his rhythm and speed, making sure he didn't slow down or cheat me out of every inch.

"Kari…" he growled with a shudder. "Fuck!"

"Let it go. I want to hear you come for me."

As if he was waiting for permission, his thrusts grew erratic, his breaths harsh, his lips at my ear, teeth gently sinking into the lobe. The way Davis said my name never sounded so beautiful as when he ground it out in time to the forceful pounding of his body against mine.

"Kari, Kari, Kari, Kar—*fuck*!"

The room was full of the scents and sounds of our shared crescendo, of the reward of release after weeks of fighting it. I pleaded, tightening my limbs around him, moaning into his ear. We rode the frenzied, feverish heights of climax, pulse matching pulse, need matching need until we shuddered against each other, then collapsed, spent and breathless. I savored the sensation of him, his weight on me, his dewy, sweaty skin slipping, his chest heaving in time with mine.

Davis rested his forehead against my shoulder, his eyes closed while he tried to regulate his breathing…and, I suspected, to hide the swell of emotion. I traced the length of his arm until I found his hand and wound my fingers with his, pulsing our hands together until he opened his eyes. I held his gaze, mentally marking the raw vulnerability that he allowed me to see. The unspoken lingered between us, communicated in a long, meaningful, unbroken stare.

"You good?" I whispered to him finally.

After a few moments, Davis nodded and cleared his throat. "I suppose I was waiting on a review of sorts."

I snorted a laugh as he shifted his body so his lips were within kissing distance. "Why are you so unintentionally funny?"

"It's not unintentional. I don't let everyone enjoy my sense of humor."

Dionne's words, when she said that Davis Scott was so

different from the man I met when I first arrived at the resort, came back to me. She had never been more right.

"So, I should feel lucky?"

"Mmmm..." He hummed, bobbing his head back and forth. "Maybe not. Vance thinks I'm corny."

"Does he know it takes a corny person to know a corny person?"

"This logic escapes him."

Davis pushed up, propping himself up on an elbow. His other hand trailed my body until he landed between my thighs, where he slowly stroked the sensitive skin and still-enlarged bud.

"How are you?"

"Satisfied and ready for rounds two and three whenever you are." I ended my sentence with a smile.

"Two...and three..." He whispered, blinking rapidly, then leaned over to lay a soft kiss on my lips. "It's time for that sustenance I offered earlier, then."

Seventeen

DAVIS

"Is this your mom?"

I looked up from the meals that the robotic delivery cart had just dropped at my door to admire how Kari's body filled out my Cornell School of Hotel Administration t-shirt. She stood at the fireplace, peering at the photos I'd set on the mantel. I was not much for decorating, but I liked to think my folks were watching over me.

"Yes, that's her," I answered, then removed the stainless-steel dome that had been placed over two biodegradable containers. I moved the meals to plates, then pulled two forks from a drawer and brought everything to the living room, setting the plates on either side of the glasses of wine I had just poured.

I then joined her at the fireplace, moving to wrap my arms around her waist and nestle my chin on her shoulder.

"That's from her freshman year at Texas Southern." Kari's fingers traced the gilded frame. Inside was a glamor shot of a stylish woman with a smile that could light up a room, her wide collar and Afro puff a tribute to the era.

"She's beautiful."

"Yes, she is." I released her long enough to point to a similar photo of my father in thick glasses and a squarish haircut. "She met my dad there. That's him. He was a good man, or so I've heard."

Kari turned in my arms at the mention of my father, likely to search my face and gauge my emotions before asking more questions.

"You look like him," she declared after studying my face. I thought so too and had heard it all my life. "Is she still in Texas?"

"No. My stepfather got a job working for a computer parts manufacturer. He's been running the factory in Shanghai for the last few years. She didn't want to live in China, though, so she moved to DC to take care of her parents. He flies back to the US every six weeks, and she goes over there a few times a year."

"Unconventional," she mused.

"Indeed. They make it work."

"Making it work runs in the family, then."

I smiled, pulling my arms from around her to lead her to the couch, where dinner and drinks were set.

"My mom passed when I was three," she said, matter-of-fact. "I never talk about it, because...well, I don't know why. I think because I was so young and my father remarried and had other children that people forget."

"Do you feel you and Reyna should get along better because you have that in common?" Kari nodded. "Do you ever talk to her about it?"

"Mmmm," she replied, chewing. "She told me not to psychoanalyze her, that she and I were nothing alike, so 'lay off that therapy shit.' She made it clear that this was not a thing we could bond over."

Kari shrugged, then dug her fork into tender beef smothered in gravy with a mound of mashed red potatoes alongside it. I followed her lead, enjoying the first few bites of oven-fried chicken cutlet while the cable TV version of *The Fast and the Furious* provided a backing soundtrack.

"Sorry to bring the room down," Kari mumbled after a few minutes.

"You didn't," I assured her. "There's only so much surface I can scratch before we dig deeper. Your emotions are safe with me."

"I swear, if you make me cry into Chef Stephen's braised beef and gravy…"

"That wasn't my intention, but Stephen would take it as a compliment."

"They should make these movies with motorcycles," she commented.

"They did, kind of. *Fast X*. It only took them twenty-three years to give us a bike chase. And there's *Hobbs & Shaw*. It's a spinoff series. With Idris—you haven't seen it?"

"Uhm…" Sheepish, she rolled her lips inward. "I've actually never heard of it."

"Oh, Kari." I scowled, even putting down my fork. "Well, we have to watch it. Required viewing."

"I hardly think I *have* to watch it."

"You think wrong."

After clearing the dishes, we bickered about what to watch, then settled on *Hobbs & Shaw* because it was my house. She sat next to me on the couch, curling into me under a light blanket.

"You've probably seen every movie with a motorcycle in it."

"Not…*every* movie."

As the movie played in the background, Kari rested her head on my chest. It felt so…*right* being with her like this, as if we had been doing it for years. As if there were not a professional boundary between us.

"So…" Kari cleared her throat, breaking the silence after a while. "Should we talk about, like…how this is going to work?"

"What do you mean?"

"Davis…" Kari huffed, sitting up just enough that she could see my face. "What do you mean, *what do I mean*? I work for you—"

"*With* me," I corrected. "It will work the same way it worked before we had sex. We will do our jobs and go about our business at work. And when we aren't working…"

I dipped to kiss her, still reveling that I didn't have to hold myself back any more. I could wrap my arms around her, kiss her, touch her, hold her against me. Take my time worshipping her body and being thankful to share the same air.

"You know, you had a lot to say on the day you arrived at the resort. About how good you are at your job. Something about 'I have education *and* experience and the energy to learn—'"

Kari burst into laughter at my impression of her. "Not you using my confidence against me, Mr. Scott."

"Mmm. I see. I become Mr. Scott when I hold you accountable."

"No…" Kari shifted, flipping back the blanket and rising to her knees, bringing us face to face. "You become Mr. Scott when you get spicy with me."

"Spicy," I repeated, badly masking a chuckle with a cough. "I iron my handkerchiefs. My ties are alphabetized by color. I have never been spicy in my life, Ms. Savoy."

The flame that ignited in her eyes spread to mine. The look that crossed her face was carnal, hungry, and unapologetically wanton.

"I beg to fucking differ," she whispered before her lips crushed mine. I moved with her as she pulled me down with her, my arousal pressed into her core. She was warm and pulsing, whipping my need into a frenzy. She writhed beneath me, her hands skimming across my chest while she pulled my t-shirt over my head. We kissed with barely restrained passion, her tongue diving into my mouth, swirling and battling for dominance.

I raised myself to full height, noting that the shirt she had borrowed had ridden above her wide hips, luscious thighs, and her manicured pussy. I licked my lips, anticipating the feel of her skin against mine again.

"We're not doing this on the couch, are we?" I panted, hovering above her.

"I don't have another alternate sex location left in me. Take me back to your bed."

I pulled her up with me, then in a sudden strike of playfulness, bent to wrap an arm around her waist and curl myself around her torso, lifting her up and over my shoulder. Kari yelped with laughter, then slapped a hand over her mouth, which did nothing to muffle her incessant giggles as I hauled her to my bedroom.

I gently lowered her into the mess of sheets that we'd left earlier. "I have to be careful what I say. You *actually* took me to your bed."

"You once told me I was very literal. I live up to my accusations." I climbed into bed next to her. "So, what does being spicy entail, exactly? I don't want to disappoint."

Kari's expression darkened, her eyes narrowing as she gazed at me. "You never disappoint, Davis. Just be yourself. You're naturally very good at this." She reached out to trace a finger across my chest.

I pulled away and looked down at her, taking her in. "Could you take your hair out of the braids? I'd like to see you in your full glory."

"If we're using terms like full glory, I will do whatever you would like."

Kari sat up and pulled out the rubber bands that Dionne had used to secure the ends, quickly unraveling the twists until her hair surrounded her face like a halo. She then pulled her fingers through her mane, trying to tame the wild, voluminous waves.

"It's a mess, but…how's this?"

"Sexy. This is my favorite version of you."

She looked so natural, so uninhibited with it flowing freely. We locked eyes, sharing in the intensity of this day, this moment. I pulled her close, capturing her lips in a hungry kiss while my hands roamed her body, exploring every dip, curve, and dimple.

Kari gasped as my fingers brushed her mound, writhing in response to every stroke of her clit, every caress of her lips, twisting in anticipation when I traced patterns around her opening.

"Davis, please. You gotta suck it or fuck it," she whined. "I can't… I can't take it."

I chuckled. "Okay, hold on."

I pulled back to open the nightstand drawer that kept several items I wanted to keep close—extra towels, lubrication, condoms, and mints. I pulled two square packages from the box I'd stored there and ripped one open. As she did previously, Kari watched me kick out of the pants I wore and roll it on, her eyes widening. I grew hard and taut at the thought of being inside her again.

I crawled back to the bed and climbed over her, watching her eyes flicker with excitement as I moved between her open thighs, then lowered my body onto hers and buried myself deep inside her.

Kari rocked against me, her nails digging into my back. "Fuck, Davis! Damn, you know what you're doing."

I laughed softly before leaning in to whisper in her ear. "Happy to hear you feel that way."

Each time I pushed into her, she met me with equal force

until we were both panting, our bodies slick with sweat. I never wanted to be without the sensation of being one with her, her limbs wrapped around me, the rising cadence and volume of her moans in my ear. Our movements grew quicker, more desperate. Her muscles clenched around me, each spasm pulling me closer to the edge. The world seemed to slow as we both approached the peak.

"Kari," I groaned, her name an exhale on my lips. "Are you going to come with me?"

"Mmmm!"

She gripped me tighter, whimpering indecipherable words, moving under me with fury before exploding into convulsions and uttering a throaty cry. The sound of her climax drove me over the edge with a force so intense that I lost my breath and the room dimmed for a few seconds. I gave over to the urge to plunge deep, then grind against her until every drop was released.

We lay there together for what felt like an eternity but was likely mere minutes, our hearts beating wildly to the same drum. I pulled out slowly and reluctantly, not wanting to let go of this moment.

I caught her gaze as she smiled up at me. "Did I disappoint, Ms. Savoy?"

"Not at all, Mr. Scott."

I laughed at her response and rolled onto my back. Kari got up to use the restroom. When she came back, I took my turn, disposing of the condom and swishing with mouthwash before returning to the bed, drawing her closer to me.

"So, you're telling me that after today—" She began counting off items on her finger. "Our bike ride, our lunch, our conversation, the two orgasms I had before we even had sex…then the sex—"

"This is a great review of our day."

"So we can be in the office together, and like…just work together?"

"Yes," I replied, to which Kari objected. "You're a very busy person," I reminded her. "And with the festival coming up, that isn't going to change. This is actually going to be very easy. Besides…"

I cupped her face, bringing her lips to mine. "You're a professional. I have every confidence that you'll be able to carry yourself with the grace and dignity you've always—"

"Oh my God, Davis." Kari rolled over me, straddling my body with hers, then leaned in to kiss me. "Just know that at the end of the workday, this is where I want to be."

"If you mean on top of me, in my bed, I would also prefer that."

"Or the inverse, in my bed, working out all the frustration that's going to build from not being able to kiss you when I want to. Don't be surprised if I drag you into a storage room to have my way with you in the middle of the day."

"I— I'm afraid that wouldn't be advisable—"

"Davis!"

"Okay, okay."

I laughed, my palms sliding up her thighs, then around to cup her breasts, admiring their heft in the palms of my hands. My thumbs grazed her rock-hard nipples, eliciting a gasp as she leaned down for another kiss.

"I am looking forward to lusting after you, holding back my urges to beat down your office door, lay you out on top of your desk, and give you the best six—seven minutes tops—of your life."

"Mr. Scott!" Kari feigned shock, then smiled down at me. "I believe you've just revealed a fantasy you've been having about me."

"I have. And I don't know how I'll be able to resist not playing it out," I murmured against her lips, my fingers gently pulling her nipples. "But I will. With the promise that I will lay you out later."

"I already can't wait."

A few hours later, Kari trudged around my bedroom, picking up her clothes so she could head back to her condo.

"I wish you didn't have to leave right now."

"I know. But it'll be easier tonight than in the morning."

I nodded, understanding. My morning routine was a constant, and as much as I liked Kari, I didn't want to throw myself out of a well-established habit. Life as we knew it would not be normal again for some time, but we needed to at least pretend that things between us hadn't changed, that we hadn't whispered tender words to each other and shared wild, passionate moments joined together.

Kari slipped her feet into a pair of canvas shoes. Her key fob clicked in her hand as she snatched it out of the bowl near the door. I pulled on a t-shirt and the same lounge pants I'd removed twice now.

"What do you think you're doing?" she asked.

I paused, confused. "Walking you home."

"No. Before I know it, you'll be in my bed. I'm already walking funny."

"We wouldn't have to necessarily… I mean, there are other things we could—"

"Hug and kiss me goodnight, then throw me out of your condo, please."

With one last kiss and a long, clingy hug in which my hands roamed her body like I'd never touch her again, I watched from the door as she walked down the hall to the elevator.

"See you in the morning, Ms. Savoy."

"Knock it off with that *Ms. Savoy* business. You know what it does to me."

"I do now," I said, then laughed. When the elevator arrived, she called out to me, then hopped on. When I was sure it had taken her away from me, I stepped back inside the condo and sighed.

Man… What the hell are you doing?

Eighteen

DAVIS

"Why didn't I get a phone call last night?"

Vance stood over me as I lay mid-bench press. He had both hands on his hips and a furrow to his brow. I grunted, motioning for him to spot me. He lifted the bar and set the weights back on the rack.

I sat up and mopped the sweat from my brow and the back of my neck. "Sorry," I panted, catching my breath, then picked up a sport bottle and downed a mouthful of water. "Didn't realize you wanted to sit on the phone and gossip like teenagers."

"Nobody said all that. But you planned to take Kari out on the bike yesterday."

"And I did. I took her to The Shack for lunch. We rode around to some nice spots. You know, our usual route."

"And then…" Vance waved an arm around, urging me to continue.

"And then, I brought her back to the resort." I shrugged,

shook my head, then lay back down. "I'm about halfway through my set, if you don't mind."

"No, brother. I don't mind at all. But let me tell you something." He bent over me again, catching my eye. "I know you. I almost know you better than you know yourself. Whenever you're ready to talk, you know my number. Might as well come on up because you know Athena wants to hear about how she was right about you and Kari."

I wasn't sure how I thought I could fool Vance. He was closer than a brother and knew me better than anyone. I didn't want to share this budding relationship with anyone, though. The time I'd spent with Kari meant a great deal to me. I couldn't cheapen it with gossip and speculation, no matter how much Vance and Athena had been hinting about what a great connection we would have.

They'd find out about us in time. For now, I wanted to enjoy having a secret. The more people knew, the faster it would spread around the resort, and I wanted to avoid a situation.

Vance grew tired of hoping I would spill more details and walked away. I finished with a few miles on the treadmill before going home to shower, dress for work, complete my rounds, and have breakfast at Breakers. Like every other day.

But today certainly *felt* different. I looked forward to a chance glimpse of Kari around the resort, unknowingly tempting me in whatever fashionable curve-hugging outfit she wore. I waited to hear her in conversation with her staff when I went to my office. I longed to sniff the scent of her perfume when she just dropped by.

Work was going to be interesting for a while.

Hours later, I was deep into reviewing the reports that Justin had dropped on my desk. The resort had reached our highest ever occupancy over the weekend, thanks to spring break crowds. We were even under contract to sell two condos. Thankfully, the upcoming week looked to be lighter than it had been in the past month. We needed the time to be ready for the festival, which was due to kick into high gear.

Kari and her team were already packed with planning meetings since we had our marching orders from Fontaine, Wade and Gage. It was up to Kari to fill up the event venues and promote the rest of the festival, as well as the regular events around the resort. It was my job to keep the wheels on this train that could run off the tracks at any moment.

Three meetings later, my stomach protested how long it had been since I'd had breakfast. A glance out of the window told me it was a sunny, warm day. The largest pool on the property and the swim-up bar were both busy with moderate crowds and about half of the beach cabanas were occupied. According to the events log, today was the first day of Spring Fling, a weeklong slate of events for owners and guests at The Pearl, beginning with a garden party luncheon. I decided to forego another meal at Breakers and invented an excuse to see Kari.

She was in her element, drifting around the garden in a sundress that hugged her shape, setting floral arrangements and making sure each table was exactly as she envisioned.

The garden at The Pearl was one of my favorite spots on the property. Combining artful landscaping with naturally occurring foliage, it boasted lush greenery, trellises covered in vines, and paved paths that meandered through the space. The flat, grassy area in the center was a perfect pad for small tables of two or four seats. Kari's team had outdone themselves, transforming the spot into an oasis. White linens with pink and blue runners draped each table. Small bouquets of roses, purple iris, and deep blue pansies were fragrant centerpieces.

A roped-off bar was set up at the far end of the garden. I recognized the bartender as one of the staff from the Bistro Cafe in the Paradise tower. He wore a flowing white shirt over a sleeveless t-shirt, khaki shorts, and a white fedora.

Guests were already lined up for drinks, shoulders bumping to the beat of tunes from Sabrina Forrest, a jazz vocalist known for adding flair and rhythm to popular favorites, from a raised stage nearby.

"You actually came out of your office." Kari's teasing tone carried above the din of the activity around us. "I'm touched, Davis."

"I had to come find you since you don't seem to know me today," I drawled, coming to stand beside her.

"What happened to being busy, doing our jobs? I had a garden party to throw." She waved her hand in a flourish, showing off her hard work.

"I see. It turned out great. Actually so nice, I'm afraid to see the final cost."

"I'm within budget, Scrooge," she said. "I spent most of the money on the band, but I've kept a tight rein on our spend."

"Alright. We will see."

"Yes, we will," she replied, brows raised and lips pursed. She eyed my robin's egg blue linen suit, nodding appreciatively. "By the way, you're *wearing* that suit, and you obviously lined up your beard like I would be paying attention. It's not fair that I can't climb you like a tree and tongue you down until you can't see straight."

I glanced around, making sure no one could have heard her. "I know it's difficult, given the cut of this suit, but control yourself, *Ms. Savoy*. Working hours behavior is still in effect."

"You are egging me on, Mr. Scott," she said, smirking. "If you didn't come out here to take me behind a building and push my dress up—"

"I'm going back to my office." Sure that my face_was developing a pink pallor, I turned and headed back the way I'd come. "Send me a plate."

"Davis!" she called, laughing. "Come back! I'll be good."

"No," I called over my shoulder.

"Seriously! I bought us a table. We could talk about the festival."

I stopped and turned, cautious. "If you promise to behave yourself."

She rolled her eyes in petulance. "I mean, I can *try*."

Kari guided us to a table for two, away from prying eyes but with a clear view of the garden. The breeze from the Gulf rustled the branches of the trees behind us as we settled in and waited for the plated lunch.

I nodded my head to a table across the garden. Surprisingly, seated together were Lillian and Patrice...and *Carl*. "Hope you added a bouncer to the budget."

"I heard they're besties again," Kari muttered. "I wouldn't be surprised if there wasn't some threesome action going on over there. Anyway, I wouldn't sell them tickets unless they promised to get along. We'll see what promises get us."

"We will, won't we?"

She shrugged, then brought a glass of sun tea to plump lips coated in a beautiful berry shade. I wished we were alone so I could kiss her lipstick off. Then I shook my head, admonishing myself for such immature thoughts.

That didn't stop them from coming. It also didn't stop my body from reacting to the thought of kissing her. I picked up my glass of tea and sucked down half of it, then wiped my mouth with a napkin.

"So...what about the festival?"

"Oh! My team and I looked at all the space against the hours that we want to operate, giving us time to clear out and turn over staff between day and evening activities. We have feelers out to people who would volunteer their time and services, and some who would pay for space and time. The best part is that Fontaine agreed to lower his fee in exchange for full control over the concert series."

"Sounds like it's coming together. Is there anything you need from me?"

"Well…" she said, emitting a sigh. "I'm still working with IT to update the website so we can start selling tickets. It's going to be pricier than I budgeted, but it has to be done. Also, Fontaine sent over a preliminary rundown, and the performance times aren't going to work. We have ordinances we have to follow."

"I don't want to undermine your authority as the lead on this event, but I'm ready to step in whenever you need me to."

A week ago, the smile that Kari gave me would have only been a symbol of our growing respect for each other. Today, that smile meant so much more.

"I appreciate that. I'll loop you in if I get pushback."

Our meals arrived, looking and smelling delicious. The starter was a mixed green salad with bacon, avocado and a creamy dressing, paired with crab cakes and grits. The recommended drink, a sangria blend with rum and fruit juice, was refreshing, perfect for a hot afternoon.

As we ate, we chatted about everything and nothing, practically like old friends instead of formerly reluctant colleagues and secret lovers. Our dessert arrived, a decadent Key lime pie with billowy whipped cream piled high. I watched as Kari closed her eyes after her first bite, a look of bliss spreading over her face.

"Oh my God," she moaned.

"Sounds familiar," I commented, taking a bite, then catching her eye. "Holy shit, this is good."

"You curse when you get emotional."

"I am emotional about this pie," I confessed, eating the entire slice in a few bites.

After a break, Sabrina and her band took to the stage again. The beat—and the volume—of the music ramped up, and a few guests rose from their seats.

"I'd better get out of here before I have to judge a twerking contest," I said, removing my napkin from my lap.

"You don't want to show them how it's done, Mr. Scott? Vance and Athena are out there."

I searched for my friends and there they were, front and center, leading the crowd in a spirited merengue to Elvis Crespo's "Suavamente."

"I definitely need to go, or Vance will have me out there looking like a newborn deer." I stood, buttoning my jacket and straightening my tie. "So you like this suit, huh?"

The light bend to her lips was seductive and teasing. "The color looks nice on you. That tie and your shirt buttoned up to your eyelashes is a bit much, though."

"Don't bite on my style. I like to *look* like a property manager."

"You *look* like you're dying of heat stroke. It's okay to let a little neck show. I've made it my personal goal to help you relax, Davis."

"I'll take those lessons *personally*, thank you."

"See, there you go, teasing me when you have no intention of following through."

"I have *every* intention of following through."

Kari stood, dropping her napkin on the table. "We'll see. I need to check on my staff and say hello to a few owners."

"I'd like to see you later, Ms. Savoy."

"Yes, sir, Mr. Scott."

Kari sashayed away, hips swaying in time to the music. I watched her go, enjoying the view. Once she was out of sight, I headed back to my office.

On the way, I removed my jacket and unbuttoned my shirt at the collar.

A few hours later, I logged out of my computer and picked up my phone to text Kari. In my experience running a secret relationship, it was better to text about our plans than go to her office, where I would have to fight the temptation to kiss her.

Or do more.

The device rang in my hands. On screen was Justin's wide grin.

"Scott," I answered brusquely. Just as I picked up the call, Kari showed up in the doorway of my office. I waved her in, pointing to the phone. She came in and closed the door behind her, then leaned against the desk.

"The ride must have gone bad," Justin said, not even giving me the courtesy of a greeting.

"On the contrary. The ride was fine. Mission accomplished."

Kari closed her eyes, rolling her lips inward to keep from laughing.

"Mission accomplished? So, y'all hung out and..."

"Went to lunch, toured the island, talked as people and not coworkers. That was the mission. Why do you ask?"

"No reason, I guess." The disappointment in his voice was palpable. I almost felt bad for not coming clean, but Justin was the one person who would not be able to keep our secret under wraps. "I guess I hoped it would like...be a jumping-off point."

"A jumping-off point to what, Justin? You thought I'd make a move on her?"

Kari was quietly laughing, her head dropped low so I wouldn't see her and be distracted.

"Kind of?" He sounded sheepish, as if the idea now seemed silly. "The chemistry between y'all is off the charts, man. But I guess if you aren't into it, after a whole day with her..."

"It would be inappropriate for me to be *into it* with a member of my team. Would it not?"

"I mean, yeah. But nobody would say anything about it. There's not even a rule against it. It's just something some old dude at Cornell told you, and you think it's set in stone."

"For now, it is." I glanced at Kari, who looked away. "I'll let you know if my rule on that changes and I decide to...I don't know...take a member of my team to bed. Until then, this discussion is closed. Am I clear?"

"Yeah. Clear," he replied, then hung up.

"Davis, that was mean," Kari scolded.

"And necessary. He'll forgive me when he figures it out. I'm having a hard enough time lying to Vance. How are you doing with Dionne? And Athena?"

"I haven't talked to either of them. I can't... I can't see Dionne. I can text her lies, but I can't lie to her face."

"So...maybe we share with one person?"

"Then that person lets it slip, and it gets around. And suddenly, I slept my way to this position and you're playing favorites. We need to keep this on the low as long as possible."

"I agree. I don't know how long that's going to be since we both have friends that know us too well."

"Then we'll enjoy it as long as it lasts. Speaking of..."

She straightened, putting her full breasts in my line of sight. Flashes of the evening before when I had her nipples in my mouth and parts of her body in my grasp raced through my mind, then through my groin. I licked my lips, then dragged my eyes to hers.

She smiled, noting my reaction. "When...and where would you like to meet, Mr. Scott?"

"I hosted last night, so..."

"You can come to me, then. I'll cook. I think too many nights of ordering dinner for two from Breakers is going to tell on us."

"Good thinking," I agreed. I was already looking forward to our evening. "I didn't know you could cook."

Kari laughed, reaching for the door handle. "I raised teenagers. Surely, you didn't think we existed on takeout for twelve years. See you around seven?"

"I will not be late."

Nineteen

KARI

Three weeks later...

"Fuck, fuck, fuck, yes! Keep going...right there..."

I flung my head back, gripping the leather bar stool at the counter that separated my kitchen from my living room. Davis' hands were busy—one kneaded my breast while the other was between my thighs, stroking my clit in rhythm to the forceful thrusts he delivered from behind. He gripped me tightly, holding me close to him as he pounded his body into mine, sending every salacious and filthy thought he could muster into my ear.

Never in all of my random thoughts about Davis did I imagine him bringing me to climax in my kitchen.

"Let me hear it. Come for me, Kari."

The restrained growl in his voice was so erotic and did me in every time. My eyes fluttered closed as I ground against him, taking him in deeper each time he slammed into me. The slap of skin on skin echoed through my condo, punctuated by moans and grunts as the late afternoon sun filtered through the blinds.

"Ahhh…yessss…" I hissed as my walls milked him.

"That's it, Kari, take it. Take it all."

I squealed, finding it hard to contain myself. Davis was giving me such good dick, and I wanted it all, but I couldn't hold back any longer. The sweetest ribbon of pleasure wove through my core.

"Yes, yes! Fuck, oh my God…"

Davis let out a loud, guttural grunt, his grip on me tightening as the speed of his thrusts ramped up to a breakneck pace. He stiffened, then shuddered against me. The deep, chesty sigh and moans of relief that he pushed out after climax had become my favorite sound.

In a brief span of time, Davis had taken a crash course on how to make me come undone. His skilled tongue, gentle hands, and the sexual instrument that was his body were all tools in his arsenal. He knew what to say, how to drag out the orgasm, and when to send me over the edge.

Starting a scandalous secret affair with my boss was probably not the wisest choice, especially since we both lived and worked on property. Davis' strict rules about work hours quickly fell apart. Within days, he gave in to reckless behavior when he could get away with it—stealing kisses in dimly lit corners, following me into empty spaces on the resort, and sneaking to my office before or after hours.

There was a thrill, knowing there was something between us that no one else knew about, that was just for him and I. We were playing with fire and we both knew it, but the excitement only added spice to our trysts. I had never felt more alive than in these past few weeks of learning the ins and outs of Davis Scott. My heart raced when I recognized his footsteps approaching or saw his broad shoulders coming down the hall because I knew it would be a race against time to steal a few moments together before someone would knock on my door or his or come around the corner and discover us.

We tried to be discreet, but we couldn't keep our hands off each other. Every day at five-thirty, whether or not the workday was complete, we met up to exorcise the pent-up desire and sexual tension between us.

Davis nuzzled my neck before he dropped a hot, sweaty kiss on my cheek, then pulled out and headed to the bathroom. My blouse and heels and his pants and loafers were unceremoniously scattered across the entryway and kitchen. That was as far as we'd made it before we couldn't hold back any longer.

I bent to pick them up off of the floor and dump them in my bedroom to deal with later. My evening was set aside to work on the festival while Davis went for a ride with Jason and Vance.

I reached to unzip the skirt Davis pushed up over my hips while I dug for my phone, which buzzed incessantly inside my tote bag. When I pulled it out, Dionne's photo popped up on screen.

I winced. I was already on thin ice with her.

I still hadn't seen her in person, and I could only get so far with late responses and vague texts, especially to her pointed questions about Davis. For the past few days, Vance had been giving me long, questioning glances. I was avoiding him and Athena, and so was Davis.

"Hey, girl," I answered, hoping I sounded as breezy and casual as I thought I did. "What's up?"

"Buzz me up is what's up."

Panic shot through me. "Buzz you up where?"

"I brought dinner, but I can't get upstairs in this top security, fancy ass building you live in. Let me up!"

Fuck. A glance around my condo told a story that I was not ready for Dionne to know.

"Uh…okay. Give me a few minutes. I'm… I just got in from work, and—"

"Don't even worry about hiding whatever it is you got going on. We need to get it out in the open so I can stop pretending I don't know you're fucking your boss. Let me up, bitch."

Fuuuuuuck. The time of keeping our dirty little secret from our best friends was coming to an end.

———

In the few minutes I knew I had before Dionne would show up, I pushed Davis out of the door, ripped off my skirt and the bra that was just barely on, and changed into a comfortable t-shirt and yoga pants. I took the last few seconds to whip through the condo, picking up various items that Davis or I had left sitting around—two wine glasses from dinner the night before, two mugs in the sink from that morning, an extra toothbrush in the bathroom and a pair of his shoes in my closet.

I thought I had done a great job of resetting the place—or at least making it presentable—except for the one item I hadn't even thought to look for. Dionne's eyes landed on it within seconds of coming through the door, dropping a plastic bag that held two containers of food that smelled amazing.

"Don't even try to lie, my friend in hoe-tivities," Dionne said, bending to pick something up off of the floor, then holding a traitorous condom wrapper between two fingers. "And in the kitchen, too. Did you at least spray the counters down, or do we need to eat somewhere else?"

I rolled my eyes, then nodded toward the couch.

"Girl…" She snorted, then picked up the bag and shuffled to the couch.

I pulled out the last two clean plates in the cabinet, a few forks, and two bottles of water and joined her as she unpacked, feeling exposed and vulnerable.

"Any time you want to get started, I'm all ears. Don't make me ask."

"Obviously, Davis and I are sleeping together. What else do you want to know?"

"All the good shit!" she said, dishing up chicken parmigiana and noodles with garlic and cheese breadsticks. "Stop acting brand-new. How did y'all go from work, work, work to fuckin' in the kitchen?"

I cut into the chicken, swooning at the golden-brown crust. "I'm going to need those yoga and Pilates classes you're teaching during the festival this summer. This looks good, Di—"

"Focus." Dionne pointed her fork at me, then smiled. "And thank you! You know I like to cook, and I always make too much food. Now spill. How long have you and Davis been together? Y'all are *together*, right?"

"Since he took me out on the bike. We had one of those breakthrough conversations where he was real with me, not formal and stiff. It was like talking to a friend. We acknowledged the attraction between us, and we decided not to fight it. That may or may not have been our best decision because we can't seem to stay away from each other. Even at the office."

Dionne took another bite before asking, "So, did you test how sturdy a motorcycle is, or…"

I almost choked on the bread I was trying to swallow but nodded. "Uhmmm…he took me to some empty beach. We didn't have sex on the bike, but let's just say we fully tested the stability."

"I know where that is," she replied, nodding. "It's romantic at night, with the breeze off the water and no lights anywhere around." Dionne winked at me. "Have Davis take you back after dark. It's a good time."

I tilted my head in curiosity. "I'm learning so much about my best friend right now."

"Same, friend. *Same*. So listen..." Dionne set her plate down, then twisted to face me, her expression turning serious. "Real girl talk right now— if he can't pin your knees to your ears, you need to take this new yoga class I'm designing."

My jaw dropped. "My knees to my *what*? And what does it have to do with yoga?"

"Yoga improves flexibility by lengthening your muscles and strengthening your abs. Then you can do shit like tuck your ankles behind your head. This enables him to go *extra* deep."

She paused, lowering her voice and leaning in. "Trust me. There's a reason I started taking yoga. If that man ain't sending you to God and back, there's a yoga position that'll get you there."

"Okay, slow your roll, Dr. Ruth. Davis is not lacking there." I blinked slowly, shaking my head. "*Whatsoever*. I'm on the frequent flyer plan."

A Cheshire cat grin spread across her face. "Okay, Davis! Mans is putting it down! To be honest, I could tell by the way he walks that he's packing more than confidence."

"Okay, that's..." I groaned, hiding my reddening face with my hands. "Entirely true, but can we please talk about something else? *Anything* else? Davis is going to ask what we talked about, and I cannot tell him I discussed his girth and confirmed his ability to send me into orbit."

"Fine, fine." Dionne raised a hand in surrender. "But I brought that up because I wanted to talk to you about teaching an adult yoga class as part of the festival."

"Adult yoga, where you teach us how to have our knees up by our ears?"

"Not in those exact words, but…yes, actually. It would be a paid class, a limited number of signups, so it's intimate. A private, adults-only, mature exploration of the body and how yoga and Pilates can enhance our sex lives. It's a new class I'm designing, and I need participants."

"And…you want our family-friendly festival crowd to be your guinea pigs?"

"Hey, friend. I delivered an opening act and a whole concert series. It's your turn." Dionne dabbed her mouth with a napkin as if she were a most prim and proper lady in that moment. "You have a daytime and a nighttime schedule, right? And you need to fill spaces, right? Did I mention I'm paying for the space I'd use?"

"Since you put it that way…" I was half-joking, but her idea was growing on me the more I thought about it. "If you're serious, write me up a proposal on what you would need, how often you'd teach, what kind of space would be necessary. I'll work on a way to get it past Davis."

"Yay!" She clapped. "I'll email it to you in the morning. I'd want the room blocked off to ensure privacy—blackout curtains, sexy music, a little liquid or green encouragement… the whole nine."

"Blackout curtains are a must if you're going to be talking about sex-enhancing yoga poses."

"So…is this thing with Davis going somewhere? Or are you just having fun? And is that enough for you?"

I let my answer roll around in my head before giving it a voice. "I like Davis way more than I should, given that he's my boss and I haven't known him long. It's not enough in the long term. I'm inching closer to forty. Davis is almost *fifty*. But it *is* fun, and that's enough for now. We can't be anything more than what we are at the moment, and we haven't had important, defining conversations yet."

Dionne's head bobbed in understanding. "You always have your head screwed on tight and your eyes wide open. You rock at this job, and I can tell you really love it. But…may I speak?"

I held my hand out, urging her to continue. She grabbed it, giving me a reassuring squeeze.

"I told Ameenah and I'm going to tell you—it's going to get real serious, real quick. Even if I wasn't looking into your big, beautiful brown eyes, I knew it when you avoided me for weeks instead of just calling to say you fucked your boss. Davis is not a guy that does casual conquests. He doesn't collect notches on his bedpost, and I can already tell that you mean something to him."

"Now you tell me, after you encouraged me to ride the pony."

Dionne laughed at my indignation. "You know good and well it was only a matter of time before you two fell into each other's beds. All I'm saying is enjoy it, but don't be afraid to advocate for you, for your needs. And make sure you know what he wants and that you match. If this becomes too hard, or not fun, or a challenge to how you want to live your life, you and Davis have to get on the same page about it."

"I hear you. I just don't think either of us knows what this is yet. We don't even have labels. Or pet names. Even in the heat of passion, he calls me…*Kari*. I'll tell you what, though…" I paused, smiling. "When he calls me *Ms. Savoy*?"

I let out a lusty grunt, pulling my bottom lip between my teeth.

"I told you that could be hot."

"And you were right."

"Enjoy the booty calls and the clandestine meetups. But don't let fear of where this could go or how fast it's going stop you from getting what you really want whenever you discover you want it."

I heaved a heavy sigh, eyeing my half-full plate. I was full, and the conversation was sobering.

"That sigh usually means *get off your soapbox, Dionne*. I'm done. Do you want to talk about something tame?"

"Like a sex-themed yoga class?" I suggested, laughing. "I'm pretty sure I have some sorbet I saved from dinner a few nights ago. Want some?"

Twenty

DAVIS

Revving engines and the smell of gasoline met me as I pulled into 3B's Biker Bar. The lot was a sea of leather-clad riders, chatting and admiring each other's machines. Vance and Jason leaned against their bikes, bulky arms crossed and helmets off, in deep conversation.

I parked next to Vance's neon yellow Ducati, then cut the engine and took off my helmet. He broke from the huddle, turning to peer at me with a curious glance, then clapped me hard on the back.

"Well, well, well. Look who decided to grace us with his presence this evening."

"Hey, watch those bear paws." I pulled off a pair of finger-less gloves, stuffing them in the compartment on the back of the bike. "Apologies, I was held up with some last-minute tasks. I'm only twenty minutes late."

"Hah," Jason shot out. "See, the Davis I know has never been late. In fact, he's always early and waiting for us. So that begs the question..." His eyes narrowed, and he tilted his head. "What last-minute tasks were you…you know… *doing*?"

"I have suspicions and theories," Vance offered.

"No one's interested in either of those. I'm starving. Are we eating or what?"

"Wait, I'm interested," said Jason.

"Yeah, Jason's interested."

I heaved a sigh, rolling my eyes. Kari had rushed me out of her place, mumbling something about Dionne being onto us and that we would not get away with hiding our relationship much longer. I could only guess what was happening in her condo, but the time had come to reveal our secret.

"Fine, if you just have to know my business. But not until I have a burger and a beer in front of me. Let's go."

The scent of fried food hit me like a wall. I'd worked up an appetite and was looking forward to dinner with friends. I was glad to return to our weekly ride, to have some normalcy after the chaos of my work schedule. Adding in a love interest meant I had virtually no time for a life outside of the resort.

We found a booth in the corner of the bar, away from the crowd and especially away from the speakers that alternatively blared country and rock music. I slid in next to Vance. Jason sat across from me. The server appeared with menus and took our orders before disappearing into the kitchen.

"Alright. Food's on the way. Beer is pending," Vance said, prodding me in the side with his elbow. "Out with it."

"I already know why Vance is chomping at the bit to hear this. At least Jason is subtle, with his smug married ass."

"Oh, it's a love life update, is it?" Jason's smirk told me all I needed to know.

"Both of you deserve Oscars for these performances where you pretend you don't know I'm seeing Kari."

"Finally!" Jason huffed, pretending to wilt. "Dionne has been asking nonstop. I kept telling her you hadn't said shit about it."

"Well, now you can have conversations with your wife about us. I'm sure she's shaking Kari down for all the details right now."

"It's been a month, man," said Vance. "Took you long enough."

"I could have gone much longer, but it would have killed you two."

Vance leaned in. "It was the tour of the island on the bike, wasn't it?"

A smile crept to my lips, thinking about the day I put Kari on the back of my bike and rode with her around to my favorite spots on Black Diamond. The conversations we had, the meaningful stares, the soft touches, the fiery kisses and moments bringing each other to the edge of ecstasy... That afternoon changed everything.

"A large part of our connection was the bike tour, yes. Honestly, Kari took great pleasure in making me feel like a fool for being worried about her knowledge and experience. She's owned the role and transformed her department. It's like night and day. I've been able to breathe, to enjoy my job again. I've gained a great deal of respect and admiration for her—"

"And," Jason interrupted, "it doesn't hurt to have something pretty in the office to look at."

"Ay, man, I work in that office!" Vance protested.

"Like I said..." Jason shot back. "Why do you sound like you're reading a PowerPoint presentation? You good with this?"

"I'm very good with this," I assured him, working hard to keep a dreamy, delirious smile off my face. "Once I realized I couldn't ignore my attraction to her, I decided to pursue her, but only if she was interested. She was more than interested."

The server stopped by with frosty glasses of Blue Moon pale ales and left again. Jason slid his beer closer. "Sounds like the chemistry is real. So, are you going to make it official, or keep it on the low?"

"Given my history, I don't want to deal with the politics of dating someone who works with me. Any advancements she makes would be seen as something she earned on her back. We haven't put a label on us, and I don't know that we're in a hurry to—"

"Women like to know who they are to you," said Vance. "Definitively."

"Kari knows who she is to me." I shrugged my shoulders. "We're still in the can't-get-enough-of-each-other stage." I bobbed my head side to side.

"If you play it right, that stage never ends, brother. By the well-fucked look on your face and the tumbleweeds in my text message inbox, plus the empty seat you used to occupy at my dinner table, you two have been getting it *in* and having a very good time."

I laughed. "That would be an accurate observation."

"That would be an accurate observation," Vance mocked. "Nigga. Please tell me you don't climax in full sentences."

"Not that that would be a bad thing," added our server, who had appeared at our table at the most inopportune time, carrying a tray with our dinner orders.

Jason choked on his beer, coughing out, "Oh God…"

"Sorry, guys. I have terrible timing. I've got a Triple-B burger for our prolific climaxer, a fried seafood platter, and a chicken burger."

She set the plates in front of us, giving me a wink as she walked away. Part of me wanted to crawl under the table. Part of me could eat my burger in two bites, I was so hungry.

"If you all are done being nosy, let's move on. I want to still have some daylight left to ride."

"My advice is to enjoy it, man," said Jason, ignoring my suggestion to change the subject. He picked up a lemon wedge and squirted it over a selection of golden fried shrimp. "Your face doesn't depress me for once."

"Kari is a big reason for that."

"Which, I believe, Athena and I told you would happen."

"Yes, you did, Vance," I conceded. I picked up my burger, determined to fill my mouth with food so I could stop talking about my love life in a biker bar.

The conversation moved to our regularly scheduled bike maintenance day, then the upcoming festival. Both Vance and Jason had been talked into running a vendor booth. *Game On!* and Wanderlust Travel would alternate sponsoring and staffing the information station, where festival attendees could pick up a map, ask questions, and get directions.

"The website goes live in a few days. I'll be happy about that. Kari has been working with a web designer for the past week to put it together. It cost way more than I budgeted, but it was necessary. I'm ready for this festival to show Calhoun what we're capable of so he can loosen the purse strings."

"Have you heard from him lately?" Vance asked, swirling the last few fries on his plate in ketchup. "Seems like he's gone silent."

"He's been suspiciously quiet. Then again, occupancy has been up since Kari started, and if finance is right, we're not drowning anymore. Can't say we're turning a profit, but we're not hemorrhaging. I see that as a positive."

"Yeah, but will he?"

"I need him to. My meeting with MGMT is coming up, and I'm about to ask them for provisional funding to pay summer staff. I need about a hundred more people to work this festival, or life is going to get very difficult."

"Put me on the payroll, man," Jason offered. "I'll give you any hours and manpower I can spare."

"Thanks. Now I only need ninety-nine people."

"This is how you know Davis is getting pussy," said Vance. "He's relaxed enough to make jokes."

After dinner, we climbed onto our bikes, donned helmets and gloves, and sped into the orange glow of sunset, engines whining. The next hour revived my soul as I thought of nothing except the wind in my face, the vibration of my bike under me, and the beauty of the Texas landscape whizzing by in a blur of color fading into darkness. We held back from tapping in full throttle, rolling along back roads familiar only to locals.

By the time we split off—Vance and I toward the resort, Jason to his house—I was tired but satisfied. I pulled into a spot next to Vance and killed the engine, then removed my helmet.

"It was good to get out tonight," I told Vance. "I didn't realize how long it had been since we were out together."

"That'll happen when you get caught up with a good woman. Suddenly, you only want to spend your free time with her."

"You think I'll get corny like you? Make eyes at my girl like you do to Athena? Wait, is Kari going to have me reading romance novels?"

"If you're lucky," said Vance. "Listen, I spend an hour a night on the chaise lounge with Athena, reading whatever sappy, lovey book she picks out. Right now, we're deep into bell hooks. I read, she reads, we talk about it. And then, my brother?"

Vance's arm slung heavily over my shoulder as we loped toward the elevator together. "We hit that bed and set. It. Off."

My grin was shy. "Sounds like a strategy for keeping a relationship strong."

The elevator arrived. I swiped my fob. We each selected our floor, then waited for the cube to rise.

"I know you see how happy my lady is. My goal in life is to keep her that way. It's worth being called corny for loving her out loud. My prayer for you is that you fall so hard, you won't even realize it's happened. You'll wake up one day looking forward to doing shit like sitting in a bubble bath reading aloud to her about female pirates falling in love with muscle-bound men."

"I'm not sure pirates are her thing...but I get it."

As the elevator doors slid open, Vance slapped me on the back. "Later, man. Say hey to Kari and tell her to stop avoiding me."

"Yeah. Tell Athena I said hey."

I swiped through the door and dropped the key into the bowl. My brain was buzzing from the ride and conversation, so it took a few moments to notice Kari's key ring at the bottom of the bowl.

A soft light poured from the bedroom. I frowned, walking through the living room, then rounded the corner.

Kari lay in the middle of the bed, wearing one of my shirts and nothing else, her body on display in the low light. Her eyes were open, and her lips were curved into a gorgeous, tempting smile. The balcony door was open, the curtains billowing in the breeze.

At that moment, I could have been convinced to do something corny.

"Hello, Mr. Scott," she purred.

"Evening, Ms. Savoy," I said, unable to tear my eyes away from her shapely, delectable legs, her supple thighs, her round breasts and taut nipples.

I pulled the riding shirt I wore up and over my head, then unzipped my jeans and kicked out of them. "How was dinner with Dionne?"

"Eventful. She's happy she doesn't have to pretend not to know about us anymore. How was bikes and beers?"

"The bikes were fast, the beers were cold, the food was greasy. Vance and Jason also know about us."

I quickly joined her, my exhaustion forgotten as Kari

straddled my thighs and pressed her mouth to the hollow of my neck.

"You just felt like coming up tonight? Or is anything wrong?"

"I knew you probably had to tell Vance and Jason about us, and I assumed you would want to talk."

"Mmmm. Good assumption." My palms traced the contours of her body, committing every curve to memory as she arched into my touch. "Do *you* want to discuss that? Or do you want to talk about why you're wearing a shirt I *just* had dry-cleaned and pressed?"

"Hmmm. Tough choice. Talk about how your friends probably uttered some piggish grunts about you finally getting some? Or," she said, scratching her nails down my chest, "tell you how *sexy* I feel in your freshly pressed dress shirt and how much wearing it makes me want you to rip it off and fuck me hard."

"You want me to *rip* my shirt—"

My words were cut off by her lips. Kari's silky thighs entwined with mine as she ground her warmth on my erection. Her eagerness, her hunger for me was heady and intoxicating. I groaned, gripping the curve of her ass, and pulled her closer to me, no longer caring about anything but making her feel as good as she made me.

Without breaking the kiss, I flipped her onto her back. Her legs wrapped around me, her body moving in sync.

"God, Kari," I panted into her neck. "I want to fuck you so bad."

"Stop wanting and do it!"

I cursed myself for not grabbing the condom beforehand. "Okay, hang on."

Kari stretched her limbs, luxuriating like a cat as she watched me lunge out of bed, pull a condom from the drawer, rip it open and roll it on, then dive back into position. Before I could even get comfortable, she had me deep inside her.

Sex with Kari was always sweet and spicy, more than I could have ever dreamed of yet never enough. I lost myself in her wet heat, her taste, her scent, her sounds, muffled as they were to not give us away. I couldn't get enough of her, couldn't stop rocking my body against hers.

Kari came first, stifling a back-bending moan as she pulsed around me. I followed, collapsing next to her.

"You...wanna hear something funny?" Kari panted into the air next to me.

"Maybe," I answered, catching my breath.

"Dionne and I had a conversation tonight about yoga poses that help you have better sex. After she left, I looked some of them up online and, uhm...I might try some."

"Was that the funny part? What are you trying to say?"

"Well... Dionne is proposing an idea to *teach* that class during the festival."

"That is completely out of the question."

An adorable peal of laughter rolled from her. "The funny part is that I *knew* you would say that."

———

Every employee on the management staff was gathered around the meeting table as I entered Kari's office. We'd all received a calendar invite for a momentous occasion, one that would kick open the doors and start the clock on the festival.

Vance stood off to the side, leaning casually against a table and scrolling through his phone. He caught my eye and winked before going back to his screen. I walked over to Kari's desk, anxiety prickling my nerves. This was going to be a monumental event for us; I couldn't wait to see how it all played out.

"Good morning, everyone. What's the latest?"

Kari looked up from her computer. Her eyes were red, the

bags under them evidence of the late nights she'd put in this week. I had done my part, but she had been the driving force.

"IT is waiting on my signal to go live, but I wanted you to be here."

"Great. I can't wait to see it."

I took the seat next to Kari and gave her a resolute nod. She sent a ping to her contact, who confirmed that he was updating the website. After a moment, he replied we should refresh the browser. Kari tapped a few keys on her keyboard, then duplicated her monitor on the screen on the wall.

A stunning aerial shot of the resort came into view, showcasing a vibrant landscape filled with the lush greens of the gardens and the golf course, the sparkling blue pools, the guest and residence towers, and endless stretches of white sand against emerald waters. Bold text scrolled, announcing the highly anticipated Beats & Eats Festival at The Pearl Resort and Residences. The image beckoned visitors to immerse themselves in paradise, where every sense would be indulged in the ultimate summer experience.

Each page loaded with fluid transitions and lively background music. Featured prominently were a course of plated dinners exploring worldly cuisines and cultures designed by Chef Stephen and the concert series sponsored by Tuneage Records, accompanied by an action shot of Gage and Wade mid-concert, followed by the monthly schedule of events and activities available for all ages.

"I see Vance got Wanderlust on the website." The not-so-subtle blurb and logo from Vance Griffin, Wanderlust Travel in the corner of the screen brought a laugh from everyone.

"If I'm not the official travel agency of not only this festival but the resort, we need to evaluate our friendship."

"Davis? What do you think?" Kari looked over at me, her eyes searching mine. It was cute that she sought my approval, as if I'd declined any of her ideas.

"Well done, Kari. Looks amazing." I laid a hand on her

shoulder, wishing I could be more open with how I felt about her in that moment. I'd reserve that for later. "Now we just have to pull it off."

"Thank you. It's been a long few weeks, and I can't even rest," said Kari, flipping over to the event schedule. "We have guests arriving tomorrow for a conference. I'm going to have everyone on their toes for a while."

"I prepped a newsletter to go out to my customer base as soon as the website was updated," Vance said, walking over to join us by Kari's desk. "Okay to tell my folks it's a go? I want to start promoting."

Kari nodded eagerly. "It's a go. Ours is going out this morning, and the ads in the Bullhorn and Corpus Christi Gazette go live tomorrow. I'm filming a spot tomorrow that'll air on the local channels. Let's get to work."

The staff dispersed, leaving Kari and me in her office. I closed the door, turning the lock on the knob to ensure we would be alone with no surprises.

"No turning back now," I said quietly, returning to her. I pushed the keyboard aside and leaned against the desk, close to her.

"No pressure," said Kari. "It's been madness, but it's actually happening."

I leaned in, my lips meeting hers in a soft kiss. "I've missed you," I whispered as our lips parted. She had been holed up in her office for most of the week, juggling tasks for the festival setup and maintaining responsibilities at The Pearl. She was overworked and exhausted.

She let out a sigh, a hand landing on my thigh and slowly climbing higher. "I've missed you too."

I trailed a finger down her neck, then over the swell of each breast, outlining her cleavage in the silk blouse she wore. I watched goosebumps rise in its wake.

"Your presence is requested at my place tonight. We'll eat, drink…celebrate…"

Kari bit her lip as her nipples rose in response to my touch. "By celebrate, do you mean some activity that I need a sex yoga class for?"

I laughed, but not too hard. It took her *days* to talk me into letting Dionne run an adults-only yoga and Pilates seminar. Kari made several great points and convincing arguments, namely that we had wine tastings and alcohol flights and I let Jason pitch a monthly poker tournament, so we were already hosting adult-themed events. After agreeing to a long list of rules, Dionne finally wore me down and I gave my consent.

I pushed up from the desk just as my phone buzzed in my pocket. "It's your lucky day. That's exactly the kind of celebration I had in mind. Limber up."

Twenty-One

DAVIS

"Mr. Scott, come in."

Gavin Palmer's voice cut through the cacophony of noise in the pavilion as the midday sun beat down on the crew setting up the concert stage. Fontaine and his army had descended on the island, and work had been nonstop ever since. The resort was slowly transforming from a sleepy beachfront retreat to a bustling hub of activity.

"Mr. Scott, come in," Gavin repeated.

I stepped away, ducking into the main building. The air conditioning hit me like a cool caress the moment I crossed the threshold. I closed my office door behind me, pulling the radio from my belt.

"You'd better be dying, Gavin," I bit into the radio. "I've got people everywhere and a hundred things going on."

"Not dying, just stuck. Kari has me out in Corpus Christi looking for lumber for some damn thing. I need you to release a couple of people to load out extra chairs from storage for a meeting in the conference center ballroom tomorrow. Kari is gonna be on my ass if she can't check it off tonight."

I frowned. "You didn't schedule your team for setup? That's not like you, Gavin."

"Thing is, that Fontaine nig— Pardon, that gentleman from the record label has them all jumping. They don't want to disappoint anyone or jeopardize anything by pulling off to set up some chairs. I need you to play bad guy—or good guy, whichever fits. If they can pull the chairs, I'll set the room when I get back, but we've got to get going on it."

I rubbed my hands over my face. "What do you need?"

"A hundred and thirty of the soft seat leather chairs. Most of them will be covered in plastic and already on pallets. They can load them up in stacks and move them over with a dolly. Then two of the big chairs for the stage, and a podium and mic stand while they're at it."

"Is that all?" I asked, only halfway joking.

"I've got a whole list if you're serious, but I know you're not."

Sighing, I tried to hide annoyance and frustration. I simply did not have enough employees to staff the resort. I couldn't wait for my meeting with MGMT. They were coming to the resort for once since I insisted I did not have the time to fly to Dallas.

"I'll see what I can do, Gavin."

"'preciate it," he said, then hung up.

I paced my office, scanning the list of employee assignments for anyone I could pull off. I almost called Jason to see if he was available but thought better of that. Instead, I removed my jacket, then began unbuttoning my shirt cuffs and rolling up my sleeves. From the desk drawer, I pulled a set of keys and set off for the storage area.

"I know that look. I peep that stride." Vance caught up with me, then fell into step. "Must be something serious—you took your jacket off and got your arms out. What kind of trouble are we getting into?"

"I need some chairs moved over from storage to the conference center for a meeting tomorrow, and I'm short on staff. I could use some manpower if you're into moving more than your mouth."

Vance raised an eyebrow. "I don't spend all that time in the gym looking at myself in the mirror."

"Try not to get crushed by anything. Calhoun's worker's comp insurance is probably not the best."

I led Vance to the storage area, unlocked the door, and flipped on the lights, revealing a gaping space full of extra furniture, temporary cubicle walls, hotel art, and other miscellaneous objects.

"Damn, how much shit y'all got in here?" Vance whistled under his breath.

Calhoun had, at one point, purchased inventory from a hotel in Miami that had closed. Much of the decor was outdated, but he wouldn't give the nod to discard it.

"We don't use much but the chairs. They're in pretty good shape."

"Well, where do we start?"

We counted out the chairs we would need, separating them from the rest of the inventory. Vance grabbed a dolly and loaded a stack of ten chairs, then did the same with the second and lugged it out of the room.

After an hour of lifting, stacking, moving, and unloading, we were both dripping in sweat.

"Is it me, or is it getting humid out here?" Vance swiped at a bead of perspiration rolling down his forehead.

"I thought it was just me." I cringed at my reflection in a nearby window. I had wet patches under my arms and a damp spot around my waist where my shirt met my slacks. "Kari picks on me about being all buttoned up all the time. I see her point now."

"You should really invest in a forklift," Vance commented, tipping his dolly again.

"Maybe I'll ask for one if Calhoun is in a good mood tomorrow."

We dropped off our next load and headed back to storage. In the distance, I saw Kari approaching, arms waving wildly, so we waited for her to catch up.

"What are you two doing?" The look on her face read confusion, disgust, and amusement. "And why do you look so...*sweaty* doing it?"

"Bailing Gavin out. He needs to set up the conference center for tomorrow, but Fontaine has all my people busy. He didn't want you to rip him a new ass if it wasn't done."

The way her face fell and her eyes widened was near-comical. "I did not tell him to ask the property manager to move chairs from storage!"

"And he didn't. He asked me to release some people from duty, but I didn't want any issues with Fontaine. I roped Vance into helping."

"For which he owes me several of those fancy beers he hates buying."

"We didn't discuss that."

"Too late. We have a couple stacks to go." Vance started to head back down to storage, but Kari held out her phone.

"Hang on. We are going to have a large problem soon."

"What do you mean?" I asked, grabbing the phone, then blanching at the screen. "Shit," I hissed. "Weather alert."

We'd been blessed with pleasant weather for the past month or so, but our luck appeared to be changing. A tropical storm that I'd been watching, hoping it wouldn't veer toward us, was doing just that.

"Tropical Storm Deirdre has shifted," Vance read over my shoulder.

"And who knows how long it's going to last, or if it takes the bridge out—" Kari began to rant.

"Hey. It'll be fine." I grabbed her arms, almost pulling her to me by habit, but forced myself to stop. "This is why we have emergency procedures, right? Alert the crews and Fontaine. I'll call Gavin and ask him to pick up extra tarp or plastic sheeting while he's out. We'll cover up tonight. Unless the power cuts out, we can work indoors tomorrow. Got it?"

"Okay. Should I let Justin know since you're busy?"

"Yes. He should inform the staff and begin storm procedures. I hope no one is expecting deliveries tomorrow. This will for sure slow down traffic at the bridge to the mainland."

"I can manage the rest of this if you need to head to your office," Vance offered.

I shook my head. "I need to finish. Justin and Kari will find me if they need assistance."

After making a few phone calls, we moved the last few loads in silence. I watched the staff quicken their steps around the resort, making their initial pre-storm preparations. They'd been trained well, and I was confident that Justin would lead every department through their paces. He would also notify guest and resident services to release a prepared safety statement.

Gavin pulled up to the loading dock behind the storage unit, his truck full of materials. "I got all the tarp and plastic sheeting I could get my hands on."

"Thanks, Gavin. Get a few members of your team to pull lounges from the pool, disassemble the cabanas, and cover electrical equipment in the pavilion. Send Fontaine to me if he has anything to say. I want everyone safely at home by nightfall. Understood?"

He nodded, pulling his radio off of his belt and barking orders into it.

"Thanks for your help." I held out a fist to Vance, and he returned the bump.

"Anytime. I'm going to call Athena and make sure she's headed home."

"You two get somewhere safe and stay there. Call if you need anything."

Vance headed toward the Paradise tower, phone to his ear. I went in the opposite direction to my office. Before I could get there, my phone rang. Justin's grin greeted me. I picked up the line.

"How are things?"

A deep chuckle gave away his nervousness. "Depends on which things you mean. The resort is fine. Everyone knows what they're doing. But, uhm…"

Justin hesitated, which gave me pause. He was not a person who bit his tongue or held back, a personality trait that was equally amusing and annoying.

"What's up? Anything you need me to handle?"

"Davis, there's a tall man in a white hat and cowboy boots in your office."

Fuck.

———

"Mr. Calhoun. This is a surprise, sir."

I entered my office, reaching out to shake the hand of a man I'd only interacted with through phone calls and virtual meetings. His sandy blond hair was slightly dented from the white Stetson resting on the corner of my desk. His bright blue eyes stood out against his otherwise pale complexion, save for ruddy red cheeks.

He'd made himself at home at my desk, in my chair and in his usual position—legs clad in heavily creased indigo blue jeans crossed at the ankles, feet in the air so everyone could see his gray and white gatorskin cowboy boots.

"Davis Scott!" he called out through a heavy Texas twang. "How the hell are ya?"

In his grubby fingers was one of my Harley models. He set it down to shake my hand, gripping tightly, pumping vigorously before releasing me, but didn't get up or remove his feet from my desk.

"Fine, sir. Surprised…but fine."

"MGMT said they were called down here for a meeting, so I decided to see for myself how my investment was doing."

He gestured at the window that overlooked the pool outside the main building and, beyond that, the Gulf. "Not bad. Place looks alright, mighty fine. I tell you what, it's nice having a private plane at my disposal when I need it. Glad I got in before the weather shit on us."

I took a small measure of pride in his brief compliment. "Thank you, sir. And yes, a tropical storm is imminent. It could still redirect, but our teams are preparing just in case."

Finally, he dropped his feet to the floor and stood. I wasn't a short man, but Harlan Calhoun and his broad shoulders nearly towered over me.

"I like the proactive approach. I don't need to remind you how much money I've invested in this place."

"That's why I'm doing what I can to protect your investment."

"We'll see about that. I want a full report tomorrow. Stem to stern, lay it on me. Right now, though…"

He took a moment to grunt through a long stretch before grabbing his hat. "I've been up and moving since the asscrack of dawn. Your assistant set me up in a suite and had my bags sent to my room. Join me for a drink and dinner at Breakers tonight, if you can spare the time. If not, no worries. I'll be around."

He'll be around?

Those words twisted in my gut like a knife. I pictured him as a meddler, constantly questioning and interfering with my team's decisions—like now, the restaurant had to be open instead of closing for the safety of the staff.

"Thank you for the invitation, Mr. Calhoun. Weather permitting, I'd like to invite Ms. Savoy to join us. She was an excellent hire, and the recent turnaround has been due to the work she has put in."

He shoved a pinkie into his ear and wiggled it around, as if his ears were plugged. "I had hoped to meet that gal while I was here, actually. I want to discuss the economics of this festival she's throwing. I need to understand how it makes me money."

"I'm sure she can answer all of your questions and more. I have a few matters to manage due to the storm, if you don't mind…"

"No sweat. I'll see you both tonight." He set his hat on his head, hiked up his jeans, and stomped to the door. As soon as his shadow crossed my threshold and I heard his footsteps down the hall, I picked up my phone and scrolled for Kari's number.

"Hi, Davis. What's—"

"Major diversion," I said as soon as she picked up. "Calhoun is on property."

"What?! In the flesh? In person?"

"Boots and all. MGMT told him they were coming down for our meeting tomorrow and he decided to surprise me. He wants us to join him for dinner tonight at Breakers. He's already picking apart the festival. He wants to discuss the economics."

"I'm supposed to pitch an event that's already underway to the billion-dollar owner of this hotel? Tonight?"

"Whatever you're doing right now, delegate it and get to my office."

I ended the call and began resetting my space. I straightened my desk, then all of my Harley models since it was obvious he had manhandled more than one.

The door to my office opened without a knock, startling me from my thoughts. Kari stormed in, breathless.

"What the hell? Why is he here?"

"I don't know."

"Why does he want to meet with me? I just came up with the idea."

"I...might have suggested that you join us."

"Davis!"

"I'm not having dinner with that man alone when all of his questions are going to be about the festival."

"So you threw me to the wolves?"

"I did not throw you to any wolves. I'll be with you. The festival was your brainchild. I want you to pitch it. I want you to take all the credit. We have already booked entertainment, taken deposits, signed up vendors—he can't cancel it. But we need him to see that we know what we're doing, and we need a budget to do more programming like this."

I reached for her, pulling her to me like I wished I could have earlier in the middle of the resort. "I have every confidence in you, Kari. Please know that."

"I'm not worried, Davis. Just irritated. Though..." A slow smile made her lips curve deliciously. "I was looking forward to our date this evening. You know how I love to relieve the stress of a work day, *Mr. Scott.*"

"Don't get distracted, *Ms. Savoy.* Work hours rules are in effect."

Her fingers grazed over the buttons of my shirt. Slowly, she undid them. "A rules reminder from the man who came to my office at 9:23 a.m. to feel me up?"

I smiled at the memory of our hurried, quiet session of groping and grinding in her office. "That was a...check-in."

"Mmmhmmm. Your fingers checked into my—"

"You are a *terrible* influence. We should prep—"

"Davis, relax. I know this festival forward and back, inside and out."

Mesmerized, I watched her fingers work. "I know something else you know forward and back, inside and out."

Kari gasped, her brows high. One of her hands slid across

my thigh, then between them and up the inside. She gripped me from outside my pants and squeezed.

"See? Flirting with me! During work hours!"

"Are…are you unbuttoning my shirt? Is your hand all the way around my d—"

Without warning, the door to my office flew open. "Knock, knock. So I put Mr. Calhoun in—"

Justin stood in the doorway, his mouth agape. His eyes flicked from Kari's hand around my dick to our stunned expressions and back again.

Kari jumped out of my arms, then stood in front of me while I buttoned my shirt.

"Justi—"

"I knew it!" Justin glanced around outside the door, then stepped into my office, pushing it closed with a thud. "You two have been a little too cozy and a lot too friendly lately. I *knew* something was up."

"Justin, we—"

"No, Davis!" he broke in, index finger in the air. "I asked you point blank what happened between you and Kari, and you lied to me." He waved his hands around, sputtering in frustration. "This is *bullshit*."

"I know. We…" I cleared my throat, searching my mind for the words to say. "Kari and I—"

"We just thought it would be better if the staff didn't know," Kari said, jumping in.

"I'm not *the staff*," he protested, using air quotes. "I'm your second-in-command. I'm the one you call when you need to get shit done. I know you both personally, way better than you think I do. I have three sisters. I know perfume. I smell her on you, Davis, especially in the morning. Sometimes Chanel, sometimes Versace, sometimes Yves St. Laurent."

I stared at Kari. She stared at me. We were both speechless for a long span of time.

"Kari, you sometimes smell like Tom Ford when you shouldn't," Justin continued, shaking his head. "I'd bet I'm not the only one who has put it together."

"Look, I'm sorry, Justin. We…" I glanced at Kari, mentally begging her to jump in with the best way to explain why we'd hidden our relationship from him.

"We underestimated your level of investment in our relationship."

"Yes. And…we didn't want it to get around. I wanted Kari to stand on her own, and for the staff to not assume that she was doing well because she's sleeping with me."

"Please," he scoffed. "Anyone who has worked with Kari knows better than that. You can TedTalk me all you want. You two need to remember that I'm the best ally you'll ever have on this property. You haven't been as discreet as you think you have."

Justin stared us both down, then blew out an exasperated sigh. "How far behind am I? Who else knows?"

"Vance and Athena…" I began.

"And Dionne and Jason," Kari finished.

Justin nodded, rolling his lips in. "Mmmhmmm. So literally all of your friends but me."

"Because you work here. Surely you understand."

Justin's Chris Tucker-like countenance and sense of humor reappeared. "Don't hide shit from me, man. I've earned the right to be treated like an adult."

"Of course, Justin. Again, we apologize."

I stepped away from Kari and headed back to my desk. "What were you saying about Mr. Calhoun?"

"I put him in the biggest suite in Elysium. There's no one else up there. But I came to tell you that he doesn't have a check-out date."

I sighed, remembering his parting shot— *I'll be around.*

"Yes, he mentioned that. I have no idea how long he'll be on property, which means we have to be on our toes."

"The staff has been notified," Justin said. "And he'll get the service he's not paying us enough to provide."

"Thank you. You've led the staff well, not just today but in recent months. You've really stepped up, and it hasn't gone unnoticed."

Justin squinted with a frown. "You tryna start an affair with me too?"

"I think I have my hands full where that's concerned, don't you?"

"Agreed. Can I have a raise, then?"

My eyes narrowed. "Do you not have duties to attend to?"

He let out a long-suffering sigh before heading to the door, closing it behind him as he left.

"That was *your* fault," I whispered to Kari when he was gone.

"Guilty." She grinned. "I'll meet you at Breakers at six-thirty. We can roll through the highlights and be ready for Calhoun."

"Let's not drag this out. I want to be out of that man's face by nine o'clock."

"Deal. I've got something I want in your face by nine-thirty."

She winked, then walked out, leaving me in my office to pick up the pieces of my shattered workday.

Twenty-Two

KARI

This dinner was not a good idea.

Not only because it was silly to justify an event that was already underway and would very likely put the resort on the map, but because Tropical Storm Deidre was already blowing in like a wrecking ball. Breakers, along with every other amenity on property should have been closed.

If Calhoun was not slumbering away in a high-rate room in the tower directly across from Paradise, all non-essential staff would have been sent home. The bridge between the Texas mainland and Black Diamond washed out at the thought of a heavy downpour.

Davis and I bitched to each other about the situation via text, debating if he should do the right thing and shut the resort down or cater to Mr. Calhoun. In the end, Tim and his staff insisted they were looking forward to serving him, and he wanted to keep the bar and restaurant open so people could eat, drink, and watch the news.

Since it looked like I'd be going to dinner after all, I

dressed in a roomy blouse and dark jeans with comfortably low heels. I put my hair into a ponytail and tossed my phone, wallet, and key fob into a clutch. Then I donned a rain poncho, grabbed my tote bag full of notes, photos, and a full project plan, and rushed across the property to Breakers.

By the time I arrived, it was so windy, palm fronds were whipping back and forth like Willow Smith's hair.

Davis and I set up at the bar and ran through the highlights. Calhoun was a money man, so he wouldn't be interested in ambience and marketing approaches. He'd want to see cold, hard numbers—the spend versus the profit. As a bonus, I could show how a projected year-over-year of exponential growth could come from introducing a customer base to the resort and giving them reasons to return.

If I didn't tire him out with the numbers, I'd dive into the aesthetics.

"Have a drink," I encouraged Davis, nudging him with my elbow. He looked nearly ill, tapping his fingertips on the wood grain of the bar.

"I think I should have all my wits about me. I want to see his shit coming from a mile away."

I hid a smile at the infrequent use of profanity. He was trying hard not to show it, but Davis was getting worked up. His dirty tongue always told the tale.

"Well, you need some water or some caffeine or something. You're making me anxious."

My mobile phone chimed loudly in my tote bag. It was the tone I'd assigned to Reyna. I picked it up...then silenced it and dropped it back in the bag.

Reyna had been ignoring me for a long while, only talking to me when she needed money, then being surly and entitled in her request. She was likely calling to tell me she had officially failed out at Southern Methodist and expected me to fix that situation somehow. I'd call her after I'd met with Calhoun and Davis was not quietly hyperventilating.

Except that she called back. Then texted.

> Lil Sis: Hey, Reyna has this number saved as Big Sis.

> Lil Sis: I'm hoping this is Kari. This is her roommate Jeanette. She's been arrested. Please call back!

My heart dropped into the pit of my stomach as I read the text message. Everything else faded away as my deepest, darkest fear sprang to life.

"Fuck. I do not need this right now."

"Who is it?"

"Reyna's roommate. She said Reyna's been arrested."

"What?! For what?"

I stabbed at the notification to call her back. The line rang twice in my ear before a panicked, high-pitched voice picked up.

"Kari?!"

"Yes, I just got your text. What happened?"

Through tears and a shaky voice, Jeanette ran through the story. Reyna's boyfriend Ronelle had been kicked out of his apartment, so he'd been bunking at their place, a nice but expensive complex near campus. Earlier in the day, Jeanette had come home to sheer bedlam. The police had rolled in like an army, busting into the apartment with force and a lot of noise. Ronelle had drugs and paraphernalia on him, and Reyna was taken into custody.

I let out a deep exhale, using up the last bit of air in my lungs. "So, where is she?"

"County jail, probably. I don't know if police really do that one phone call thing or if that's just TV, but I have her phone. Ronnie will probably get a public defender and…" She hesitated, pushing out a pensive sigh. "I don't know, Kari. This isn't his first rodeo. He's the type to turn this on her because she'd get a lighter sentence."

"Yeah, I'm afraid of that, too. Thank you for letting me know about Reyna. I'll see what I need to do. Please let me know about damages or anything. I don't imagine your folks are impressed."

"I'm packing to move out. I told Reyna that I didn't want to live with her drug dealer boyfriend. She said she wasn't kicking him out, so my parents found me another place."

"I fully understand and don't blame you. Save this number, and please call me if anything else comes up."

"Is it bad?" Davis asked as I disconnected the call. When I nodded, he waved the bartender over and asked for a shot.

"What's your poison?" asked the bartender. I recognized him from the garden party a few weeks prior.

"Just make it strong and brown." When a butterscotch bourbon shot appeared, I threw it back, seething through the burn.

"So, what happened?" Davis asked. "How long is she in jail?"

"All I know is that she's at the county jail. I don't know how to find out more. I don't know how to get her out. I don't know what she's been charged with. I don't know what to do. We have this big ass meeting, and I can't even concentrate—"

"No, *I* have this big ass meeting," Davis broke in.

"We cannot lose this event."

"And we won't. Leave all of this"—he nodded at the stacks of folders and pages that covered the bar—"with me. I'll make sure Calhoun understands the work and thought you've put in—"

My phone buzzed again. The caller ID read *Dallas County Jail*.

"This is Kari," I almost yelled, picking up the line.

A mechanical voice recited, "You have a collect call from

an inmate at Dallas County Jail. Press '1' to accept charges." I pressed *1*, then waited through a few clicks.

"Kari?"

Her voice was so soft, so small, so timid. I hadn't heard Reyna so vulnerable since just after our parents died. For a moment, she was a frightened nine-year-old again, curled up into me and shaking in fear. I wanted to be furious with her. In fact, I *was* furious with her, but the tone of her voice told me it was not the time or the place for a lecture.

"Reyna, honey… I just talked to your roommate. Are you okay?"

"Not really," she answered, her voice warbling as she burst into tears. "I'm sorry, Kari. I didn't… I mean, I knew he was selling, but I wasn't, I swear!"

"First, these calls are recorded. *Hush!* Second, have you been arraigned? Charged? What do I need to do?"

She sniffed. "The cop said *distribution*. They said I have a right to an attorney, and they were going to give me a free one, but I don't want a free attorney because what if Ronnie tries to say I was the one selling because it's my first off—"

"Reyna!" I glanced at Davis while hissing into the phone. "Listen, alright? You are going to be a model prisoner right now. You are going to zip your lips. You are going to wait for an attorney that I will choose to represent you. And you are going to pray to sweet baby Jesus that you don't get jail time because as tough as you think you are, you cannot handle that. Tell those people that your attorney is on the way, then don't say shit else. Got me?"

"Yes," she replied through heaving sobs. "How long do I have to be in here? It's gross!"

"That's what I'm trying to find out. I'm—"

The operator broke in to tell us that the time was up, and the call disconnected.

"Kari, you need—" Davis' eyes diverted to a spot just over my shoulder.

I spun in my seat to watch a tall, blond white man in jeans and a long white dress shirt, untucked and hanging under a suit jacket, walk into the restaurant. A pair of mirrored shades hung from the collar of his shirt. His blue eyes darted around the place, taking in every bit of scenery and atmosphere.

"I don't even need an introduction. Calhoun sticks out like a sore thumb on this island."

"You need to get out of here, Kari," Davis said, spinning me back around. "Maybe you can make it off the island tonight."

"Bridge is already closed," said the bartender. "Might make it over if you've got a bike."

"Shit! If she's arraigned tomorrow, I can't make it—"

"Can her brother make it before you?"

I shook my head. "Moses took a group of kids to tour Howard University this weekend. He's further away than I am."

"Okay, then listen to me." Davis took my face in his hands, his expression tender, his eyes soft. "Go home. Start making phone calls to find an attorney. Book the first flight to Dallas you can find. Then pack a bag and put on some riding gear. I'll get you to the airport."

"Davis, you have—"

"My meeting isn't more important than getting you where you need to go. I'll handle Calhoun. You handle your sister. Go," he said, then turned me around, handed me my poncho, tote bag, and clutch, and pushed me toward the door.

On my way home, I called Dionne to fill her in. Her father was a Dallas-based attorney. If he couldn't represent Reyna, he'd know someone that would. She promised to make a few phone calls and call me back.

I pulled out a carry-on bag and opened it, laying it out on the floor of my bedroom. What does one wear to bail their sister out of jail and attend an arraignment hearing?

"Shit, I should probably book a flight," I mumbled to

myself, then flopped onto the bed with my laptop. After a few minutes of scrolling, my heart sank. Even if I could make the last flight out to Dallas, it was already canceled. The earliest I could get out, if the weather broke, was six in the morning.

My nerves were fried. I got up and paced, alternately cursing myself for ignoring her so much.

Then Reyna for getting herself into this mess.

Then Moses because he told me to leave her alone.

I was just about to book that hatefully early flight when my phone pinged with a text from Dionne.

> Dionne Woods: Don't book a flight yet if you haven't!

> Dionne Woods: You owe me so many yoga classes, bae. Until the end of time.

> Dionne Woods: Dad is calling the jail. He'll text me with info when he gets it but...

> Dionne Woods: I told Ameenah what was up, she called Gage. His plane was supposed to return to New York this afternoon, but they held it over.

> Dionne Woods: His pilot will fly you to Dallas as soon as the weather breaks. In the meantime, my dad is headed over to the jail to meet with baby girl.

I wanted to cry, I was so relieved.

> Kari Savoy: DIONNE. Oh my GOD, I love you forever and ever.

> Dionne Woods: Hoe, just be ready to get into plow position.

Kari Savoy: I might get into it right now as
homage.

> Dionne Woods: I heard the bridge is already
> closed. I assume Davis is putting you on the
> bike to get you over.

Kari Savoy: I wish he wouldn't. He needs to
be at this meeting with Calhoun tonight.

> Dionne Woods: Girl, HUSH. let that man
> show his love.

> Dionne Woods: Ok go pack. Call me when
> you make it to the airstrip so you can brag
> about flying private. Love you the most.

I smiled through tears at our old college sign off. At some
point, we'd fallen out of using it. It was a great time to bring it
back.

Kari Savoy: I can't thank you enough. Love
you the most.

I packed in a hurry, tossing panties, bras, socks, shoes, and
random articles of clothing into a bag. I shoved my iPad and
charger and a few books Athena had lent me inside and
zipped it up. Then I changed into warm riding gear: a black
sweater over a thermal top, leggings under my jeans, thick
socks inside my boots.

I rolled my bag out of my bedroom as soon as I heard a
distinct knock. I flung it open, greeted by the sight of Justin
and Davis outside my door. Justin was sleek and aerody-
namic in his riding gear, a helmet tucked securely under his
arm. Meanwhile, Davis, who was soaked, held a small black
helmet in his hands. He shivered slightly in the breeze.

"I was saving this to give to you as a gift."

He shrugged, handing me the helmet. It was midnight black with built-in speakers and a mic. He'd had my name emblazoned along the side, mimicking my signature.

"This helmet has Bluetooth. You should be able to communicate during your ride. I bought a new one to match. When you're back, we'll try them out together."

If Justin wasn't standing there, I would have jumped him. Davis was *adorable*.

"Thank you, Davis. I'm sorry to ruin the surprise."

He motioned toward the handle of my carry-on suitcase. "Dionne called to fill us in. Justin is going to ride you over to the hangar. He's better at navigating the wet roads, and...let's just say it's better that I stay here and smooth things over with Calhoun. The pilot needs clearance to take off, but we'll get you to the hangar to wait. Did you find an attorney?"

"Dionne's dad is working on it."

"Good. So, let's get you to Dallas."

I grabbed my phone, keys, and wallet, stuffed them into the crossbody bag I had used on our last ride, and slung it over my head and across my torso, then slipped on my jacket and the rain poncho. Davis reached over to pull up the hood and snap the front closed.

Then he leaned in and dropped a lingering kiss on my lips. He said so much without saying a word.

"You two need to get on the road," he said softly when he pulled back.

I steeled my resolve, stepping out of my condo and into the storm. We mounted the bike, and after a last wave from Davis, Justin started his engine, and we set off. The wind whipped around us, icy rain pelting my body. I clung tightly to Justin, trying to ignore the low rumble of thunder echoing in the distance.

The ride seemed long, probably because we were moving through a storm. Leaves and branches littered the deserted roads leading up the bridge between Black Diamond and the mainland. Justin was a skilled rider, dodging debris and other obstacles with ease, maneuvering the bike expertly across the bridge and into Corpus Christi through the darkness and less-than-ideal conditions.

"Made it," said Justin through the mic some time later. "Record time, if I may say so myself."

Gage's plane had been holding at Atlantic Aviation, the fixed base operator that ran private flights into and out of the city. The Cessna Skyhawk was parked on a strip of tarmac, ready to whisk me away to Dallas.

A burly man in a pilot's uniform greeted us in the waiting room. "I'm Clayton," he said, extending a hand. "I'll be flying you to Dallas soon as the weather clears up. You must be some kinda precious cargo."

"I guess. Why do you say that?"

"Gage called me about an hour ago and told me to get my tail over here and be ready to fly his friend to Dallas for an emergency as soon as we safely can." Clayton shrugged, a nearly empty cup of coffee in one hand. "Don't matter none to me. I'm on his dime. I'd planned on heading out in the morning anyway, so I'll roll on home after our pit stop."

Clayton led me into the lounge area where the air was warm and carried the scent of freshly brewed coffee. A row of soft, comfortable chairs lined each side of the room.

"Make yourself comfortable. There's donuts and coffee, the vending machine over there takes cards. Pretty good food. TV gets just about every damn channel, but I've been watching the weather. There's a pilot's lounge around the corner. I'm going to catch a catnap so I'm bright-eyed when we need to take off."

Clayton disappeared, leaving Justin and me alone in the quiet lounge. He sank into a chair, glancing around the room and giving a low wolf whistle. "This is how the other half lives, huh?"

"Looks it. You don't have to hang out with me. I'm fine to wait alone."

"I'm under strict orders to not leave your side until you're on that plane. I suddenly don't mind waiting. Have a seat."

I sat, realizing how tired I was from the flurry of activity. "Thanks for getting me here, Justin. You didn't have to."

"Yes, I did. Davis is a cool dude. I'd do a lot of shit for him. And you've become one of those people I'd do a lot of shit for, too. I'm glad he called."

He paused, pulling out his phone and dialing Davis up on speaker. "I never said there wouldn't be compensation, though."

I laughed, pulling out my phone to text Dionne. "I can't wait to hear what you demand."

Twenty-Three

DAVIS

"Back in my day," Calhoun drawled, swirling golden liquid in his glass, "people were dedicated to work. Know what I mean? I'm real tired of playing second fiddle, Davis."

Calhoun was fuming—again or still, I couldn't tell. I had briefly stepped away to arrange for Kari's transportation over the bridge to the private airstrip and returned to Breakers to take over for Tim. He was clearly unhappy with being left in the care of a restaurant manager. I was not at all concerned with what Calhoun was not pleased about.

He grunted, finishing his drink and pushing away the plate of meatloaf and vegetable medley. "I'm supposed to wait for her *personal issues* to clear up so she can tell me how she's wasting my money? Because that's how I see it, and it's unacceptable, Davis."

He crossed his arms over his chest, his face set in petulant displeasure.

"Your frustration is heard and understood. Your business is my responsibility; it runs whether or not Kari is here. I'm familiar with the numbers and I offered to review the festival specifics with you."

He'd waved me away when I brought out the stacks of spreadsheets and documents Kari had left behind. He was already bored with conversation about it; I surmised that he only wanted to have a pretty woman entertaining him. In his mind, Kari was grateful for employment, and he wanted to be praised for bringing her on. He also missed an opportunity to threaten her job.

"I don't need you to read a spreadsheet to me and guess at the numbers, Davis. I hired her to run marketing and events here, and I'd think nothing could keep her from reviewing the first large event at this resort with the man that owns it. You know…"

He paused, absentmindedly rubbing his eyes with this thumb and forefinger. "I think you underestimate how serious I am. This place better blow up this summer."

An eyebrow rose at the threat that had come at such regular frequency that it no longer frightened me. How many times had he said he'd replace me with a manager who would do his bidding without question?

"Or what, Mr. Calhoun? You'll hire another manager to exploit, to work seven days a week for criminally low pay, to run this resort on a ragged shoestring budget? My review with MGMT is going to highlight a great deal—chiefly how you've provided inadequate funds for staffing and upkeep."

I slid out of the booth and stood, pulling at the still-damp jacket, my body shaking with the buildup of adrenaline.

"You won't find a better, more dedicated team to run this resort. Kari is a key member of that team, and much of its recent success is due to her. So yes, if she has a personal issue that keeps her from entertaining you, that takes precedence. Unfortunately, I need to step away to check on the staff that have been held over because we've kept the resort open. The kitchen will close in about an hour, so order anything you think you might like now."

As I stepped out of the restaurant and into the storm, I felt Calhoun's piercing gaze at my back, but I refused to let him get to me anymore. I had a more than sneaking suspicion that he was talking out of his ass. I wasn't quite willing to bet my job on it, but if I lost the job, I'd be free. I'd take Kari with me and…

I froze mid-step. Take Kari and…do *what*?

Force her to quit a job she loved and excelled at?

Move her away from a premier resort on an island just to appease my ego and, more importantly, my libido?

Was I ready to admit to myself that I cared deeply about her? That my feelings for her were more profound and intense than I'd ever felt for Charlotte, even though we'd dated far longer? That the time I'd spent with Kari had made me far happier and that I was evolving into a different, better person just by knowing her?

The storm mirrored my own turbulent emotions. It would be the first time in over a month that I'd be sleeping alone, and I was not looking forward to it. How was I supposed to rest without her next to me?

The muted sounds of music and chatter lured me toward the maintenance wing. I pushed open the door to find a room full of people, some gathered around a table where a lively card game was in progress, the air around them hazy with smoke from half-burned cigars. Others were busy in Gavin's makeshift kitchen, running two electric skillets where tortillas were toasted before being filled with savory beef and fillings.

Above the din, a boombox thumped upbeat music.

"Ay, Mr. Scott!" Gavin called to me from the table, a smoking cigar in one hand and an array of cards in the other. "You play poker? We got room for one more!"

Ben, a guest services employee, filled tortilla shells with

cheese, lettuce, and tomato. "Hungry, Mr. Scott? We have plenty of tacos."

"I appreciate it, Ben. Thanks, though. Are these people stuck here tonight?"

Ben shook his head. "I live close, but it sounded more fun to ride out the storm here. Justin made sure we have access to a few guest rooms for those that need them."

"Good…" A bout of laughter erupted from the card game. The sounds, scents, and energy of people determined to make the best of what they had filled the room. "Sounds good," I finished, stepping back toward the door.

"Leaving so soon?" Gavin had laid down his cards and crossed the room. He gripped my shoulder and squeezed. "You stuck here just like we are. Come play a round."

"Gavin, I told you I wanted people gone before sunset."

"And I relayed your message," he replied, adding a bit of attitude likely aided by the beer he took a swig from. "They shut down the bridge early, though, so some didn't make it. They came on back, and we decided to hunker down here. This building is stone with no windows, so it's not likely we'll blow away, and the guests can't see or hear us."

"Good thinking. Ben said Justin made sure we opened a few rooms for people. Is everyone okay?"

"We got shelter, heat, liquor, food, cards," he said, counting off on his fingers. "We got all we need. Come on, play a hand. We're only betting pennies."

"You don't need me at that table, Mr. Palmer. But thank you for the invite."

"Ain't scared, are ya? There's a reason we're only betting pennies."

I was tempted. I hadn't played poker in years, but when I played, I was pretty good.

He grabbed my arm and pulled me over to the table. "Take off that jacket, roll up those sleeves, have a drink. You don't have to be Mr. Scott tonight. You can just be Davis."

I nodded, sliding into the seat that Gavin had pushed me to. The dealer shot me some cards from the stack. I picked them up, arranging them.

"We don't have time for you to alphabetize them, Davis. Play or fold!"

I chuckled, picking a card and tossing it onto the stack to a chorus of cheers from the table.

I lost count of how many rounds we played, but I was having a great time. And winning. It was refreshing to let my guard down for once and just be one of the guys. The crew members surrounding me were a diverse group, ranging from young adults in their late twenties to seasoned veterans in their mid-fifties. They joked easily with each other as they played. Inside jokes were rampant, the shit-talking wild and unfiltered.

"Davis!" Gavin yelled, breaking my concentration. "You playin' or you sleep?"

"I'm contemplating. Don't rush me." My hand was strong, and I was confident. "I'll raise."

Gavin grimaced, matching my bet. We went back and forth, increasing the stakes until he eventually gave in. "Shit!" he yelled, tossing his cards onto the table.

"Y'all don't *have* to let him win," Sarah called out from her spot on the couch across the room. The skillets had been turned off and now they were all gathered around the small television set.

"He's actually not bad," one player replied.

"What do you mean, *actually not bad*?" I asked, stacking my cards. "You thought I wouldn't be good at poker?"

"Not really," said Gavin. "Either you've been holding out on us, or you got lucky."

My phone vibrated in my pocket. I pulled it out to read a text from Justin. Kari's flight had finally departed, thanks to a window of clear weather. He was heading home to check on his family.

Relieved, I slid the phone back into my pocket. Kari was safely on her way. Her departure meant the countdown to her return had officially begun.

"I didn't get lucky," I told Gavin as I pushed back from the table and stood. "I'm excellent at poker."

"Now you tell us when you took all our pennies."

"You encouraged me to play. I'm going to head up. Tomorrow will be a long day."

"Surely will," Gavin replied. "Tell Ms. Kari we hope she's doin' alright and hurry back to us."

I blanched as I nervously scanned the table. "I... I will. When I speak to her."

"Which we all assume will be tonight. That scene down at Breakers earlier is flyin' around this place faster than a forest fire. Made it real obvious there's something goin' on. I kinda thought you two were getting close, and...well..."

Gavin shrugged, only the slightest bit ashamed of what he was about to admit. "I'm a gamblin' man. I won the pot."

I laughed, feeling my skin flush. "Do not tell Ms. Savoy that you placed a wager on whether she and I were dating."

"My lips are sealed, and they're smilin'. Y'all make a nice lookin' couple. Do what you got to do to keep her around."

"I hope we will see her back in a few days. In the meantime, reach out to me or Justin."

I left the room, the sounds of laughter and conversation fading. Once I swiped my keycard to enter my condo, I opened my laptop and accessed the surveillance system, clicking through the various cameras placed around the property. So far, we appeared to be intact, but it would be better to assess in the daylight.

Content, I logged off my computer and headed to the bathroom. I turned on the shower and, in the heat and steam, began remove the clothing that had dried against my skin and stepped in. The hot water spray beat against my neck, and I relished in the pulsing sensation as it rinsed away the dirt and tension.

I emerged from the bathroom wrapped in a towel after completing my evening hair, teeth, and skin routine. A notification lit up my phone. I lunged for it, hoping it was Kari.

> Kari Savoy: Just landed. Like, the wheels just hit the tarmac.

> Kari Savoy: Thanks for getting me here. I can't see Rey until tomorrow, so I'm going to the hotel. Dionne booked me a room close to the courthouse.

> Kari Savoy: I wish I was seeing you tonight.

I grinned and thumbed out a message:

> Davis Scott: I'm pleased that you've landed, Ms. Savoy. Travel safely and call me when you arrive at your room. I look forward to speaking with you.

> Kari Savoy: Why is that so sexy to me?

> Kari Savoy: Talk soon, Mr. Scott.

I fell onto my back, grabbing the pillow that Kari normally slept on. It smelled like her. I shut my eyes, picturing her soft skin against mine, imagining her warmth pressed against me, her gentle breaths tickling my skin.

The silence around me was no longer as comforting as it used to be. I couldn't wait for Kari to be back.

Twenty-Four

KARI

I rested my head against the cold glass of the car window as I watched Dallas city lights streak by. Exhaustion hit me like a ton of bricks, but my mind raced, my emotions flip-flopping by the second. I'd had a long time to think while waiting for a break in the weather so we could take off, then the short flight and deboarding.

I was angry at Reyna for being so reckless.

And scared that she was in real trouble.

And ashamed that I hadn't been able to keep her from this.

My phone buzzed in my lap. Bradford, Dionne's father, and I had been exchanging texts throughout the evening, but now he was calling.

"Hey, Bradford. Tell me something good."

"That, I can do. I pulled some strings and had Reyna moved up to the first block of the day. Arraignment begins at 9 a.m.—she'll be tacked on to the end, probably. I went over to the jail earlier and met with her to explain what'll happen.

I'll meet you in the courthouse lobby at 8:30. You drink coffee?"

"Lots of cream and sugar."

"Just like Di drinks it," he replied. I heard the smile in his voice. "I'll see you in the morning."

"Thank you for all of your help, Bradford."

"Of course," he replied, as if he never had a choice but to help us. "You're family. Reyna is going to be fine."

I was almost afraid of the answer, but I asked anyway. "How is she?"

"Scared. Trying not to show it. She was short with me until I explained what could happen if she didn't play this right, then she simmered down."

That sounded like Reyna Savoy. "Let's hope she can sleep and that she won't get smart tomorrow. Do you think they'll keep her?"

"They know me well around there. I'm confident I can argue a distribution charge down to possession, which is a misdemeanor. That's a fine as opposed to a few years, and she should have no problem getting bond."

"What about her boyfriend?"

"He's going away for some time." I had figured that. It was nice to hear someone else say it. "Reyna expressed concern about getting stuck with the charges since she doesn't have a record. That's not happening."

I heaved a sigh of relief. The car slowed, then pulled into the driveway of a brightly lit hotel.

"I just got to the hotel. See you in the morning."

The knot in my stomach shrank a little when he confirmed Reyna would not be taking the fall for her boyfriend's charges. I could only hope that she learned her lesson. Despite desperately wanting to protect her, I wasn't sure if I could go through this again.

I paid the driver via app and stepped through the entrance doors. The hotel lobby was deserted since it was well past normal check-in time. After signing for my keycards, I rode the elevator to my floor.

I suddenly wished I was riding up to Davis' condo or getting ready for a night in with him.

I entered my hotel room, the scent of bleach and generic hotel smell greeting me. The decor was bland and understated, but comfortable enough—just nothing like my beachy, cozy abode on Black Diamond.

I kicked off my shoes and headed straight for the shower, turning the knob to hot and peeling off my clothes. When I was nude and the bathroom was steamy, I stepped into the spray. The longer I stood there, the more I could unclench my jaw, roll my shoulders, release the stress. I lathered up with body wash and let my mind empty, just for a moment.

In place of thoughts about Reyna came thoughts about Davis.

Followed by worry about the resort, about the meeting with Calhoun, about the review with MGMT, most of which I should have been on property to support Davis. Instead, I was in Dallas, hoping my sister wasn't going to jail. I was still a new employee, still in a probationary period. Were I not sleeping with Davis, I wasn't so sure I'd have received such concern and care about my sister and this situation.

After my shower and body oil rubdown, I slipped into a plush robe and ran a few pumps of moisturizer through my hair, then pulled it into two braids. Feeling refreshed, I crawled onto the bed with my phone and called Davis on FaceTime.

After two rings, he answered. He was propped halfway up in bed and shirtless. "Hey," he said, his voice thick with sleep or want of it.

"Hi. You said to call, but I wanted to see you."

"No, it's fine." He reached over to set the phone on the charging dock and rolled over to face me. I noticed he had a towel wrapped around his waist. "I wanted to see you too. How are you? What's the latest?"

"Hey, remember when I thought the storm and Calhoun were going to be the hardest things I had to deal with?" I started to tear up but cut it off. "I'm sorry."

"Don't be sorry. We can talk about whatever you like."

"No, I'm okay. Dionne's dad went to see Reyna. She was a jerk, I'm sure. He arranged for her to see the judge in the morning, so I have to be at the courthouse at 8:30. Just pray she gets bail, and I can take her..."

I paused, rolling my eyes. "Take her where? I can't leave her in Dallas. Too many of Ronnie's friends are around, and she's obviously gullible. I can't take her to Austin and leave her at the house alone. I have a job four hours away that I love, and I don't want to leave because I have to take care of my sister."

"Sounds like a tough spot. You could bring her with you."

"With me *where*?"

"To the resort. Bring her to The Pearl."

I scoffed. "Davis, be serious."

"I am serious," he protested. "We could give her a job, some responsibility. We need people to work the festival—there's plenty to do. You can let her work off what I'm sure she owes you for bail, damages...pain and suffering."

"That sounds like punishment for *me*. She'll hate working for me."

He laughed. "She can work for me—I'll be the bad guy. Justin would love having a lackey. Let her fill in wherever she's needed—catering, guest services...maintenance. Gavin would scare her straight."

A tired but evil cackle rolled from my lips. "She has to know she will not be on her own for a while. Not after this year, not after this stunt. I haven't even spoken to Moses yet. He's going to be pissed."

Davis' eyes softened. "Sometimes it's a good thing that family is, well…family."

"Exactly. Would I do this for someone I didn't love so much, that wasn't a blood relative and a part of me?"

"Of course, you would. That's what I like about you—you wouldn't even think about it."

I smiled and adjusted, getting more comfortable. "You really like me, Davis."

"You say that like I don't know that. I'm realizing, now that you're gone, how much I like you."

"Oh? And…how much is that?"

He chuckled. The sound tickled my insides. "Do you want *me* to tell you, or do you want *Mr. Scott* to tell you?"

"First one, then the other."

"Well, Davis from Houston, Texas would say something like, 'I'm really diggin' you, Kari, and I miss your face,' because Davis from Houston says corny shit like that. But Mr. Scott, Cornell School of Hospitality graduate, would say, 'I care for you a great deal and your presence is missed.' We both hope you'll be back soon."

"If I bring my sister back, how are we going to sneak around to see each other?"

He groaned, scraping a hand down his face. "I don't think we have to worry about that. Gavin told me that scene at Breakers is all over the resort."

I smiled at the lingering memory of his fingers caressing my face, his gentle insistence that I leave to take care of my family. "Don't know how, but I forgot about that. Seems like eons ago."

"He sends his well wishes, and he hopes you're sticking around."

"Does *Calhoun* hope I'm sticking around?" I almost dreaded the answer.

"He doesn't know it yet, but he does. Later, I'll tell you about how I snapped on him tonight and we might both be out of jobs tomorrow." He ignored my wide-eyed stare and went right past it. "Right now, I want to talk about what you're wearing under that robe."

"What do you think? Brown skin and *nothing* else."

"Mmmm," he moaned softly. "I miss your skin. I want to see it."

"Not my bare-chested king over there telling me he needs to see something. Do you have anything on under that towel?"

Davis chuckled on the other end of the line, his deep voice rumbling through the phone. "You know very well that I'm naked, Kari."

My brows rose, a smile bending my lips. "I have to make sure. You're not going to show me?"

"Mmmm…no. As you can imagine, seeing you and hearing you is doing things to me."

"I *can* imagine that. I'm not opposed to seeing it. Probably close to what's happening over here."

"I'd like to see that."

"Are we really bickering over which of us is going to show their naked body first to a person who has seen every inch of them for the past few months?"

"We aren't so much bickering as stalling," he replied. But then I watched his hand move to his waist.

Slowly, agonizingly so, his fingers dragged the cotton towel down his body, revealing that V and the line of hair that I'd licked on so many occasions. When the towel was pulled away, he was in full view. Erect, thick, and curving upward, with a few drops of moisture at the tip.

"Davis. You miss me. A *lot*."

His pleasure rumbled over the phone line as he gripped his length in one hand. "You miss me?"

"If I was in that room," I began, dropping my tone to a low, seductive murmur, "you'd already be in my mouth."

A low moan rolled from him. The sound of his palm

stroking with increasing speed was such a turn-on. "And then?"

"I'd tease you a little…jack you off for a few. I'd swirl my tongue around the head the way you like me to. Lick it like a lollipop. Suck it, soft and sweet, then hard, until you're about to bust. Then, when you're about to come, I'd straddle you and take it slow. Drag it out until I couldn't take it anymore."

He licked his lips, then shuddered. "You…you've done this before."

"I have not!"

"You sure? Don't leave me hanging."

"Oh, well. Nothing left but to ride that dick so hard, my titties bounce against your chest."

"Fuck!" he moaned, dragging out the word. "Why are you so far away? I want to see you."

"See me? What do you want to see? Be specific."

He laughed. "Your titties, your pussy, those thighs, that ass. Show me all of you, Kari."

"Good boy. I like when you express yourself."

I propped the phone against the lamp on the nightstand and pulled the robe from my shoulders. My skin tingled in anticipation of my first virtual sex session. Noah was never this adventurous.

I shifted so he could see me laying on my side with one leg bent, caressing my clitoris in sync with him. The other hand gripped a breast and flicked the nipple that stood on end as if yearning for his lips.

"You like what you see, Mr. Scott?"

"Mr. Scott went to bed," he replied, breathless. "Davis thinks you're so *fucking* sexy. He wants more of you. All of you."

I gave him more. More of me with each stroke of my clit, each gasp and moan that rolled from my lips. His eyes didn't leave the screen as he watched me bring myself closer and closer to climax. His pumps grew faster, his grip tightening on his length.

"Use your fingers. Match me."

I felt the first tremors of orgasm and bucked my hips, encouraging the surge in my body as I inserted two fingers. "Yeah, that's it. You're making me come."

He sped up his strokes, pumping his hips and moaning in time with me. "I wish I was deep right now."

"Me too. In my mind, you're there. I'm so close…"

I moved faster, egged on by watching him pleasure himself, his actions sending ripples of erotic electricity down my spine. His breathing grew heavier, and I knew this wouldn't last much longer for either of us.

"Come for me, Kari," he gasped. "I want to watch."

We locked eyes as I rolled my hips and arched my back, calling out his name as I rode out my orgasm.

"Oh God, Davis! Shit, I'm coming!"

"Kari…"

His deep, shuddering breaths, the pure lust shining in his eyes, and the grip around his dick growing tighter and faster told me he was on the cliff, about to fall over.

"Come for me," I urged him, my voice like silk. "Let me hear it."

"*Shhhiiiiitttt…*" His eyes rolled back, and his body stiffened. Davis spilled his release onto the towel as he let out a hoarse, satisfied groan.

We lay there, panting together. My heartbeat thumped between my ears and my legs like frantic drums.

"I'll take the real thing any day, but that was…" I heaved a sigh, too tired to finish my sentence.

"Outstanding," he offered.

I giggled. "Did Mr. Scott wake up?"

"Briefly. He sensed someone having fun. I put that nigga back to sleep."

I howled at that. "Davis! I didn't think you knew that word!"

"Oh, but I do. Only a few people know the real Davis Scott. You're getting a crash course. Sorry if it's a rough one."

"I like this ride. Remember what you said when you put me on your bike? I'm always safe with you."

I curled up, feeling the cool air of the room as sweat dried on my skin. "Thank you for the helmet, by the way. I can't wait to try it out with you. Dionne said to go back to that spot where...uh—"

"You let me get you off on the beach?"

"Yes. At night."

"She would know. Jason was the one who showed me that spot."

"I'm looking forward to trying that out."

"As am I. I can't wait to show you all the places you haven't seen. And some you have, just not with me."

My heart fluttered at the thought.

"You look cold," he said. "And tired. You should get under those covers and get some rest. Let me know what happens tomorrow. And when you'll be back so we can resume whatever it is we're doing."

"Wait. Hold. Pause. *Whatever it is we're doing*?" I repeated, working to keep irritation out of my tone, especially after I'd defended not having a label to Dionne. "That's what you call us?"

"Well, what do you call it, Kari? Fucking your boss?"

"Of course not. I just... *Whatever it is we're doing* seems casual for a man as intense as you are. I guess I'm surprised. Am I just something to do, or...is it more than that?"

The line went eerily quiet for a few beats. I was afraid Davis was about to cut off our conversation. But then he picked up the phone and rolled to his back, bringing the device close to his face.

"This thing between us," he began slowly, meting out his

words. "Our mutual attraction, our physical connection, the way my body feels like it's with you, even though it's not. Even my concern for your sister, a woman I haven't yet met… It's my favorite thing, actually. I just wanted to tread lightly. It's awkward with us working together—"

"It's not awkward, Davis," I protested. "I mean, we could make it awkward, but it isn't. I like you, you like me, we like being together. It's a risk, but it's working. Really well. And now everyone knows that's how we feel about each other."

"Well…maybe I…"

He blinked through a pause, then continued.

"Maybe I don't just *like* you. Maybe I can't get you off my mind. Maybe I miss you when I'm not touching you, when I'm not with you. Maybe I want more than just to be with you on an appointment basis. Maybe I want to be with you every day, every night. Maybe…I'm in the middle of what Vance warned me about. Athena has that man reading romance novels, and he swears he doesn't mind."

This moment of vulnerability and honesty made me want to reach through the screen and pull him close to me.

"Athena lent me some of her favorite romances. You're thinking about reading them with me?"

"If that's a thing you like doing, I…I want to like doing it with you. I wanted to give you the new helmet and take you out on a ride and tell you I'm falling in love with you. Quickly. And that I'm not afraid of it; I want you to be comfortable."

"You could still do that."

"This is obviously not an ideal way to hear it." He rambled as if I hadn't said a word. "But I see this as an opportunity to be honest about my feelings and future intentions. I'm excited to share my ideas for what life could look like, and I wanted to plan a special event for us to discuss them."

I bit my inner cheek to not laugh at this adorable man.

"So, Mr. Scott is preparing a thesis to present? Will this be in PowerPoint, or…"

"Don't tempt me," he replied. "Laugh all you like. Mr. Scott is never ill-prepared. So…you would be okay with all of that?"

"Yeah." I smiled. "I would be more than okay with all of that, so long as Davis from Houston gets a say. My feelings mirror yours, and I am prepared to discuss your proposal for the future."

He sighed, relief evident in the way his body relaxed. "Excellent, Ms. Savoy."

"Were you nervous I'd say something different?"

"I am confident enough that I was not truly worried," he said after a beat. "Hearing the words is confirmation of a few things, though."

"Things like I care for you, and I respect you and the work you do? That the way I feel means I'd never throw you under the bus for a job?"

"Yes, Kari. Things like that. Charlotte used me to get ahead and when I was useless to her, she threw me away. I will not waste more time and pieces of my heart mourning her or what could have been."

"Her loss. I could not imagine a more supportive person to have in my corner. You really let me shine, Davis."

"I didn't have time to stand in your way," he said, laughing. "I was just grateful that you came to take over the tasks that you manage much better."

We fell silent, content to stare at each other. Until I started yawning. And shivering.

"I told you to get in the bed. We need to get some sleep," Davis said.

"I don't want to. I want to lie here and stare at you."

"That is not advisable, Ms. Savoy." Davis laughed when I groaned. "We'll see each other soon, Kari. Go to bed. Big day tomorrow."

We disconnected the call, and I curled up in bed, clutching a pillow to my chest like I was plastered up against Davis. This trip couldn't end soon enough. I longed to be back in his arms again, feeling the heat of his skin against mine without the barrier of a screen dividing us.

———

Reyna and I crowded Bradford after sitting through hours of cases before she appeared before the judge for arraignment. It was worth the wait because soon after her case concluded, Reyna was released from handcuffs and walked out a free woman.

"Thank you so much, Bradford. I don't know what we would've done without you."

He shrugged, humble. "I'm happy I could help. Keep up your end of the bargain, Reyna. Stay out of trouble. Any questions, any issues, you and your sister have my number. Call me, alright?"

Bradford had moved mountains, getting the charges reduced from felony distribution to misdemeanor possession. He also convinced the judge to allow Reyna to leave the county in exchange for surrendering her passport, meaning I could take her with me to Black Diamond. As I predicted, she was not at all happy about her summer plans, but I couldn't leave her in Dallas and I refused to leave her at home alone.

"I will make sure she stays out of trouble," I promised.

"Great," Reyna drawled. "She's gonna be up my ass all the time."

"After this stunt, I'll be so far up your ass I'm going to file a change of address."

Reyna rolled her eyes. I ignored it. I could tell she was relieved to be free. She had only been an inmate overnight, but that was clearly enough for her. The past few hours had been such a whirlwind—her arrest, my rushed trip to rescue her, meeting with lawyers and trying to figure out a plan. I was anxious to get back to real life, however different that might look for the next few months.

"I've got to head to my office," Bradford said. "Can I give you two a ride?"

"Thank you, no. You've done so much already."

"Alright. Give my daughter a hug for me when you see her, and good luck with that festival you told me about."

"I will. We hope to see you this summer. Dionne has been bailing me out right and left—she's the reason we're even having a festival."

"That's D, bringing people together. See you soon." He gave us a wave, then headed to the parking garage.

As soon as he was out of sight, I grabbed Reyna's arm and steered her toward the exit. "Let's go. We have a lot to do and only a few hours to do it."

"Okay, handsy!" she complained, trying to shake free of my grip. "What do we have to do?"

"You need to pack so we can get out of here. We'll come back in a few weeks and deal with your apartment and your car and online enrollment for summer courses. Right now, I need to get back to work."

"You were serious?" Her lip curled in abject disgust. "I don't even get to say goodbye to people?"

I halted my march toward the exit and turned to her, nearly towering over her petite form.

"Did *people* hop on a plane to bail you out of jail, Reyna? Have *people* been putting up with you failing out of school, spending your money on pot, letting a guy move in with you and sell shit out of the apartment I pay for?"

She said nothing but dropped her gaze. I huffed, practically dragging her out of the courthouse to the parking lot.

"You weren't thinking about *people* when you were hanging around a grown ass man that let you get arrested. I just spent a lot of money to get you out of trouble, so yes, little sister. You are leaving today."

"I don't see why you can't let me clear things up here and come back for me in like two weeks."

I logged into a rideshare app to arrange for a ride to Reyna's apartment. "Because I don't trust you, is why. Did you really think I'd ask Bradford to beg the judge to let you leave the county for no reason? Be so *fucking* for real."

"Okay, not so much on trying to sound cool, Kari."

I sighed. "Do me a favor. Shut up, Reyna."

While we waited for our car, Reyna sulked, her thin arms folded tight across her chest and her lips in a permanent pout. I sent out a few texts to keep interested parties informed and checked in with my team at work.

Our car arrived just as Justin's status bulletin appeared in my email. The resort had weathered the storm, resulting in minor cosmetic damages. I loaded my bag and my sister into the car and read through the update, relieved that the repair schedule did not seem to be extensive.

The festival was still on, and setup would continue.

Reyna was sullen and withdrawn during the ride, staring out the window as the city passed by. I was not looking forward to an entire summer of the silent treatment. She needed structure and supervision, as much as she wanted to deny it, and I did not want to provide it.

I wrinkled my nose at the cloying stench as Reyna unlocked the door to her apartment. Amid boxes stacked up in the middle of the living room, furniture cushions and trash were strewn about. Dishes were piled high in the sink, and remnants of multiple meals were spread across the counters.

"No wonder your roommate is moving out. This is gross."

Reyna kicked a box out of her way as she stormed through the apartment. "She acts like it's always like this. We didn't have time to clean up before the police busted up in here."

"This is, at minimum, a week or more of food and dishes just sitting out. I'm so surprised you don't have flies."

"If it bothers you, big sister, then clean it up."

"That's your answer to everything, Reyna. You make messes and then tell me I can clean it up if it bothers me. I'm sick of cleaning up your mess."

Reyna heaved a deep, loud sigh and rolled her eyes hard. "This don't have shit to do with you, Kari. Mind your fucking business—"

"Excuse me?" I rounded on her, trying not to scream at the top of my lungs. "You called me, crying from *jail*, after you had been *arrested*. I could put a down payment on a car with the money I just paid to hire a lawyer, then bail you out and pay your fine. Your roommate is so sick of your shit that she's moving out, so I have to cover all of your rent for who the fuck knows how long because this is how you maintain a house."

"You act like that money is coming out of your fucking pocket!" she screeched. "God! I'm so *sick* of your martyr persona, like you deserve sainthood for taking care of us. Meanwhile, you pay my bills, my tuition, Mo's tuition, and his bills out of money you got because our parents died. Don't talk to me about how much you had to pay for shit—it's not your money."

"That money has to cover everything that's involved in taking care of you and Moses, from the insurance on the house you smoked pot in, to the tuition you're wasting, to that expensive ass shampoo you buy. I work so I don't spend *your* money. And because I work I have to get back, so I don't *fucking* have time for this, Reyna. We have to get your passport over to the court, and I have to get us to Black Diamond. Go pack or I will do it for you."

Reyna glared at me but didn't argue, stomping to her room and slamming the door shut behind her. A few seconds later, thumping bass and rough, lewd lyrics blared from behind her bedroom door.

I picked up the cushions from the floor and put them back on the couch, then plopped down with my phone.

Kari Savoy: Remind me that I love your sister.

> Moses Savoy: You love my sister. She being Reyna?

Kari Savoy: She's Reyna-ing like she's never Reyna'd before. I'm just trying to get her out of here.

> Moses Savoy: She'll be a'ight. You want me to swing through on my way back to school?

Kari Savoy: Nope, we're heading out as soon as I can get flights. Probably sometime tonight. I have to get back to work.

> Moses Savoy: Damn, you not playin.

> Moses Savoy: Deep breaths, Kar. She's gonna fuss, but she knows you're right. She just has to be obstinate about it first. When she gets to the beach, her tune will change.

Kari Savoy: Maybe, maybe not. She's going to work.

> Moses Savoy: That will be good for her.

Kari Savoy: How was the tour at Howard?

> Moses Savoy: Nice. Kinda wish I'd chosen Howard, but I'm happy at Xavier. For now.

Kari Savoy: We can talk about a transfer if you want to.

Moses Savoy: Let me contemplate and get back to you.

Moses Savoy: Love my lil sis down, a'ight. She's hurting. I wish I was there, but I'm thankful you got her.

Moses Savoy: You always got us, and we owe you everything for that. We both love you, even though Rey is allergic to showing it.

I sighed, wishing Mo was in the room so I could hug him —then make him deal with Reyna.

Kari Savoy: Stop making me cry, little boy. What time are you heading out?

Moses Savoy: Hitting the road in a couple minutes, actually.

Kari Savoy: Ok. Love you. Drive safe. Check in, and text me when you make it back to school.

Moses Savoy: K. I'll see you both when I come out for the festival. Love you.

I closed down the app and looked around the apartment, feeling overwhelmed. The mess made me anxious. I hated myself for it, but I got up and headed to the kitchen. We couldn't leave dishes and food out for weeks, and I wasn't leaving the mess for Jeanette. I also knew Reyna would not do it.

I loaded the dishwasher, hand-scrubbed the pots and pans crusted with caked-on, dried-on, burned-on food, and disposed of the empty boxes and cans that littered the cabinet. An hour later, the kitchen was presentable, if not sparkling.

I had just finished sweeping the floor and emptying the dustpan when the music cut out and Reyna's door opened. She had showered, changed clothes, refreshed her makeup, and pulled her waist-length braids back with a headband. She rolled a suitcase and a backpack stuffed full out of the room and lined them up in the hallway.

"Feel better?"

She shrugged in response, then held out a small blue book. Her passport. I took it, walked it over to my bag, and zipped it away, then pulled out my laptop to search for flights.

"Moses texted me," she said plainly. She dropped into the chair across from me, tucking a leg up under her body.

"I didn't tell on you."

"I know," she snapped, nostrils flaring. "I'm just saying. I talked to my brother, like you care."

"I do care, actually. I know how much Moses means to you, and it's been hard not having him around. I miss him too." I went back to the laptop screen and the search for affordable same-day flights. "So…what did he say?"

"Stay my behind out of jail. Ol' Captain Obvious ass."

I snorted. "He has a point…"

"Whatever," she mumbled, pulling out her phone, which her roommate had left for her, and beginning another session of mindless scrolling. "He's sick of my shit too, I guess. That man cussed me out about getting myself in a situation where you had to come get me. He said you take good care of us, and that I gotta stop being…like I am. Like imagine if you didn't give a fuck. Could have just left me to rot in there."

"Now you know your mama and daddy would come up out of the grave if I did not go get their little girl. Not to mention your brother. Hate me all you want. I don't play about you."

She grinned from behind the screen. "So you're saying I have power. Influence."

"If only you could use it for good."

"That takes the fun out of everything."

A few clicks later, I had booked us on a late afternoon flight to Corpus Christi and messaged the flights to Dionne so she could meet us there.

"We have a few errands to run before our flights this afternoon. Is there anything you need to do before you leave?"

"Nope. Ready to get out of here since you're kidnapping me."

I drew the lid of the laptop shut and slid it back into my bag.

"I'm going to say this every time we talk, even though you roll your eyes and suck your teeth at it. I love you. I *really* do. I really want the very best for you. You can believe that or not, I don't give a shit. You heard it. I wish we could be best buds, actual sisters. All I can say is I am here. I lost my parents too—twice. And I know, I know, you don't want to bond over our common parental loss, but—"

"'kay, so, actually…" Reyna sat up and set her phone down. "I think about that a lot. You lost your mom when you were a baby. You almost never knew her. And then your dad married my mom, and he had other kids. You never treated us like your half-siblings. And when mama and daddy…"

She teared up and swallowed hard. I reached across the table and squeezed Reyna's hand. For the first time, she gripped my hand and squeezed me back.

"I know," I whispered. "And you know I know losing them was hard. I can't even promise it's the hardest thing you'll ever make it through—"

"A night in county jail was no picnic."

"True. But you handled that too."

"Thanks to you."

"As long as you let me, and sometimes even when you won't, I'll be here. If you're interested, you can spend this summer getting to know your big sister. I'd also like us to start therapy."

She cringed. "Therapy? Me and some nosy ass mother-fucker asking about my daddy issues?"

I chuckled before I could stop myself. "Well, no. We'd actually find a *good* therapist. It's something I've needed to do for me, so let me do this for us. We can go together. You can go alone. But I want you to be able to talk, to express yourself in a way that I don't have to come and get you."

"I'm sorry." She sniffled, not meeting my eyes. "About... everything. I never want to go through jail and court and all that shit ever again." Reyna looked up, her eyes rimmed red. "This year has been a blur. I wasn't ready for SMU, for being in a new city. I feel so alone right now. I made everything such a mess."

I swung over to her chair, forcing her over so I could be close. Then I wrapped my arms around her. When she leaned into me, tears sprang to my eyes.

Reyna sobbed into my shoulder for what felt like an eternity. I held her tight, letting her release the pain and anguish that had built up over so many years. As her sobs quieted to sniffles, I stroked her hair and said gently, "It's going to be okay, Rey. You are not alone. We're going to figure this out together."

We sat in silence for a bit. I knew opening up was hard for her, but I was glad she felt comfortable enough with me to be vulnerable. Eventually, she sat up, sniffling and wiping away tears.

"Shout out to waterproof mascara and setting spray."

"I'm proud of you for letting that out," I said gently. "I

know it's not easy. Don't let that be the last time you open up to me, okay?"

Reyna nodded, swallowing hard. Her countenance was already softer. "I'm just...tired, Kar. And angry. Depressed. And tired of feeling like that, and pretending I don't, and pushing everyone away. Especially you. Mo was like, *Rey... what if she decides she don't want to deal with you anymore? Then what?* And...the thought of not having my big sister around kinda scared me."

"See, Moses likes that tough love approach. I'm not going anywhere, I swear."

Reyna gave me a small smile. "That means a lot. I'm sorry I've been such a brat."

"It's...it's not okay. But I get it. And it stops. Right now."

"Yes, ma'am."

"Now, what is it with you kids calling me *ma'am*?" Playfully, I pushed her away, then pulled her to me and dropped a loud, sloppy kiss on her cheek. "Love you, Rey."

"Ewwww!" she squealed, but giggled and didn't pull away.

"Are you ready to go? I'm dying to show you the resort and my beachfront condo."

"Yeah. Thanks for cleaning the kitchen. Housework isn't my ministry and Jeanette would just...do it. I don't blame her for moving out."

She stood, stretching while a long, loud yawn rolled from her. She'd probably slept very little in jail and would pass out on the plane ride. "Mo told me to ask about your crush on your boss. He said he's some puckered dude."

I stopped short, my head whipping around. The innocence in her expression didn't fool me at all. My siblings had been talking about me.

"Who said you could have a boyfriend? Me and Mo gotta inspect him first. We're not having any more dusty ass Noah situations."

My jaw dropped…then I gathered myself. "Uh, well, it's officially more than a crush. Given the situation I just rescued you from, you don't have much room to talk. My boyfriend might be your new boss, so talk to him nice."

Twenty-Five

DAVIS

Calhoun had already sent my day to the shredder, and it wasn't even noon.

He was hungover, surly, and impatient, refusing to learn how to order room service from the delivery robots. Instead of falling into the comfort of my usual routine, I was at Breakers manually placing a breakfast order, then sending the machines to his suite. I dressed, then rushed to my office to help Justin manage Kari's events staff.

At the office, issues mounted relentlessly: a mix-up with room assignments, a florist error, and a guest that repeatedly locked himself out of his suite. With Calhoun's presence looming over the property, every issue was amplified. I applied Band-Aid solutions, but Kari's absence left a notice-able void.

I was so happy to read her text that she and Reyna were on the way to the airport and would be back on property in a few hours. She would not, however, return in time to dazzle the suits from MGMT and Harlan Calhoun as planned.

Considering that our management company and owner had been dancing on my last nerve, perhaps it would be best that I handle the conversation.

I headed to the conference room, armed with the binder that held months of reports and analysis as a paper shield against the skepticism I was about to face.

Three stoic, stone-faced men in jackets and slacks sat side by side, their backs to the amazing view of the resort's largest pool and the beach in the distance. Each had a copy of the presentation in front of them and were flipping through the tabbed sections with interest.

Calhoun, dressed in the rumpled shirt and jacket he'd worn the evening before, sat fuming, his copy untouched. *What a clown.*

"Good morning, gentlemen," I greeted. My gaze met Calhoun's cool, steely one.

"No need for pleasantries. Get on with it, Davis," Calhoun said, his fingers drumming an impatient rhythm on the polished mahogany table.

I set the binder down, flipping it open with a practiced hand, and launched into my presentation, guiding the group through the numbers page by page, detailing the steady increase in revenue, particularly in recent months.

"The bottom line is that this resort is operating at its highest level of efficiency since I took over. Even more so since Ms. Savoy joined the team. Occupancy rates are up by over fifty percent," I said, pointing to the graph that showed a steady climb. "Facility rentals have doubled just since the last quarter. Every department is running within budget and achieving revenue goals—"

"Even labor?" one of the suits asked.

"It's painful, but yes. Even labor. That's something I want to discuss—"

"These numbers mean jack if we're bleeding funds elsewhere." Calhoun's words cut through the room like a knife.

"Which is precisely why the festival is critical," I countered, moving around the room. "In the next section, Kari has outlined several strategies to continue our growth and stay ahead of our competitors. The first of those strategies is an annual festival, an investment that will pay off year over year in publicity and future bookings. Kari is of the belief, and I agree with her, that we will break even this year—if we have the funds we need to run it well. If we don't, we'll overspend trying to bridge the gap. In future years, the festival will make us money. It'll have some history behind it—"

"Well, what you call critical, I call frivolous," Calhoun cut in sharply. "If we're overextended, we should cut costs, not plan parties."

"Sir, this is a world-class beachside resort within an hour of the Texas coast. Planning parties, conferences, and events should be our primary job, and we should have the funds to do this well. We are professional hosts, and without events like this, we risk stagnation. We have no real way to draw people to this island, to this property. The concert series, as well as a few private events that are planned for the end of summer, are serious bait that will open the door to high-dollar and celebrity events. No other hotel on this island would be suitable to host such an affair. We have a prime opportunity to put The Pearl on the map."

"Your passion for this festival is understandable," said one of the suits, "but we need to see evidence that it will be profitable for the property."

"There is a detailed budget and Kari's marketing plan in this section of your presentation," I replied confidently, flipping through the binder.

Calhoun picked up his copy and began flipping through the pages, scowling.

"The budget includes partnership deals with local shops," I explained. "Yoga classes, a poker tournament, the bookmobile; all have applied to present booths or activities, and all will be sponsored by Black Diamond business owners. This allows us to recoup operating expenses. The numbers also project ticket sales and potential revenue from food, drink, and entertainment. The concert series is an added bonus— we're planning monthly shows managed by Grammy-winning recording artists with a stable of talent waiting to grace our stage. Kari has established a rapport with the stake-holders, and we've given them the reins to book the talent. We sell the tickets and split the profits."

"What about marketing?" one of the men asked. "You're talking celebrities here. You'll have to spend a mint on advertising."

"The festival and our guests have sold themselves thus far. Kari has several ads running in major music publications and the local newspaper. She had a low-cost but very good-looking television spot recorded and social media influencers are picking up on the excitement, especially surrounding the concert series. That's a lot of free promotion."

"This is all cute, I guess. So, what happens when this little gamble fails?" Calhoun leaned back in his chair, his beady, bloodshot eyes trained on me. "When you've spent all of my money and come back with your hat in your hand, begging for more?"

"Then you lose more than money. You lose the confidence you had when you hired me that I could dig you out of the hole you were buried in. Kari and I are doing that. This gamble won't fail," I said firmly. "I need your trust on this."

"Trust is earned with results, not promises," said one of the suits from MGMT.

"And I have given you results!" I said, tapping the report emphatically. "I refuse to let this group gaslight me into thinking I'm not running the hell out of this place. So, if you're done peeing on my leg and telling me it's raining, as Mr. Calhoun would say, I'd like to talk about how we can make this year and next year an enormous success at The Pearl."

I flipped ahead in the binder to a section that Kari, Justin, and I had spent weeks poring over and perfecting.

"If we don't plan ahead, we'll fall behind," I began. "We already know we'll do more at the resort this year and next. There's no sense in waiting until we're drowning. I'm proposing a substantial increase in the operating budget, beginning immediately. Making up this year's shortfall is essential if we're to continue the growth we're seeing."

"An *increase*?" Calhoun's disdain was palpable. "You've got a set of brass balls, don't ya?"

"Yes, sir, I do. I can account for every penny—where it will go and how it will grow us. The staff we've worked hard to train, who are integral to the experience here at this resort, will walk right out the door to another hotel where they can make more." I paused for a few beats, locking eyes with him, letting my words sink in. "And I'll lead the way. If it starts with me, it'll domino down to the waitstaff in the restaurants."

Calhoun's posture stiffened. His lackeys from MGMT mimicked him. "Is that a threat, Davis?"

"No, sir. However, it is a reality check. I have worked these people to the bone for your benefit. It's time to give them some relief. You have a very simple choice: invest in the success we're building, or watch this place end up like the Tropicana in Vegas. They're imploding it this summer. An entire legacy— gone. After all the money you put into building this resort and the millions you've spent to keep it operational, do you really want to see it abandoned, shut down, turned into a parking lot?"

Calhoun's stare could bore holes through steel, but after a moment, his shoulders slumped ever so slightly. "Depending on the recommendation from MGMT, I'll approve additional funding, but don't think you have carte blanche. I still hold the checkbook. Don't launch another ridiculous event like this festival without approval."

I wanted to huff the biggest sigh of relief, but I fought to keep my cool. At least until I was alone.

"Understood, sir," I replied, feeling the victory settle in my stomach. With Harlan Calhoun, there would never be a winner...only survivors of another skirmish in an ongoing war.

Today, though, The Pearl came out on top.

———

Restless, I moved around Vance and Athena's living room, unable to stand still and constantly checking my watch.

"Anxious much?" Vance chuckled from a chair near the chaise lounge. "You might explode if I tell you to sit your nervous ass down."

Athena perched on the arm of Vance's chair. "Leave the poor man alone. He's probably just figured out that he's in love. You'd be just as bad if it were you."

"How do you think I know how he's feeling? That's why I don't let you go anywhere without me."

"A watched pot never boils," Justin chimed in from across the room, scrolling his phone. His long legs stretched out under the coffee table and were crossed at the ankles. "Davis, chill out. Pacing won't make the plane land faster."

"You can no longer talk about how I act about Athena. I don't think I've ever seen you this twisted up over a woman before. It's not like she was gone for weeks. It hasn't even been a full day, man."

My face grew warm at the teasing from my friends. The past twenty-four hours had felt like an eternity without Kari. I'd been counting the hours, then the minutes until she would be back on property. I was happy to turn her department back over to her. More importantly, I was happy that she'd be back in my face, in my life...in my bed. Talking on the phone and texting wasn't the same as having her with me. I needed her close.

My phone buzzed with a text.

> Kari Savoy: Landed! Finally. Headed that way.

Relieved, I tapped out a response:

> Davis Scott: Tell Dionne to drive fast.

> Kari Savoy: She said she is not your employee and to sit down somewhere.

I resumed pacing, willing the hands on my watch to move faster. My friends exchanged knowing looks while they engaged in casual banter.

"I'm going downstairs," I announced after twenty minutes. "They'll be pulling into the parking deck soon."

I made it to the deck just as Dionne's sporty coupe slowed to a stop. The passenger door flew open, and Kari leaped out in jeans and a t-shirt, a wide grin splitting her face. She was never more beautiful as she rushed me, jumping into my arms. I held her close, lifting her off of her feet.

"I missed you so much!" she squealed, making no effort to keep quiet or hide her emotions.

"I missed you too," I murmured into her hair. I set her down gently but kept my arms around her.

Kari leaned back to look up at me, her eyes shining with amusement. "I'm sure you did. I saw Justin's end-of-day report in my email. You had to do all of my job today."

"That is but one reason I'm happy to see you." Our eyes locked, and I leaned in, kissing her slowly. She returned the kiss, her hands coming up to cradle my face.

For a blissful moment, nothing else existed except her lips on mine.

"Not that I don't appreciate this romantic ass scene, but let me out of this clown car!"

I took my time ending the kiss, then bent to peer inside the vehicle. Large, almond-shaped brown eyes that were undoubtedly Savoy stared back. "Reyna, I presume?"

"You presume right. Can you move this seat so I can get out?"

I reached in to pull the seat forward so Reyna could slide out. She unfolded herself from the backseat, grumbling and stretching dramatically as if she'd been trapped back there for hours.

"Oh, Reyna. This is Dav—"

"Aht!" she barked, holding up a hand. "Stand back. I'm on a mission—I have orders from Moses Savoy to check this dude out."

She looked me over with an appraising eye, scanning my footwear, then rolling her eyes up to my tailored suit, pressed shirt, designer tie, and close-cut hair. I withstood the scrutiny, curious about her opinion as if the rating of a nineteen-year-old could move the needle.

"So…this is the man that has my sister sprung? Rushing back to work, smiling at her phone with that dewy glow and shit?" She shrugged a shoulder, then glanced at her sister. "Not bad, Kar. He cute. I approve."

"That's as good an opinion as you're going to get." Kari moved to stand next to her sister, who was only slightly shorter. "This is my baby sister, Reyna. Rey, this is Davis. He is the General Manager and everybody's boss."

"You got no more times to call me your baby sister."

"You are so very late on that, baby sister. Act like you have manners, please."

"Pleasure to finally meet you." I extended a hand. Reyna shook it firmly. "I've heard a lot about you."

"I bet you have," she replied, a gleam in her eye. "Just so you know, I've recently turned over a new leaf. Forget everything you've heard."

"That pleases me because we will be working together this summer."

"Don't stick me with grunt work. I'm not here to fetch coffee."

Kari laughed, moving to the trunk where Dionne was retrieving their bags. "You might actually beg to fetch coffee."

"We'll make sure you get hands-on experience across the resort. My goal is for you to understand how a property like this works from the inside out."

"Yeah…don't put yourself out. My goal is to find the beach and work on the *toasted* part of my toasted caramel skin tone." She pulled a pair of shades from a crossbody bag and slipped them on. "Point me at it."

"First, we unload the car," said Kari. "Then I'll show you around."

I stepped back at the sound of the elevator doors sliding open. Vance, Athena, and Justin spilled out onto the parking deck, shouting out loud greetings and throwing open arms as if Kari had been gone for months.

"Justin will be your supervisor," I said, introducing them. "He handles staff management."

"We'll drop off your bags," Justin said, "and I'll give you a tour of the resort. Might as well get your paperwork started."

"Already shoving me off onto a lackey," Reyna mumbled, limply shaking his hand. "This lowers your rating, Davis."

"Actually, I'm the *assistant* property manager, second in command here at The Pearl." Justin's brows shot up and his chest puffed out, as I knew they would. "I'm the buffer between Davis and everyone else, so I'm the one you need to suck up to. If we lost Kari because she left to rescue you, I was going to be very upset."

"Mmhmm." Reyna sucked her teeth and, I was sure,

rolled her eyes. "Mkay, then, Mr. *Assistant* Manager, second in command. Kari is here, and so am I. Show me around, or whatever."

"Whew, I don't know if we can handle two people with attitude around here," said Kari.

I grabbed Kari's hand, winding my fingers between hers. "Let's meet up at Breakers for a late dinner," I proposed. "I'd like to catch up with my...girlfriend?"

I winced, hating how young that word sounded coming out of my mouth. My plans for a future with Kari involved an adult, mature relationship.

"Woman? Partner? What are you?"

Kari smiled up at me, squeezing my hand. "We can discuss terms later. When we're *alone*."

"Yeah, let these two get some time together. Davis has been pacing for hours." Vance dropped an arm around Athena's shoulders as we headed toward the Paradise tower. "We, uh...are about to have some alone time as well."

Reyna audibly gagged. "How can you stand all of this syrupy sweet lovey-dovey crap?"

"You get used to it," I replied, stepping into the elevator with Kari, Vance, and Athena. "Tell Tim we'll be in around eight o'clock."

———

I kicked the door of my condo shut as we shed clothing. My suit, her jeans, my shoes, her sneakers, my boxers, her bra— all were strewn throughout the kitchen and living room. I slid my hands across her skin, drinking in the supple smoothness of the soft canvas.

"I missed you so fucking much. The operative word being *fucking*."

Kari laughed as I dragged her to the bedroom. "Leave it to you to identify an operative word."

We tumbled onto the bed, limbs tangled together. I wasted no time pulling her close to me, my hands cupping her breasts. She arched, moaning softly. I lowered my head to take a taut nipple in my mouth.

I lavished attention on her breasts before trailing kisses down her stomach. Her body responded instantly to my call. I paused at the juncture of her thighs, breathing in her scent, taking in the view of her wet warmth before popping my head up to make sure she was ready for me. Her eyes were dark with need, her lips drawn in so tight her cheeks were dimpled.

She spread her legs for me, then gripped the back of my head and pulled me to her. I dove in, lapping, kissing, sucking, teasing. Kari bucked her hips against me, her fingers gripping my shoulders. I circled her clit, pulling it between my lips.

"Unh, fuck yeah!" she yelped, grinding on my tongue. I loved seeing her this way—open and uninhibited, all her defenses down. Knowing I could bring her here, that I could elicit this response from her was intoxicating. I slipped two fingers inside her, picking up the pace as I flicked my tongue over her clit.

Kari panted, her body tensing. I doubled down, determined to push her over the edge. With a wail, her climax hit, thighs clamping around my head as she convulsed, trembling through wave after wave. I gentled my movements, helping her ride it out until she collapsed back on the bed, chest heaving as she worked to fill her lungs.

I kissed my way back up her body until we were face to face. "Welcome home, Ms. Savoy," I murmured against her mouth. She smiled and pulled me in for a deep, sensual kiss, licking her juices off of my lips.

"I was only gone a day, Davis."

"I missed you like you were gone for months."

"Aww. You're sweet," she purred, reaching down to stroke me, then guide me to her. "I missed you, too."

"Wait, I don't have a condom on—"

"Don't stop. I'm protected. And I trust you."

I wasted no time, sinking into her unencumbered and pushing deep. Her head rolled back, exposing her neck to the light nibbles I spread from shoulder to shoulder. We both groaned at the decadent feeling of being joined skin to skin. I moved with slow, deep strokes, savoring every sensation until my need for her took over.

Hard and fast, I pounded my body against hers. She met me thrust for thrust, her nails raking down my back as the tension coiled tighter.

"You feel amazing," I panted against her neck. "Made for me. I love this feeling. I love us, right here…right now."

Kari locked her legs around me, pulling me even deeper. A few more powerful strokes and she shattered beneath me, head thrown back, her inner muscles fluttering around me, crying out my name as her release washed over her. Feeling her pussy clench around me like a vise was my undoing. I buried my face in her neck as I spilled inside her with a gut-level, shuddering grunt.

Spent and sated, I collapsed, my full weight on her body. She did not argue; rather, she enclosed me completely, folding her arms around my neck. We clung to each other as we floated down from the high of climax. Her lips found mine, and we rewarded each other with kisses and caresses until I had the energy to roll to the side, pulling her with me.

"I'm not saying this because we just had amazing sex—"

"Because we did just have amazing sex," she interrupted.

"I'm definitely in love with you, Kari."

"You think?" She giggled. "How in love are you?"

"Mmmm…" I shook my head, wracking my brain. "So in love, I might consider doing something I'd pick on Vance about."

"You're pretty far gone, then?"

"I am. He mentioned something about taking a bubble bath and reading about pirates, if that interests you."

Kari cackled, throwing her head back in laughter.

"I don't know if pirates are hot to you. I'm just saying I'd consider it if they were. Whatever gets you there."

"I'm not really a 'reads romance novels with my man' kind of girl but..." She propped herself up on an elbow, finding my eyes and stroking the wayward hairs in the beard I hadn't had time to trim that morning. "If you put me on your bike and take me for a nice ride, then bring me back here for food, wine, and sex while we ignore a movie about motorcycles, I could get into that."

"You're not going to make me watch a show about people who get married to strangers?"

The cringe I felt my mouth curling into fell away as Kari laughed.

"Dionne would be pissed if I watched our show with someone else. I like that you're thinking about it, though."

"I really missed you, Kari. I missed you being here—not just here in my bed but around the resort. You're a part of this place. So much that I told Calhoun if we didn't get what we need, we'd walk. All of us."

"I assume we still have jobs, so he didn't call your bluff?"

"I wasn't bluffing," I confessed. "I'd definitely find jobs for us where we're valued and we can still work together. Thankfully, though..."

Rolling to my side, I prodded her to lie on her back and hovered over her. She grinned, accepting my body and my lips on hers. "We don't have to look for jobs. At least not this year and maybe not next year. I made him pay up, so your ideas won't go to waste. Now the festival can be the success you imagined it to be."

"Davis..." I smiled at the moisture that gathered in the corners of her eyes. "You really love me."

"Yes, I do. All of me loves you. Mr. Scott, Davis from Houston…whoever else might be in there. We're all big fans."

She tipped her head up for a kiss, pressing her mouth to mine. "I love you too. Even though none of you know what to call me."

"Well, let's negotiate. How about Paramour?"

"No."

"Lover."

"Absolutely not. I'd feel like I'm in an '80s cable movie."

"Boo thang? Davis from Houston likes that one."

"He would. Next."

"Head giver? Soul Snatcher?"

She sighed, letting her eyes slide closed. "Davis, be serious. I can't introduce you as that."

"I have never been more serious. I'd love that. Or we could go with Dick Groper, especially in my office—"

Her eyes flew open. "Mr. Scott!"

I laughed. She paused, then snorted before asking, "What if I called you my *Manfriend*?"

"Well, now you've ruined the spirit of the whole exercise."

"But Dick Groper was an option?"

"If you had a dick that was being groped, it would be." I smiled, leaning in to kiss her again. "At least we intend to come up with something. We'll figure it out, baby."

Her brows rose at that. "You could be on to something. The way my body reacts to you calling me *baby* is the same way my body reacts to you calling me *Ms. Savoy*."

"And…what happens when I call you *Ms. Savoy*?"

She sat halfway up, pushing me over to my back, and climbed on top of me. "It makes me want to go through your closet and put on one of your clean, freshly pressed dress shirts."

"Go on." My hands settled on her hips as she gripped me, holding me in place as she slowly sank down, enveloping me in her heat. A lusty, sultry moan rolled from her as she rocked her body, slowly at first but quickly building up speed, her breasts bouncing with her movement.

"It makes my heartbeat thump in my clit."

"And that's good?" I sat up to take a nipple in my mouth, flicking it with my tongue as she moaned with pleasure.

"Fuck yes, it's so good." She sighed, closing her eyes, letting her head drop as she ground her body on mine. I gripped her hips tighter, thrusting up to meet her.

"It makes me want to ride you until my legs give out. It makes me—"

"Ms. Savoy?"

She paused, opening her eyes to find my amused gaze. "Yes, Mr. Scott?"

"I don't need a dissertation. Ride, baby."

Epilogue

KARI

The Beats & Eats Festival consumed my summer, and I'd never been happier.

Local businesses took advantage of the expected crowds, transforming Black Diamond from its northern boardwalk to its southern tip. Colorful tents and booths lined the streets, offering a selection of mouth-watering food and one-of-a-kind merchandise. Dedicated fans of Tuneage label artists waited in long lines for ticketed events—meet and greet gatherings, exclusive listening parties, and concerts that had them swaying and singing late into the night.

Davis and I spent every moment that we weren't working checking out attractions across the island. We sampled gourmet food from all over the world, watched street performers dazzle crowds with their talents, and tried our hand at some of the carnival games. Davis even competed in the Sips & Chips Charity poker tournament and won the third-largest pot. He convinced Calhoun to match the winnings and donated the entire sum to a local children's organization on behalf of our resort.

Once he was convinced that Davis wasn't running his hotel into the ground, Calhoun hopped on his Gulfstream and headed back to Houston, leaving us to enjoy the summer without the added headache of having the owner on property.

Having my sister by my side made the summer even more satisfying. Reyna and I put in hard work to build our relationship, prioritizing one-on-one time together, often after our joint therapy sessions. Her attitude and perspective made slow but sure turns.

Moses was a frequent weekend guest and part-time employee. Despite being granted additional funds for temporary help, we needed every hand we could get and gladly welcomed him and some of his friends in exchange for concert tickets.

The festival culminated in a sold-out concert featuring Wade, Gage, and their label artists. Fontaine, as always, ensured we had the best seats and VIP access. Two weeks later, we hosted the event of the season.

Once the rumors of a surprise wedding had been allowed to spread like wildfire, nearly every room and event space at the Pearl was booked solid for weeks in advance. We hoped for great weather, and our wishes came true as the sky was a cloudless cerulean blue. A soft ocean breeze carried the sweet melodies of a string quartet playing while guests mingled.

Ameenah's maternity gown was stunning as it draped gracefully over her belly. She glowed as she grinned at Wade in white Armani. A burnt orange lily was pinned to his lapel, adding to the pops of color that matched the sunset-inspired theme of the wedding—and Wade's favorite Tikis & Cream creation, Frozen Sunshine.

"This is the type of throw down I want when it's my

turn," Reyna whispered, standing beside me as we watched the scene from the penthouse rooftop.

"Absolutely," I muttered under my breath. "When you have a cool million to spend on a weeklong party on an island, I'll hook it up."

"Okay, never mind."

I chuckled, drawing an arm around her to pull her close as we watched the ceremony. Reyna had stopped by on her way to work the wedding reception. I fought back tears, trying not to think about her turning in her uniforms, her badge, and her fobs in a few days. After a long summer of working nearly every department at The Pearl and completing her summer courses online, she would return to Southern Methodist University as a sophomore...*barely*. Moses would drive Reyna back to Dallas on his way to Xavier.

"By the power vested in me by the state of Texas, I now pronounce you husband and wife. You may kiss your bride!" the officiant declared, lifting his arms in a grand gesture.

Wade leaned in to seal their commitment with a tender kiss. The crowd erupted in joyful screams as the couple was introduced as Mr. and Mrs. Wade and Ameenah Marshall, and string instruments began playing a beautifully arranged version of Natalie Cole's "This Will Be an Everlasting Love."

"Alright, that's enough slacking, Reyna," Justin said, annoyingly snapping his fingers. "The catering crew is moving into place."

"Hang on a second! Damn," said Reyna, a quiver in her voice.

I glanced at her, surprised to see her wiping away tears. "You okay?" I whispered.

She nodded. "That was just...really nice. I'm moving into my soft girl era. It's still shout out to holding spray and waterproof mascara."

"Okay. Have a good shift. I'll see you..." I pursed my lips. "Probably tomorrow."

"Ugh," she grunted, rolling her eyes. The tender moment gave way to faux annoyance. "I'm glad you and Davis break the headboard at his place and not ours."

"Mind your business, Reyna," said Davis, rounding the corner. "Or you won't get any more plum assignments."

"I have two days left. I have given up hope of a plum assignment." Justin and Reyna took off for the reception hall, loudly harassing each other all the way.

"Hi, baby," said Davis, leaning in for a lingering kiss. His hands slid down my back, pulling me close against him. When he released me, his eyes sparkled. "You look…"

He grunted, shaking his head. "That dress makes me want to take you home and call you *Ms. Savoy* over and over and over."

I smoothed my hands over the fitted bodice of the cocktail dress I had splurged on for the occasion. "You clean up nicely yourself, Mr. Scott."

Davis wore a linen suit that accentuated his build, his signature Tom Ford scent tickling my nose as he drew me in for another kiss, this one deeper and more urgent. A quiet moan rolled from me as I melted into him.

"Alright, break it up," a familiar voice called out. Vance and Athena walked hand in hand toward us.

"What a beautiful ceremony, absolutely gorgeous!" Athena gushed, grinning ear to ear. "You did such a great job with this event, Kari. I'm so impressed."

"You're just saying that because your wedding is next," I teased.

"Not at all," Athena insisted. "I just love watching two people pledge their lives to each other. I teared up."

"Beautiful gowns, tears of happiness….we're going to miss the toast," said Vance.

The crowd flowed gracefully into the ballroom, a sea of bright colors and elegant attire. Each guest seemed eager to get the celebration underway, the smell of decadent food and sounds of lively chatter and music in the air.

Gage, Wade's best man, wore a crisp white suit, his vest and handkerchief matching the wedding theme. He motioned for the microphone, making sure the room saw the glint of diamonds in his custom cufflinks. Using a knife, he tapped his champagne glass to get everyone's attention.

The room quieted as all eyes turned to him expectantly. Fontaine handed him a microphone, mumbling, "Keep it brief, man."

Gage chuckled. "He thinks he's in charge." In response, the room burst into laughter. "A'ight…so, I've known Wade for more than half of my life. He's been my A-1 since high school, when we would pass rap lyrics back and forth in sophomore English. He's been by my side for some of the biggest moments in my life— when I met my wife, when I married her, the birth of my children."

He paused to toss a glance at the head table where his wife nodded and smiled.

"He's also been there for some of the tough moments. Fighting record labels to do the music we want to do, the way we want to do it. Through it all, Wade was only ever concerned about me. How I'm doing? Do I get my cut? Do I get to use my voice and my talent and my skill? That's just the way Wade is. So…"

Gage sauntered across the room to stand in front of Wade and Ameenah, who blissfully beamed from their seats.

"Believe me when I say that I've never seen this dude happier than when he is with Ameenah. The love they share and model is an inspiration to me and my family. Ameenah… I mean, I'm a rapper and I write most of our songs but I wish I could have come up with some poetic shit like *you're the wind beneath his wings* or whatever…"

The room tittered in laughter for a few moments.

"For real though? The love you have for him makes him a

better person—and that's a feat because if I know anything about Wade, it's that he's a real good dude. Now with a little one on the way, life can only get better."

He turned to address the crowd, a smirk falling to his lips. "I'm tellin' y'all, I can't *wait* to see my bro hauling a little dude around Brooklyn—"

"Gage!" Ameenah and Wade shouted in unison, drowned out by cheering and clapping.

"What I say?" Gage asked, brows furrowed.

"You weren't supposed to tell everybody we're having a boy, man!" Wade replied.

"Aw, my bad!" Gage called back with a grin. "I got carried away."

"Never thought I'd say this," said Fontaine, "but somebody cut that man's mic off!"

"A'ight, before they sit me down, everybody put your glasses up. Raise 'em high so we can toast my best friend and wish him all the happiness in the world." Gage lifted his glass. "Cheers to the newlyweds and my lil' nephew!"

A chorus of cheers echoed through the ballroom as everyone clinked glasses and sipped champagne. As the evening progressed, the celebration was in full swing. The dance floor was packed, with guests of all ages dancing to Sabrina Forrest and her band doing every line dance ever invented, and a few I was sure they made up on the spot.

Later, Wade and Ameenah swayed together during their spotlight dance, lost in their own world.

"They look so happy." I leaned against Davis as we watched from the edge of the dance floor.

"Because they *are*," he agreed. "Today was perfect, and you had everything to do with that."

"I'll take that credit, but I didn't do it alone. Ameenah had a very expensive and demanding wedding planner to help me. Wade wasn't going to agree to any of this unless it was stress free for her."

"Are you thinking about how one day, this could be us?"

"This scene exactly?" I sighed. "All these people, all this decadence, all this *money* for a few hours? I hope not. But yes, I think about how some version of this could be us."

"A version more like..." He turned, pulling me into his ams and swaying to Sade, By Your Side blaring through the speakers above us. "A deserted beach. Our family and friends. A few drinks to toast us, then we hop on the Harley and ride off into the sunset."

"That's more like it," I replied, closing my eyes. Then they popped open again. "Before it's us, it's your best friend. And I'll admit I'm scared."

"You should be. They might recite sonnets to each other."

I bit my lip to keep from laughing. "Stop. Seriously?"

Davis rolled his eyes. "I told you he's corny. You know I'm never ill-prepared, so be thinking. I'll want a full project plan—"

"A dissertation, if you will?"

He bobbed his head in a deep nod. "Preferably in one of my shirts and nothing else."

I sucked my teeth and turned in his arms, elbowing him in the ribs. "You are always teasing me. If you're not pulling me into a back room to push my dress up and show me something, I need you to hush."

"I'm not a tease, baby. I'm a sure thing." He nipped my ear before sliding an arm around my waist. "I'm going to start my rounds. You know how I do—out of here by nine o'clock—"

I grinned. "And into me by nine-thirty?"

We circulated the ballroom, saying our goodbyes and well wishes to the bride, groom, and other guests. I checked on my staff to ensure everything was on track before I disappeared. After thanking Ameenah and Wade once more and wishing them a wonderful honeymoon in Belize, Davis took my hand, and we slipped out into the warm evening air.

As soon as we swiped into the condo and the door closed behind us, Davis backed me up against the wall, his warm hands roaming under my dress, pushing it up and over my hips. My hands gripped his shoulders as his lips crushed mine.

"Pursuant to your request, Ms. Savoy," Davis whispered, breaking the kiss to trail his lips down my neck. "I am here to push your dress up. And I've got a lot to show you."

Acknowledgments

I'm probably going to forget someone. As the old saying goes, charge it to my head and not my heart.

First to the fam I was born into, the fam I chose and chose me: *I love you all the most and then some.* I thank you so much for your support and enthusiasm for me and these books I write.

Specifically to my pockets of friends and friends in my pocket- the Wordmakers, the PDubs, the Trollops, my Girl-Time pals: thanks for entertaining my nonsense and believing in me.

Special thanks to those who provided inspiration for characters and...*activities*... in this novel. *looks at Erin*

Thank you to **AdotK Edits** for always getting me together and leveling up my books. If you find any mistakes, they're mine.

Thanks to _me_ for this *amazing* cover —the image is courtesy depositphotos.com. Full wrap print cover designed by AuthorMya.

Also by DL White

Pick up my titles in eBook, print or audio at my store-
Payhip.com/booksbydlwhite.

Brunch at Ruby's, a Ruby's novel

Dinner at Sam's, a Ruby's novel

Unexpected, a holiday short

Beach Thing, a Black Diamond Romance

Elysium, a Black Diamond Vacation Romance

Leslie's Curl & Dye, a Potter Lake Small Town Romance

Second Time Around, a Potter Lake holiday short

The Guy Next Door, a Potter Lake Small Town Romance

The Kwanzaa Brunch, a holiday short

A Thin Line

The Never List

Hey, Lover